THE LAST SUPPER

ALEX CROW

Double Dutch Publishing

The Last Supper by Alex Crow

Copyright © 2020 by Alex Crow. All rights reserved.

No part of this book may be reproduced in any written, electronic, recording, or photocopying without written permission of the publisher or author. The exception would be in the case of brief quotations embodied in the critical articles or reviews and pages where permission is specifically granted by the publisher or author.

This is a work of fiction. Names, characters, places, and incidents either are the product of the author's imagination or are used fictitiously. Any resemblance to actual persons, living or dead, is coincidental and not intended by the author.

Books may be purchased by contacting the author at:
www.alexcrowbooks.com

Publisher: Double Dutch Publishing
Cover Design: Zita Harrison
Interior Design: Double Dutch Publishing
Editor: Double Dutch Publishing

ISBN: 978-0-9984309-6-6

First Double Dutch Publishing Edition: November 2020

10 9 8 7 6 5 4 3 2 1

A sincere Thank You to Chris J.:

Chris, as my most trusted beta reader and friend, you repeatedly put your life on hold when I throw a new manuscript in front of you. Even with barely any notice at all, you are happy to drop everything in order to help me out in a pinch.

You always put such time and thought into your critiques and your notes and comments are invaluable to me. Too often, I find my confidence waning and you are always there to ensure me that I'm right where I'm meant to be and doing exactly what I'm meant to be doing.

From the bottom of my heart, I Thank You! :o)

Prologue

A single droplet of hot wax emerged from beneath the cuff of the crisp white sleeve. Obeying gravity's pull, it continued across the back of the hand and along the edge of the stiff ring finger. Upon reaching the nailbed, the wax united with a thin line of clotted blood. With a fresh pink hue, the merged droplet traveled off the end of the fingertip and fell to its demise on the warm concrete.

It would be the first of many. The sun was high in the sky and every minute that passed, the shade from the three-story building receded a little more. A man of wax didn't stand a chance against the slowly rising temperature.

It was an unusually warm spring day and the streets were bustling outside of Madame Tussauds wax museum. Situated at the corner of 10th and F Street in Washington DC, it was a prime location for pedestrian traffic.

Although it was just an ordinary Tuesday afternoon, the passersby were in for a special treat that day. Set up on the sidewalk, just outside the museum doors, was a detailed three-dimensional scene.

The scene starred three life-sized wax figures. A man, a woman, and a teenage boy. They sat around a rectangular dining table complete with china plates adorned with fake food. There was room at the table for a fourth guest, but the extra dining chair stood empty and unoccupied.

It looked like a typical scene you'd see peeking in the window of any normal suburban home.

The figures were posed as if they were enjoying a nice evening meal. Although *enjoying* wasn't quite the most accurate term. Their emotionless faces more easily suited an unhappy family giving each other the silent treatment. Their blank eyes stared straight ahead and their lips pursed tightly together.

Apparently, not a single drop of conversation occurred at that dinner table. Very awkward and uncomfortable. Such a strange choice for a display.

A dark-haired man sat with one hand holding a fork over a plate and his other hand resting on his leg. The woman across from him wore a dark brown wig of jaw-length curls. She had one elbow leaning on the table while her hand rested under her chin. The blond teenage boy sat with both elbows on the table with one hand wrapped around a glass of water. Their actual positioning was a little off and unnatural, but the idea was easily understood.

"Look, Mommy. That man is melting," said a young boy, around eight years old, holding his mother's hand as they walked along the sidewalk.

And he was right.

A pool of melted flesh-colored wax had collected on the pavement next to the man-figure's foot. His hand, resting on his thigh, had several droplets running in lanes off his fingertips.

His forehead had begun to sweat as well. Another drop of wax traveled down from his hairline and hung off the sharp angle of his jaw.

"He certainly is," the boy's mother said. She stopped walking and leaned in for a closer look. "It's a great advertisement for the museum, but I'm not so sure it was a good idea to set it up in direct sunlight on such a warm day."

"Who are they?" the boy asked. "Doesn't the wax museum always do statues of famous people? What are they famous for?"

"I have no idea. We can Google it later though." The woman tugged on the boy's hand and began to walk again. "Right now, we have a birthday party to get ready for."

A smile spread across the boy's face. He turned and waved goodbye to the display. "Bye, wax people."

Just then the woman-figure's hand fell from its position under her chin and slammed onto the table. The plates jumped and clanged from the hand's impact.

The boy's eyes grew wide. "Mommy, did you see that? The lady tried to wave back at me."

The woman stopped and turned to see what her son was going on about.

The woman-figure's head suddenly dropped into a strange angle. Then her shoulders drooped and her entire upper body began leaning to one side. Farther and farther to the side until the figure toppled from the chair and landed in a heap on the pavement.

The woman with the boy gasped. She knew it was just a prop, but the way the figure had dropped with such a heavy thud unsettled her greatly.

"I should go inside and tell the manager that their display is falling apart," she said.

With the boy in tow, she made a wide circle around the prop not wanting to get too close. She reached the front door of the museum and had her hand on the doorknob when the man-figure toppled over behind her. He landed hard with a loud thud as well.

The woman yanked the door open and stuck her head inside. "Excuse me. Your wax people out here are melting," she called out to anyone who would listen.

A young woman with a short brown pixie cut walked over from behind a desk. "Hi, can I help you with something?" she said in a chirpy voice.

"No, but I can help you. Your wax people are melting. Someone needs to bring them inside. It's too warm out there. They're already falling over."

"I'm sorry, but I don't understand. What wax people are

you talking about?"

"The ones out here on the sidewalk." The woman held the door open wider and nodded her head toward the street corner. "Those wax people."

The young pixie stepped closer and peered out of the open door. "Oh my gosh!" she said, covering her gaping mouth with her hand. "Where on earth did that come from?"

"They're yours, aren't they? I mean, they're wax statues. In front of a wax museum." The woman let out a nervous chuckle. She had known something was not right about that display. She had felt it deep within her gut and saw it in their odd posture and expressionless faces. She clutched the boy's hand tight and drew him closer to her.

As both of the women stood there dumbfounded, a crowd had begun to form.

"Whoa, I thought those were dead bodies at first," a young man on a bike said as he passed by the scene. "I couldn't even tell that they were wax." He laughed and peddled down the sidewalk and off the curb.

"They *do* look like dead bodies, Mommy," the little boy said, staring down at the sidewalk.

"That man was just kidding, sweetie."

"But that one's bleeding." The boy pointed his finger at the man-figure that laid in a heap in front of him.

The mother leaned forward to examine a crimson smear on the figure's temple. By that time the wax had nearly completely melted away on that area of the face. "That can't be

5

blood."

On closer inspection she could clearly see that, not only was it most definitely blood, it had originated from a deep head laceration on the side of the figure's head.

The woman gasped and jumped back.

She stared down at the man lying on his side on the pavement. It was an extremely awkward position. A true wax statue would have broken into pieces if it fell onto that hard of a surface. Or at the very least, flattened one side of its face and body.

This figure displayed limbs that had moved into different positions upon impact, but still appeared every bit intact. His eyes were open and staring blankly ahead.

Her eyes shot over to the woman-figure sprawled on the concrete on the other side of the table. Her limbs were bent in unnatural positions as well. Her lips parted as if she were about to speak and the woman knew for a fact they were not like that earlier.

Wax statues didn't have movable jaws…but bodies that were coming out of rigor mortis did.

The woman straightened and pulled her son close. "Someone call 9-1-1."

♦♦♦

Less than ten minutes had passed before a squad car pulled up to the curb, lights flashing and sirens blaring. A moment later, another one. Four uniformed officers, two from each car, exited their vehicles and snaked their way through the crowd.

One had a roll of yellow crime scene tape and immediately went to work. He rolled out a perimeter that encompassed the entire street corner, wrapping the tape around every signpost that stood.

Another officer directed the crowd, nudging them backward and outside of the new yellow boundary. He then whipped out a small notebook and a pen.

"So who discovered the bodies?" he said to no one in particular.

"Everyone," someone replied back.

"Okay, then who got here first?"

No answer. Just every single person looking around at each other and shrugging.

"Can someone please tell me what happened? Anyone. From the beginning."

The woman and her young son stepped forward. The young pixie followed.

"Thank you," the officer said as he flipped open his notebook. "Now let's get started."

In the meantime, the remaining two officers walked over to the two downed bodies and knelt next to them. They stuck out their necks and moved their heads around for different viewpoints, careful not to disturb anything. Look, but don't touch. That was Crime Scene 101 when it came to murders.

One officer stood and walked over to the teenage boy

figure that was still positioned at the table. He circled around it, peering into the figure's face. "Homicide will be here any minute," he said. "Along with the Medical Examiner."

"Now *that* is an exam I'd be interested in seeing," said the other.

"Man, they are completely covered with wax. They look just like statues."

The other officer knelt down even lower and looked directly into the dead woman's eyes.

"She's wearing green contact lenses. That's why her eyes look so weird."

A loud clatter rang out as the torso of the remaining teenage-figure collapsed and his face smashed onto the table.

"What the fuck!"

Every officer and every member of the crowd jumped at the startling noise.

"What the hell was that? Why did he move?" The officer's eyes widened with horror.

The little boy stepped forward as far as his mother's grip would allow.

"They're melting."

Chapter 1

The delightful aroma of freshly baked chocolate chip cookies wafted out of the open oven door. The woman sucked it all in with a deep inhale before reaching in to retrieve the piping hot cookie sheet.

"Ow, ow, ow," she whimpered as the hot pan burned right through the thick quilted fabric of her oven mitts. After dropping the pan onto the stovetop, she took off the useless mitts and threw them hard into the back corner of the kitchen counter.

Joanie Jackson, a short plump woman standing only a smidgeon above five feet, was a real estate agent. And a damn good one at that. But even she, with her vast experience and irresistible charisma, could not sell the Donovan house for its full value.

The multi-million-dollar mansion had been sitting on the

market for two full years without any takers. At that price, the buyer pool was small. And of those few that had the millions to shell out, none were willing to take on the Donovan House of Horrors.

Everyone knew what had gone on in that basement. True Crime had even filmed a documentary starring Andrew Donovan's torture chamber where he had mutilated and butchered five women. Those murders happened seven years earlier, but the stories hadn't slowed down. Actually, they had increased, mainly due to that same documentary that aired several times a year on as many anniversaries as the media could conjure up.

The anniversary of the first murdered girl, of the last murdered girl, of his arrest, his acquittal, and of course, his death.

Tyler Maddox's killing spree hadn't helped matters either. It was that whole father/son dynamic. Nature vs nurture. The media ate it up. The problem was that Tyler was not Andrew's son. But God knows he had wanted to be.

He had idolized the man. Wanted to be just like him. He would have tried to be Andrew's partner in crime had he known what he was up to. And after his death Tyler had tried his best to carry on his legacy.

But Andrew didn't make Tyler into a serial killer. It wasn't a matter of nurture winning out. A person doesn't just start killing and mutilating women because his role model did. No, Tyler was already broken inside. He was born that way. Andrew was just the key that unlocked the door.

Whatever horrors that had occurred in that house and affected the men that lived there, it was in the past and Joanie Jackson was doing her best to keep it there. It was Open House Day and she was going to sell that house if it killed her.

With that thought, she kicked her Martha Stewart vibe up a notch and flipped the cookies onto a two-tiered decorative plate and placed it aesthetically amongst the fresh flower heads scattered across the island counter.

"Don't mind if I do," an approaching voice said.

She looked up and a big smile spread across her face. "Spencer. I'm so glad you're here. I've got a good feeling about today."

"Oh yeah?" he said as he snatched a warm cookie off the plate. "Think we'll get any offers?"

"I'm betting we'll have a slew of visitors today interested in this house."

"I hope you're right because I sure am ready to get rid of this thing and get on with my life."

Joanie widened her smile as she looked at him. She had known the Donovan family for over a decade. After all, she had sold them this house back when Spencer was just a small boy. He had suffered through enough psychological trauma in that house to last him ten lifetimes. Where Tyler Maddox had longed to be Andrew Donovan's son, Spencer actually was, and the horrifying acts his father committed right under his nose was something he would never be able to get over. Add to that the fact that his father was then dissected on top of the dining room table and it's a wonder Spencer had any sanity left at all.

But he was strong and determined to spend the rest of his life making up for his father's sins. And that determination brought him straight to the Montgomery County Police Department and the youngest officer to ever make detective. He had a big heart and a brain to match and spent his days finding justice for the families of murder victims all over the county. His father's demons still haunted him though. Joanie could see that just by looking into his eyes. But he had a healthy outlet for it and it usually resulted in murderers behind bars. She was proud of the man he had become, especially amidst such harrowing circumstances.

Both she and Spencer looked up at the ceiling as heavy footsteps could be heard above them.

"Is someone here?" Spencer asked. "I thought the Open House doesn't start for another half hour."

"There were two couples waiting in the driveway when I pulled up this morning," Joanie explained. "Like I said...there's going to be a lot of interest today. I let them go ahead a start their own self-guided tour while I finished prepping. I surely wasn't going to keep them waiting outside." Her shoulders bounced as she laughed heartily. "One of them is likely going to be the new owners of this magnificent house. I can feel it."

With Spencer's help, she spent the next few minutes putting the final touches on her prep. Two glass pitchers of ice water, one with floating lemon slices, the other with cucumber.

The flower arrangements were exquisite and the brochures she had picked up from the printer that morning were fanned out in a perfect semicircle at the end of the granite counter. She was ready, and with impeccable timing.

The front door opened and a half dozen more potential buyers entered into the foyer. Joanie beamed as she watched their eyes widen and their mouths fall open as they scanned the massive foyer with its glistening white ceramic floor, elegantly arched doorways, and towering curved staircase.

Of course, she would have to disclose the unfortunate events that occurred there, but she had a new angle she was working on, and she was confident that she would have these buyers eating out of her hand in no time.

"Come in, come in, please," she sang out as she waved the group into the kitchen.

Another couple entered the foyer from the staircase and joined the crowd making their way toward Joanie. She recognized them from earlier and motioned them aside. "Well, what did you think of the upstairs? Grand, isn't it? And how about that view from the master bedroom?"

"Very nice indeed," the man answered. "I'm not sure about the statues though. I hope they don't come with the house." He laughed heartily. "Very lifelike, but an unusual staging choice if I'm being honest."

Joanie's forehead wrinkled as she pondered over what the man had said. "Statues?" She looked at Spencer for an explanation.

He shrugged. "I didn't set up any statues. I did a walk-through last night after the cleaning crew left and everything was in good shape."

Spencer and Joanie immediately set off through the incoming crowd toward the foyer and up the staircase. Spencer took the steps two at a time with Joanie's short legs trying to keep up.

Their dramatic exit caused a few visitors to follow which then led to the entire crowd following each other up the staircase, without even a clue as to why.

Spencer froze when he reached the top, staring down the long hallway which led to his former bedroom. Two figures stood directly outside his bedroom door.

Joanie caught up to him and let out a loud gasp. She remained behind him, peering around his shoulder. "What in the world?"

Spencer began walking slowly down the hall toward the two figures. It was a man and a woman. The man had his back to him and was leaning against the wall with an outstretched arm. As he got closer, the woman came into full view. She had short black wavy hair and wore a white terrycloth bathrobe. The right side of her body leaned against the wall while her hands crossed her chest, clutching the collar of the robe.

A painful knot began to twist inside Spencer's stomach. He stepped closer until he stood right next to both of them.

Joanie hadn't followed. She remained at the end of the hall with both hands over her mouth. The crowd of visitors had gathered behind her, but thankfully did not approach.

Spencer leaned in close, studying the male figure top to bottom. He was dressed in jeans, sneakers, and a long sleeve shirt. He had blond spiky hair, but it was fake. A wig. He glanced at the woman and recognized her immediately. Their faces wore no expression.

On closer inspection, he spotted three nearly invisible lines running from the tops of their heads up and disappearing into the ceiling. He circled around slightly, allowing the sun to shine fully and unobstructed through the two-story foyer, illuminating the hallway. Now they gleamed in the sunlight. Dozens of transparent lines rising off the figures and disappearing into the ceiling like spider webs. Actually, puppet strings was a more accurate description. Life-sized puppets.

Next, his eyes went to the walls. Colorful jigsaw puzzles set in large poster frames. They were similar to the ones that used to hang there years ago. Similar, but not the same. Whoever created this scene had intimate knowledge of his house and the people that used to be in it.

His attention went back to the figures in front of him. There was something about them that made his skin crawl. He looked deep into the woman-figure's eyes. They were odd. The irises were green, but the pupils were a light shade of gray instead of black. Not what you'd expect from a mannequin or a puppet or whatever she was.

He raised his hand and poked her cheek with his fingertips. It was soft yet firm. Wax.

The pressure must have been too much because as soon as he drew back his fingers, the woman crumbled to the floor. The numerous strands of fishing line stretched and then ripped through her scalp, shoulders, and wrists.

Spencer stared in disbelief at the figure at his feet. The wax had cracked and pieces had broken off where the lines had ripped through. And underneath...lifeless flesh. As a homicide detective, Spencer had seen his share and he was certain. They weren't statues. They were corpses.

Chapter 2

Rebecca black lay sprawled out on her sofa enjoying the first half of a lazy Sunday. It had been five years since her friendship with Tyler Maddox ended with her injecting an empty syringe into his carotid artery. It was one of several traumatic events in her life and she had only just recently been able to sleep through the night without seeing his murderous face.

The brutal mutilation and murder of her sister by Andrew Donovan was the grenade that blew her life to pieces. She took her pound of flesh, literally, from her sister's killer, but not before unknowingly inviting a second homicidal psychopath into her circle to take his place. Tyler Maddox had picked up where Andrew left off and did far more damage to her sanity.

Rebecca was a fighter though. She had never realized how much so until faced with her own death. She has had two brushes with obsessed serial killers and managed to survive them both. And now, Andrew is dead and Tyler was currently serving out multiple life sentences at the Savage River Correctional Institution in Western Maryland. Admittedly, she had at least some pleasure knowing she had left her mark. The massive stroke she had forced upon him had landed him in a wheelchair requiring daily physical therapy just so he could learn to wipe his own ass.

She was glad he had survived. She wanted him to suffer and live out the rest of his life in a prison cell. Death would have been too easy…too nice. Although, it wasn't as if she hadn't tried. She honestly hadn't known exactly what would happen when she injected that air embolus into that bulging artery in his neck. But she knew that whatever followed wouldn't be pretty. Suffice to say, it wasn't.

And through it all, her record remained clean…at least by her definition. She had not killed anyone. Yes, she had tortured and mutilated Andrew on his dining room table, but it was his ex-wife that ripped the heart from his chest.

As for Tyler, he was actually more alive than she would have liked. Her blood boiled when she heard of the cushy private cell he had received in exchange for that exclusive tell-all True Crime interview. But at least he was behind bars and locked away from the rest of the world. She was finally able to let her guard down and move on.

And that was exactly what she did. She moved out of the townhouse where Tyler had beaten her unconscious. Where her blood had stained the walls, upstairs and down. And where Michael had been slaughtered in the parking lot just outside her door.

She moved from a townhouse full of blood and terror to a small cape cod full of love and happy childhood memories, tucked away on a quaint peaceful street in Silver Spring. Her grandmother had passed away many years earlier and Rebecca couldn't bear to lose the house she had practically grown up in. As a single career-driven woman, she wasn't ready to live in it herself at the time, but she knew someday she would. Her mother had allowed her to rent it out as long as she took care of all the headaches that came along with being a landlord. She did so with joy since it gave her ample excuses to drop by in between renters and breathe in the nostalgia. And now, with her life taking new turns, she couldn't think of anyplace else she'd rather be. Even La Croix was having a hard time drawing her away.

La Croix D'or, the upscale French restaurant that she owned in downtown Bethesda, was her pride and joy…but even her time spent there needed to change. Over the years she had been slowly turning the Head Chef duties over to Peter, her young and eager French apprentice and dear friend. She had taught him everything he knew about cooking French cuisine and he had seamlessly stepped up and taken over the kitchen when she needed him to.

Rebecca had focused her attention on the business side of the restaurant which allowed her much better hours and a lot less stress. Although, she could never fully abandon the kitchen. Cooking was her first love and she still popped in several times a week to work with Peter during a hectic dinner rush.

However, her current love was sitting on the sofa next to her. Rebecca lifted her cramped legs and stretched them out across the lap of the man at her side. Taking a backseat at the restaurant had opened up her schedule and gave her the time for all sorts of things, such as a social life.

She had met Adam Callahan three years ago at a Taste of DC festival in downtown Washington. An entire block closed down to cars so that fifty of the region's best restaurants could set up their tents and tempt customers with their appetizing dishes. Rebecca was proud that La Croix D'or had a spot on the roster every year since she had opened almost a decade ago.

The streets were packed with thousands of hungry pedestrians and Adam had emerged from the crowd toward La Croix's tent to check out what she was offering. He was a ruggedly handsome mountain of a man. Standing 6'2" with a thick powerful build. His blue flannel shirt stretched across his broad chest and shoulders and his jeans did a lousy job of hiding strong muscular thighs. His short light brown curls bounced ever so slightly as he strode up to her table. *Cowboy* was the first thought that entered her mind. It was confirmed the moment he opened his mouth.

"Good afternoon, ma'am," he said with a soft subtle drawl. "Whatever you're cooking over here sure smells good."

He flashed her an enticing smile and that was all it took. Rebecca was lost.

She showed him over to the open grill topped with cuts of duck breast and assorted sausages. The meat sizzled and a swirl of smoke drew up the mouthwatering aroma and spread it throughout the street. Rebecca leaned in, closed her eyes, and waved her cupped hand to direct more of the delicious smell up toward their faces. Adam leaned in as well.

When she opened her eyes, he was right there, just inches from her. They both stared at each other silently, neither pulling away. It should have been awkward, but it wasn't. It was clear that he wasn't there for the sausages, and that she wasn't actually trying to sell him those sausages. Yes, it happened just that quickly. Without logic or reasoning or even knowing his name, Rebecca had already mentally planned out their future together.

Their eyes remained locked as they both continued to inhale the delightful aroma. His lips curved into a smile and hers followed. And then it happened. His face suddenly contorted and he jerked away and began spinning and slapping himself on the front of his jeans. The hem of his untucked shirt had dipped into the flames of the grill and he was now officially on fire. His attempt to pat the fire out was proving ineffective so Rebecca turned and grabbed the first liquid she saw, her 32-ounce tumbler of iced sweet tea. She popped off the top, ran around the grill, and poured the cup's entire contents onto the fireball hovering on the zipper of his jeans.

The fire was doused immediately and Adam was left with a large wet spot on his crotch. Rebecca held her breath as she waited, empty tumbler in her hand, for his reaction. He looked down at himself and laughed. She let out a sigh of relief and grabbed a fistful of napkins from the table. For a moment she considered taking advantage of the perfect flirtatious moment that lay right in front of her, but she let it pass. She handed him the napkins and let him dry himself off without success.

After the fire fiasco, Adam spent the rest of the day hovering around La Croix's tent and Rebecca kept feeding him skewers of andouillette and chorizo to keep him there. Although, Rebecca knew it wasn't the grilled meat that was keeping him there. And even after he had been stung twice on the stomach by bees attracted to the sugared sweet tea that had dried onto his crotch, he still stayed.

She learned that he taught biology at the community college and coached wrestling at the high school and that he was, in fact, a cowboy, having grown up on a farm in Oklahoma. He was sweet and funny and had an adorable smile that knocked her off her feet.

Peter had taken over serving the customers and would occasionally send an approving glance her way. At the end of the night, Adam had helped her and Peter pack up and had become a regular fixture in her life ever since.

A year ago they were married, and today Rebecca browsed baby furniture on her laptop. They had just found out a few days earlier that the baby growing inside of her was a girl. After trying for almost a year, it wasn't until she had slashed her hours at the restaurant even more that it finally happened. Her body knew what it was doing.

She was barely showing. A loose shirt could easily hide the small bump on her abdomen. But she had no desire to hide it. She wanted the world to know that Rebecca Black finally had a bright innocent future in front of her. Life was good...mostly.

Adam still had no idea about her past trauma. The fact that she was, in a way, lying to him, weighed heavily on her conscious. Even though both the Andrew Donovan case and the Tyler Maddox case made national headlines, Adam only moved to Maryland a few years ago and had been spared the daily conversations that surrounded the murders. He had heard about them in passing from students or through flipping channels and landing on one of the many documentaries covering the story, but he didn't know the details and he didn't care to. It was just one more thing that Rebecca loved about him.

She had wrestled with telling him the truth on countless occasions, but the truth always lost that match. She never wanted Adam to know what had happened in her past. She wasn't the same person now as she was back then anyway. And she would never give up the way he looked at her. Never. He gazed at her with wonderment and desire. As if she was the perfect blend of intelligence, strength, and beauty. With Adam, she was able to start over with someone who didn't look at her with pity for what she had gone through...or fear for what she was capable of.

Rebecca peered over her laptop screen at him. Her legs were still draped across his lap and his hands mindlessly rubbed her feet as his eyes remained glued to the Orioles game on the television. Yes, he was indeed a keeper.

She still had a few more hours before she planned on dropping into La Croix to help Peter with the Sunday dinner crowd. And now she was trying to decide whether to spend those hours picking out a crib online or taking her husband to the bedroom. It was a good dilemma to have.

Through all of the darkness that had fallen upon her life, Adam was the ray of sunshine fighting through the clouds.

Decision made.

Chapter 3

Spencer Donovan donned a pair of latex gloves and followed the woman over to the steel examination table. Dr. Elizabeth Adler had been the Chief Medical Examiner for the state of Maryland for over two decades. She was tough, but also brilliant. Her office in Baltimore was a good distance from his Montgomery County precinct, but his friend, Ed Harmon, had given him valuable advice when he first made detective—Drive, Observe, and Develop. Make the drive to Baltimore, observe the autopsies, and develop a good working relationship with Dr. Adler.

Harmon knew what he was talking about. The breaks in several of Spencer's toughest cases had come from brainstorming sessions with Dr. Adler while she dug into various corpses. Spencer found her experience and insight to be instrumental in solving murders.

"I finished the woman not long ago," she said, motioning to another exam table with a sheet-covered body form on it. "The wax was relatively easy to remove and didn't appear to damage the tissue at all. She's still a Jane Doe as of now, but I sent her prints and photos to the lab. Hopefully, she's in the system and an ID will come of it."

"And dental?" Spencer asked.

"Don't expect much from those x-rays. Her teeth were just short of perfect. No bridges, crowns, or even a root canal. I doubt she even had braces as a child."

Spencer let out a low groan. "No one is missing her yet either. No current missing persons reports have come in that would match."

"Give it time, trust the process." She stepped up onto a stool which elevated her short stature well above the exam table and the male wax-covered body lying on top of it. She pulled a magnifying headset over her cropped silver hair and switched on the attached headlamp. Spencer stood across from her on the other side of the table, careful to stay out of her light.

"Wow," Spencer said as he took a good long look at the body. The torso, arms, and legs appeared just like any other body about to be autopsied. But the hands, neck, and face were covered with a thick layer of flesh-colored wax. It looked plastic, as if the body had been dismembered and the head and hands were replaced with those of a store mannequin. He shuddered.

Spencer remembered the way the body had appeared when it was posed in the hallway of his house. A long-sleeved shirt had covered the arms to the wrists. All of the exposed areas had been waxed while the areas underneath the clothes had remained seemingly untouched.

"How was the woman? Was there any assault?"

"None that was detectable." Dr. Adler scanned the body with her magnifiers as she answered his questions. "The killer likely redressed her in the robe she was found in, but she might have been wearing the undergarments all along."

"Why do you think that?"

"Just a hunch really. Based on experience." She gently lifted the man's wrist and studied the area where the fishing line had ripped through his flesh. "Often when a killer redresses a victim, either ante- or post-mortem, he does so for a reason. He would have picked out something special. Our Jane Doe was wearing yoga briefs and a worn-out sports bra underneath that robe. It's doubtful her killer would have specifically chosen that set."

"You think he could've nabbed her last night while she was out for a run or something?"

"Or leaving a gym or studio. Or neither. Work-out clothes are comfortable and many women wear them just to lounge around the house. She could have just been making a trip to the 7-11 for some milk when he grabbed her. We may never know. But the point I'm making is that it's likely her clothes were stripped only to accommodate the robe and not for sexual reasons. The robe is important to him."

"Yes, it is," Spencer agreed.

Dr. Adler ducked her head and peered over her lenses at him. "That sounds like you know something that I don't. Spill it."

Spencer met her eyes. He hadn't planned on disclosing his theory yet. Not until he had more to go on, but when Dr. Adler tells you to do something, you damn well better do it. "You know there's another one like this, right?"

"If you mean another posed scene consisting of wax-covered bodies...yes, I am aware. Word gets around when a case this unique pops up. I already sent in a request to the DC medical examiner to have the files sent over for comparison." She removed her headset and held his eyes locked in an intense stare. "But what do *you* know about it that no one else does?"

"I didn't know anything when the first one happened a month ago. I just thought it was a freaky case like everyone else did. But then, when these two showed up in my house..." He waved his arms at both of the bodies. "I know who they're supposed to be. This is Tyler. And that, over there, is Rebecca." His eyes widened and his tone intensified. "Whoever did this was mimicking a scene that happened in my house back when my dad was dating Rebecca."

Dr. Adler's mouth fell open. "Rebecca Black dated your father?"

Ugh, Spencer had forgotten that there were only a select few who knew of Rebecca's undercover work as her alter ego, Amanda White. He had never seen anything shock the doctor, but he sure was seeing it now. "It's a long story and I'll tell you all about it some other time."

"You bet you will," she said with a stern nod. "Go on."

"It wasn't until after I saw the scene this morning in my own house that I was able to recognize the earlier scene that happened in DC There was a young blond guy, a woman with short dark hair, and a man with black hair. That was Tyler, Rebecca, and my dad all sitting around the table having dinner. I remembered when that happened. I was up in my room and didn't come down because I was so pissed at my dad for bringing yet another new girlfriend home."

Dr. Adler was speechless. Probably for the first time ever, especially on her own turf.

Spencer continued. "Whoever did this knows specific details about what went on in that house during the time Rebecca was around. Maybe she's being targeting again. Or maybe *I* am."

Several awkward moments passed before the doctor put her headset back on and resumed her exam. "We *will* talk more about this before you leave here," she said as she glanced up and narrowed her eyes at him.

"Yes, ma'am."

"The cause of death was blunt force trauma to the head. Here, I'll show you." She slid her gloved hands along the body's temples and underneath the edges of the blond wig. It detached easily from the scalp and she placed it in a large evidence bag.

A massive indentation the size of a softball sat above the ear in the temple area. The skull had been crushed and small bone fragments protruded through a blood-matted section of dark hair, previously hidden by the former hairpiece.

"The cause of death of the woman was strangulation. She had bold ligature marks along her neck," she said. "But I'm inclined to think that was not seen as an effective method in this male victim. Perhaps the attacker is of small stature and needed the blitz attack to subdue the male. The woman is petite and strangulation wouldn't have been as much of a problem."

Dr. Adler continued her preliminary scan of the head and neck area. Suddenly, she leaned in close and zeroed her headlamp in on the body's neck. "I knew I saw something," she said, the corners of her mouth slowly lifting into a confident smile.

Spencer watched without saying a word.

Dr. Adler reached for the instrument tray and picked up a pair of long forceps. She pierced the wax under the left ear and removed a two-inch section. As she held it up in front of him, Spencer could clearly see the three hairs embedded within.

"That's good, right?" he asked.

"Very good. From the color and coarseness, I can tell you right now that this is not the victim's hair. And they did not just fall onto this body. They were pressed against the wax before it was completely dry and then ripped out. The root tag is still attached."

"So, DNA."

"We'll send it out and hope for a hit," she said, bagging the wax section. "And along with that..." She leaned in, removed another small piece of wax, and held it up with the forceps. "...we'll add in this partial print." She dropped it into a separate bag. "I love it when they get sloppy."

Dr. Adler spent the next few minutes studying the waxy parts closely in case there were any other prints or hair present. There was none to be found. The little bit she had found would have to be enough. She then returned the forceps to the tray and, with both hands, carefully began lifting large sections of wax from the body. It removed easily, just as she said it would.

Working her way upward, she was able to clear the wax from the face in two halves. Spencer tilted his head to get an upright view of the victim's face. He gasped as Dr. Adler removed the final piece, stumbling a few steps backward in shock.

"Oh, my God! I know him!"

Dr. Adler's head shot up.

"It *is* Rebecca that's being targeted again."

"Well then, who is *this*?"

Spencer's head lowered and his eyes closed. "That's Peter."

Chapter 4

Rebecca stood in her bathroom, bent over and upside-down, blow-drying her freshly washed hair. The lazy half of her Sunday was over and it was now time to get something accomplished. As much as she would have loved to stay sunken into her sofa, she always went in to La Croix to help out on Sunday evenings and Peter would be expecting her.

She flipped her hair back and stood upright, her long blonde waves cascading across her shoulders. She startled momentarily seeing Adam suddenly standing next to her, examining himself closely in the large mirror.

"Babe, you think I should grow a beard?" he asked, rubbing the curled hairs poking out of his jaw.

"What?" Rebecca turned off the hair-dryer.

"School's out for the summer. I think I should grow a beard."

"You kind of already have one."

"No, a real one. A thick, bushy, manly beard," he said, his voice lowering into a deep growl.

"Well, I do think you're super sexy when you're scruffy. But I don't really want to be sleeping with Wolverine so how about you skip the thick and bushy and go for trimmed and studly instead?"

Adam nodded, still admiring his copious amount of facial hair.

"There are clippers in the cabinet under the sink," Rebecca said, in case he misunderstood her earlier statement.

He smiled and winked at her before dropping to his knees and opening the cabinet doors. His arms disappeared inside as he rummaged through five years of odds and ends that had somehow ended up in there. Rebecca replaced the hair-dryer with a brush and ran it effortlessly through her soft honey hair.

"What a mess down here," Adam said as he pulled out old hair spray cans, broken curlers, and a slew of other miscellaneous items, and dropped them onto the bathmat beside him. "Ooh, what are these?" he asked, pulling out a gallon Zip-loc bag full of prescription bottles.

"Those are my mom's leftover meds from her knee replacement."

He opened the bag and began rifling through it. "Anything good?" He looked up at her from the floor with a sly smile on his face. "We could have quite the party depending on what's in here."

"It's nothing we'd be interested in." She chuckled as she took the bag and tossed it back into the cabinet.

"Then why are you keeping them? Huh?" He smiled up at her and eyed her suspiciously. "Aren't you supposed to throw away leftover medication?"

"You just never know if you'll need it down the road."

"Zombie apocalypse?" he said, nodding.

"You know me so well." She leaned down and planted a kiss on his forehead. "We might need antibiotics. Even expired ones."

He laughed. "What are you going to do if you live your entire life and never get to see zombies?"

"Then I'll make sure that when I die, I'll come back as the *first* zombie. And then you'll have to put me down."

He gasped. "Babe, you know I could never do that." He grabbed the clippers and stood up. "I would keep you as a pet though."

"Aww, you would? That's so sweet."

"Yep, I'd have to barricade us inside to make sure you could never get out." He set the clippers on the counter and moved behind her. Resting his chin on her shoulder, he looked into the mirror at the both of them. "And then I'd take care of you like a little puppy." He raised his hand and began stroking her hair.

She turned, took his face into her hands, and kissed his lips. "You'll make the best apocalypse partner."

"You got that right." He leaned in to continue the kiss, but was interrupted by Rebecca's phone ringing on the sink. He looked over at it and saw it was Spencer calling. "Ugh, Spencer, you're killing me." He handed her the phone and moved back over to his side of the sink.

Rebecca kissed his cheek and stepped out into the hallway. "Spencer. Hey. It's been forever since I've heard from you. I was actually just thinking about you guys the other day." She barely took a breath as she rambled on. "I've been wanting to get together with you and your mom because I haven't seen either of you for months...and Lily. What have you been up to?"

"I had an Open House today to try and sell my father's home," he said when she finally gave him the opportunity.

"That's great! I think you'll feel much better when you can finally sell it and move on." Truth be told, she wanted him to sell it so that she could move on as well. She still carried around a lot of trauma and bad memories from that house.

"Yeah."

She heard in the defeated tone of his voice the trauma he also carried. Was he remembering what his father had done to those women in that house? Or was he remembering what *she* had done to his father? Whichever it was, it didn't need to be discussed between them. They knew that both of them had become totally different people while in that house...and that was Andrew Donovan's doing. She was confident that Spencer would agree with her on that.

"Have you had any offers?" she asked, trying to keep the conversation light. "How many lookers showed up? Did they seem interested? They'd be stupid not to. That house has so much to offer. The lot alone is pristine, and the pool—"

Spencer cut her off. "I need to meet with you."

"Okay. I'm about to head into the restaurant now, but I'm free tomorrow if you want to have lunch."

"I need to see you today. Now. It's urgent."

Chills ran up Rebecca's spine as she felt the seriousness in his voice. She rarely heard that voice coming from him and nothing good ever came with it. This was not what she had in mind when she said she wanted to get together with him and catch up. But when Spencer played the "urgent" card, it meant he was serious and she had to go along with it.

"Can you meet me in a half hour at the Four Corners Starbucks?" he asked.

"Sure." She wondered why he wouldn't just come to her house since she lived five minutes from Four Corners, but she didn't question it. Perhaps he didn't want Adam involved. And since Spencer was actively trying to sell the Donovan mansion, it was a good assumption that whatever he wanted to talk about had something to do with that house—the house and the time in her life that Adam knew nothing about. Now she understood what was going on.

"I'll call Peter and tell him to start without me."

Chapter 5

Rebecca stepped through the door of Starbucks and waited a moment for her eyes to adjust from the bright sunlit outdoors to the comparably darkened room of the coffee shop. She breathed in the aroma of fresh brewed coffee. Scanning the room, she spotted Spencer sitting alone at a corner table. His eyes downtrodden and his expression strained, he hadn't yet noticed her.

She headed first to the section of the counter that held the mobile and online orders. Spotting the iced quadruple-shot espresso with her name on it, she quickly snatched it up. She had planned ahead knowing she was going to need something strong to stay focused and help Spencer with whatever he was going through.

His slouched, beaten-down posture told her to forego the usual hugs and pleasantries. She quietly slid into the table's open seat and waited for him to speak. Her heart pounded in her chest as she felt a growing sense of dread emanating from the man sitting across from her.

"I have bad news," he said. "Actually, horrible news."

Rebecca stared at him with wide eyes. "What is it?"

"There was a double murder at my father's house sometime last night."

"Wh—, wha—?" Her mouth fell open. It was such an unexpected statement that Rebecca didn't know how else to respond.

"The bodies were found this morning during the Open House," he went on.

Rebecca continued to stare at him, unblinking and mouth agape.

"They weren't killed in the house. They were killed elsewhere and then moved to the house and posed." He took a breath and then resumed. "They're similar in methodology to another murder case that happened in DC a month ago."

"That's crazy! But why the house? Was it because you were going to be showing it today?"

"These bodies were definitely meant to be found quickly and with the utmost shock value. Successful on both counts."

"Were they found in the basement? Cut up? Diamonds?" Rebecca leaned forward, keeping her voice low. "Was it because of your father?"

"Unfortunately, I think it has more to do with you than him. Actually, it has everything to do with you."

She jerked back into her chair, her eyes growing even wider. "Me? Why do you think that?"

Spencer reached down into the shoulder bag at his feet and pulled out a folder. He placed it on the table and flipped it open. His fingers thumbed through several photographs before selecting one and sliding it across the table to her. "This was the first murder scene from DC a month ago. Three victims found staged outside of Madame Tussauds wax museum. They were covered in wax to resemble statues as if they were props from the museum. Probably a hundred pedestrians passed by before anyone noticed anything strange about them."

Rebecca picked up the photo and studied it closely. The scene was so eerie, but he was right. They did look like statues. She probably would have walked right past them too.

"Does any of it look familiar to you?" he asked her.

She glanced up at him and then back down at the photo. "I don't know. Maybe. I mean, there's something familiar about it, but I can't really place it."

"What about the figures themselves? Do any of them look familiar?"

Her brow furrowed as she concentrated. And then it hit her. It had been many years since she had worn that look…that dark curly bob. That female figure sitting at that table was Amanda White. *Her* Amanda White. She swallowed down the lump that was creeping up her throat.

"Go ahead. You can say it." Spencer urged her on.

"That's me. Back then." She took a big gulp of her coffee to soothe the dryness that had overtaken her throat. "Which means that man is supposed to be your father and the other one...Tyler." She dropped the photo onto the table.

Spencer leaned forward and tapped his finger on it. "This scene actually happened. Do you remember it?"

She nodded, almost catatonically. "It was the first day I met you. I was there for dinner. And Tyler was there too." She spoke in a monotone as if her brain had shut off all emotion and switched to autopilot. "You were so angry and refused to come down. So, it was just the three of us."

He reached into the folder and pulled out another photo. "This was taken this morning."

Rebecca's eyes lowered as he slid the photo in front of her. She gasped loudly.

"This happened, didn't it?" he asked her firmly. "This exact scene. It happened, right?"

Once again, she nodded. "It happened right there. Right outside your room." Her eyes stung as the tears came. "I stayed over and when I woke up, Andrew had gone to work. I thought I was alone in the house." She swiped at the tears that crawled down her cheeks. "I was alone in the house and I went snooping. In your room." She looked up at him, her face drawn tightly with guilt. "I'm sorry, Spencer. At the time, I thought you were the one killing those women."

He gave her an understanding nod.

"I heard the front door shut and knew someone had come home so I ran out of your room and down the hall...and Tyler was there. He blocked me, just like he's doing in that picture. Exactly like that. He wouldn't let me pass." She covered her face with her hands, remembering how she had felt that day...that moment. "He was terrifying."

"Were you wearing a robe like that? The one that's in the picture?"

She nodded. "It was your father's. It looked just like that."

"You and Tyler were the only people that knew that this happened. The only ones that knew the details."

"He must have talked about it to someone. He couldn't have done this. He can't even walk. And he's in prison!" she said forcefully, garnering a few glances from nearby customers.

"No, he didn't do this. But he must know who did." Spencer collected the photos and slid them back into the folder. "Either he's using someone to get your attention...or he has divulged enough information about you to someone else and they're doing it on their own."

"Oh my God," Rebecca cried as she leaned over onto the table and buried her face in her arms. "I can't believe this is happening again." Her voice was tearful and muffled as she remained face-down in her sleeve.

"Unfortunately, I'm not done," he said in a tone so soft she barely heard him. "There's more."

She lifted her head, her eyes red and swollen.

"I just came from the ME's office. The male victim from this morning..." He paused and took a deep breath. "...it's Peter."

"What?" She popped up. "My Peter? That's impossible. He's at the restaurant prepping for the Sunday dinner rush. I just called him earlier after I got off of the phone with you."

"Did you actually speak to him?"

"I left a voicemail." Her voice trembled as she spoke, barely above a whisper. She pulled her phone out of her back pocket and dialed Peter's number. The phone shook in her clenched hand as she counted the rings. Then his voice came on the line. The same voice she had heard earlier, reciting the same recorded message. She hung up and dialed again...the restaurant this time. It rang four times before her own pre-recorded voice came through the receiver.

"I'm so sorry, Rebecca."

A flush of heat rushed upward into her cheeks. Then all color drained from her face and the flush was replaced with an icy chill that ran back down throughout her body. She couldn't speak. And then she couldn't see. And then she toppled off her chair and onto the floor.

Chapter 6

The last thing Rebecca ever thought she'd be doing that day was riding with Spencer to Baltimore to identify Peter's body. Yet, here she was doing just that. Peter didn't have immediate family in the area and his uncle, who Rebecca first co-owned La Croix with, had gone back to France several years ago.

Rebecca had always thought of Peter as family—like a favorite nephew—so it wasn't a surprise when he listed her as his emergency contact. But she never in her wildest dreams thought she'd ever be called on it. She turned toward the side window as the tears streamed down her face.

Spencer's foot remained heavy on the gas pedal and Rebecca watched as they passed each vehicle one by one. She couldn't help but think of all the lives that had been lost around her. At times the word "cursed" even entered her mind. Her life over the past seven years mimicked that of a massive train wreck, with each car just piling up behind the other until all that was left was a huge pile of rubble. Seven years of bad luck. Truer words had never been spoken.

But it wasn't *her* fault. It was Andrew Donovan's fault. It all began with him. It all began when he murdered her sister. If only she could go back in time and stop Sara from ever meeting him, then none of the rest would have ever happened. But that also meant that she wouldn't have put herself out there to him, drew him in, and slit his throat. Not literally, of course, but close to it. If he hadn't killed her sister, Rebecca never would've hunted him and he might have lived to pile up even more bodies of innocent women.

And at some point, Tyler, the idolizing psychopath that he was, would have discovered Andrew's secrets and teamed up with him. What a deadly duo they would have been. Who knows how many women would have been mutilated and murdered if she hadn't stepped in.

Yes, it all began with Andrew. The death of Sara, which in turn led to her father's death. The rise of Tyler Maddox, which led to the death of Michael and the near-death of Harmon...twice. And now Peter.

But if she were to take away Sara's murder the overall death toll would have likely been higher. However, it wouldn't have been anyone she knew. It wouldn't have been anyone she loved. It was a selfish thought, but she couldn't rid herself of the feeling. She wasn't the type of person that could shoulder all of her personal losses with that "greater-good" mentality. She just wasn't strong enough. She couldn't lose anyone else.

She felt Spencer looking at her as she swiped again at the falling tears. It was at times like this that her friendship with Spencer felt a little strained. After all, he was the son of the man that shredded her life to pieces. He shared DNA with the man that, in one way or another, had been the root of every painful trauma and loss in her life. As her previous train of thought had deduced, without Andrew, even Peter would have still been alive.

She sensed the guilt that Spencer felt in times like this. She saw it in his stiff posture. She heard it in his silence. *For the sins of the father, the son must pay.* She didn't blame him, but she knew he blamed himself. But what could he have done really? He was just a kid—an only child with a missing and presumed dead mother. His father was all he had in the world. He couldn't pull the trigger himself. He needed someone else to do it for him. Rebecca was that someone.

As for their current predicament, dead bodies were piling up at a record-setting pace. Tyler was responsible somehow. She needed to go to the prison, to see him face to face. She needed to beat him within an inch of his life until he told her who was killing all these people…until he told her who killed Peter. Or maybe she would just kill him once and for all and be done with it. If she would have done that five years ago, none of this would have even happened, she was sure of it. It was a moot thought anyway. He was safe at the prison and out of her hands.

Her mind drifted back to Peter. She admitted to herself that the thought of assassinating Tyler had distracted her from the reality of the situation, if only for a short time. But now she was on her way to identify Peter's dead body and no homicidal revenge fantasy was able to shut her mind off to that.

After nearly an hour, Spencer finally broke the silence within the car. "We need to talk about getting you some police protection. If you truly are the object of this killer's obsession, which you appear to be, then you're at risk. And so is anyone you care about…meaning your husband. We need to hide both of you away until this case is solved."

She didn't respond. Instead, the wheels turned in her head of how that conversation with Adam would go. Adam didn't even know that she knew the notorious Tyler Maddox. He surely didn't know that she was the root of his killing spree. Harmon had worked his ass off swiping her real name off the records and replacing it with a legal alias. Even the True Crime documentary that recounted the Gut Wrencher's reign of terror listed a *Paula Green* as Tyler's inspiration and downfall. The name, Rebecca Black, was nowhere to be found in relation to Tyler Maddox or The Gut Wrencher. Adam had no idea who he was married to.

"Look, I know you're overwhelmed so I'm not going to push you right now. But you don't just have yourself to think about this time. You have Adam to think about. You have that baby in your stomach to think about."

Her head snapped in his direction.

"Give me a break, you don't hide it *that* well."

She relaxed back into her seat. This killer already murdered someone very close to her and it wasn't a coincidence. Adam would be the next likely target. She couldn't accept Spencer's protection offer without telling Adam everything. Her pulse raced whenever she thought about doing that. But he'd be in more danger if he walked around carefree and unsuspecting.

On the other hand, she knew information like that would change their relationship forever. He would never look at her the same, not after knowing she was broken and partially psychotic herself. He would be scared of her. But he would survive and wouldn't be the next body she'd have to identify on a morgue table. If she took the protection offer and came clean to Adam then all three of them would be safe, including her baby.

Spencer pulled over to the curb along West Baltimore Street and stopped in front of the building marked Forensic Medical Center. "Dr. Adler is waiting for us," he said.

She sat still her seat, unmoving.

"You don't have to decide right now. Take some time to think about it." He unbuckled his seatbelt and turned off the engine. "But don't take too long. There's a killer out there and I have a strong feeling that he's just getting started."

She wasn't ready yet. The drive needed to be longer. Her mind was filled with so many questions. She wasn't ready to face Adam with any of it, but more importantly…she wasn't ready to face Peter.

Chapter 7

Rebecca shivered at the sudden drop in temperature as she followed Spencer into the cold storage locker. A strong chemical odor singed her nostrils. It wasn't pleasant at all, but she reminded herself that she was in a room full of death and the smell could have been so much worse. She took a moment to survey the space. She had been there before, in that same room. It was where she had identified her sister's body years earlier.

She looked at the short plump woman that stood along a wall full of square stainless-steel cooler doors. Dr. Elizabeth Adler. She had been there too, although Rebecca didn't remember even speaking to her back then. That entire day was just a blur now. It was the worst day of her life…or so she thought. How could she ever have imagined that things would get so much worse that she would find herself back there again identifying yet another senselessly murdered loved one?

She crossed the room and stood opposite Dr. Adler.

"I'm so sorry we have to meet again under these circumstances," Dr. Adler said.

Rebecca nodded. "I'm sorry too."

Dr. Adler pulled open the middle drawer of the cooler. A platform, seven feet in length, rolled outward and filled the void between them. A white sheet lay across the table with the unmistakable shape of a body underneath. Spencer appeared beside her and placed a comforting arm around her shoulder.

They had offered to have her do the identification through a monitor, but Rebecca had insisted that she see the body in person. She second-guessed that decision now. Her legs were weak and rubbery. A slight dizziness swept over her and she swayed forward. She reached down to grab the edge of the table to steady herself, but instead, her fingers wrapped around a surface too soft to be steel.

She looked down at her hand clutching the cylindrical form of the arm that rested beneath the sheet. She jerked it away and took a step back.

"Let me know when you're ready," Dr. Adler said.

"Go ahead," Rebecca responded. "Let's get this over with."

Dr. Adler pulled back the sheet, exposing the head, neck, and shoulders.

Rebecca's heart dropped into her stomach. It was Peter. There was no doubt. She gazed down at his face. The warm Mediterranean color that usually tinted his skin was nowhere to be found. He was pale and cold and lifeless. She had expected him to look like he was sleeping. She had hoped so much for that. But he didn't look asleep. He looked dead.

Her eyes narrowed in on the large crater in his skull where the killer had caved in his head. She couldn't look away. She had expected the flood of tears to return once she saw his face…but they were nowhere to be found. Her sorrow had been replaced with rage. Lightning hot, hulked-out fury.

Her fire had been lit and it was a fire that, once it got going, it didn't stop until justice was served…until vengeance had been taken. Her hands curled into fists at her sides and fingernails dug deep into her palms. A rush of searing heat filled her cheeks. Her nostrils flared as she struggled to take deep breaths to avoid screaming and flipping every table in the room.

Spencer must have felt the change in her demeanor. The hand he had rested on her back suddenly began to knead her shoulder while, at the same time, gently pulling her backward and away from Peter. He gave Dr. Adler a nod and she pulled the sheet up over Peter's face.

With both hands on her shoulders, Spencer turned her and slowly nudged her across the room to the double doors leading to the hallway. Behind them, Rebecca heard the drawer slide back into the wall and end with the clunk of the cooler door closing.

She hadn't even reached the exit before the decision was made. There would be no police protection for her. Hiding was not an option. She would find Peter's killer and make him pay. Whoever he was, he had no idea who he was dealing with. She was Rebecca-*fucking*-Black and she *would* get her vengeance in blood.

♦ ♦ ♦

The inside of the car was unnervingly silent on the drive back to Four Corners. Spencer glanced over at Rebecca. She sat in the passenger seat, upright and stiff, gazing seemingly spaced-out at the telephone poles whizzing past her side window. He wasn't fooled though. He could almost see the wheels turning in her head, no doubt thinking of all the ways she wanted to kill whoever did that to Peter.

Rebecca was like a time-bomb, only no one knew the count. She could go off at any moment…in an hour, in a week, in a month. She was volatile when pushed and it was his job to diffuse her before she did something stupid.

It was unspoken between them at the time, but they both knew Tyler was involved somehow. How could he not be? The details laid out in those crime scenes were only known to Tyler and her. Of course, he could have just told the stories to someone. A fellow inmate about to be released. A crazed fan that visited him in prison on Saturdays. But it was quite a stretch to think someone would commit such elaborate murders of innocent people just because of a story.

Tyler would have had to give them detailed instructions, as well as offer something in return. Respect? Glory? Notoriety? Whatever it was, Spencer was confident that Tyler was one hundred percent controlling the murders and he was also certain Rebecca was thinking the same thing.

"I want to go talk to Tyler," she said, as if reading his mind.

"Absolutely not."

"Can you really stop me?"

Spencer drew a deep sigh. "Probably. But I'd rather not go through all that red tape."

She stubbornly crossed her arms across her chest and sat staring straight out of the front windshield.

"Look, Tyler is a manipulative sociopath. His whole motive for everything is to get your attention and terrify you. He's literally the definition of a criminal terrorist."

"Except that I'm not afraid of him. He failed on that front."

"Yeah, it always starts out that way, doesn't it? And then, further down the road, all that bravado is replaced with blood and gunshots and beatings and carnage. And finally, terror." Spencer glanced over at her looking for agreement, but her stubbornness would not allow it.

He refused to give up. "You'd be giving him exactly what he wants if you go see him."

Her head slightly tilted in his direction.

"He's been alone in prison for five years without a single visit or line of communication from you or me or anyone from his past life," he continued. "His own father won't step foot in that prison out of disgrace for what his son had become. Of course he would find a way to rile you up by killing all those people and force you back into his life. For Christ's sake, Rebecca, he's doing exactly what my father did!"

Spencer's chest heaved as his voice boomed throughout the vehicle, his knuckles white on the steering wheel. Rebecca was at full attention now.

A moment or two passed and he loosened his grip. He took a few slow deep breaths and tried again. "You'll be giving him exactly what he wants and then he would have won."

Spencer knew she would rather die herself than let Tyler think he had reigned superior over her. But it wasn't enough. He needed to give her something. A task. A job to occupy her so that she was involved, but without being on the front line. She just needed to feel that she was doing something.

"I'm going to meet with Dr. Adler again in the morning," he said. "By then, she would have received all of the autopsy reports from the ME in DC regarding that first scene. Come with me and we can all go over them together."

"I can do that."

"In the meantime, I'll contact the warden and have all of Tyler's visits, phone calls, and mail correspondences monitored from here on out. If he plans another murder scene like the others, they'll intercept the plan and determine who else is involved." He waited as she mulled over his proposal. "Cool?"

"Okay," she finally answered. "I'll stay away from him for now. But if this doesn't work and more death scenes from *my* life turn up, I swear—" She cut herself off as her voice hit an infuriated pitch.

"Deal." He had no idea what he had just agreed to, but whatever it was, it bought him some time.

The bomb that was Rebecca Black stood diffused…for now.

Chapter 8

The dashboard clock read 9:03 and it was officially nighttime. Rebecca couldn't stall any longer. She had sat in her car after Spencer had dropped her off for nearly two hours. And now, parked in her own driveway, she was still having trouble taking that next step.

Adam would be inside watching tv, not even expecting her home for at least another hour. As far as he knew, she was still at the restaurant helping Peter with the dinner service. Her eyes stung as the burning tears returned. For the latter part of the day, her emotions had toggled back and forth between heart-crushing sorrow and fuming rage.

Admittedly though, her grief-stricken state was exactly where she needed to be at that moment. In another minute or two, she would walk through her front door and tell Adam where she had been. And her face of fury that had reared its ugly head earlier needed to remain in hiding...at least where Adam was concerned.

She would tell him about Peter's death. And she would break down into a sobbing mess while doing so. That much would be sincere. But she couldn't tell him about the murders. She couldn't tell him that Peter's head had been bashed in so some sick freak could play "dolls."

Yes, she would tell Adam about Peter's death. But there would be some liberty taken with the details.

She took a deep breath and exited the car, taking as much time as she could to reach her front step. Inside, Adam was exactly where she knew he'd be, lying on the sofa in front of the television, oblivious to the buckets of tears she would soon rain down on him.

"Hey, babe," he called out to her. "You're home early."

She took another deep breath, inhaling the scent of aromatic lemongrass that hung in the air. He had been busy while she was gone. The house sparkled and smelled clean and invigorating. She almost couldn't bear to take another step for fear of soiling the aura with her dirty lies.

He popped up from the sofa and crossed the room to greet her. The genuine smile that so often adorned his sweet face began to dissipate as he closed the distance between them. By the time he had reached her, it was gone and replaced with a growing look of concern.

"What happened?"

She opened her mouth to speak, but all that came out was a whimper. He placed his hands on her upper arms and her forehead fell until it landed on his chest. His thick arms wrapped around her and pulled her in close, squeezing her tight. It was exactly what she needed. Her arms went slack and she collapsed into him. With one quick movement, he lifted her off her feet and carried her back to the sofa. He sat and pulled her on top of him, cradling her while her body trembled and shook against him.

"What happened?" he softly repeated.

"Peter's dead." The words came out weak and broken.

Adam lurched backward and looked down at her.

"When Spencer called earlier. That was why." She sniffled and wiped her nose on her sleeve. "He needed me to identify the body."

"How did it happen? How did Spencer know about it? Wait a minute, Spencer is a homicide detective. Oh my God, was Peter murdered?" His eyes were wide as he rattled off his string of questions.

Rebecca shook her head, cursing how perceptive Adam could be sometimes. She pulled her head from his chest and looked up at him. Then she buried her face into his neck. She couldn't look him in the eye while she filled him with lies.

"It was a car accident. Early this morning. The police on the scene found his phone and he had me listed as his emergency contact. The officer recognized my name and called Spencer first." Her breathing had slowed and her voice leveled out as she spun the story in her head. "I guess it was good that they called Spencer. I wouldn't have been able to handle news like that coming from a stranger."

"I'm so sorry. Oh my God, I'm so sorry you're going through this." He squeezed her so tight she thought her bones would shatter. But it felt so good. "Why didn't you call me earlier?" he added.

"I couldn't. Not over the phone. I couldn't even speak." She wiped her eyes and lifted her head. "It's just so horrible. He doesn't even have any of his family over here. His dad, who I used to own La Croix with, moved back to France years ago. Peter stayed and I promised I would take care of him." The tears returned because it was the truth. She had made that promise. "I still have to call and tell him. I told Spencer that it needs to come from me. But how am I going to tell him that his son is dead?" The reality of the situation hit her again and she could speak no more. Her body convulsed and she began to cry uncontrollably.

He rocked her gently for what seemed like forever until her tears finally slowed.

"You need to eat something," he said. "You're exhausted. You need some fuel." He slid her off of his lap and laid her on the sofa. After pulling off her shoes, he grabbed the fleece blanket from the arm of the recliner and laid it on top of her. He pulled the blanket up to her neck and tucked it in snug around her sides. "I'll be right back."

Rebecca watched him as he disappeared into the kitchen. She felt awful. Her stomach was tied up in knots and physically throbbing with pain. Some of it was hunger as Adam had suspected. He knew her well…to some degree. But most of the pain was shared between the distress of losing Peter and the guilt of being dishonest to her husband.

Early in their relationship, she had simply omitted certain events of her past. She didn't consider that to be lying. But now, there was no explaining it away with deceptive semantics. She was a liar.

It killed her to keep him in the dark, especially since Spencer had pointed out that he could be the next target. She vowed it would never get to that though. It had been a month between the murders and Tyler's every interaction was now being monitored. Her and Spencer would find the fucker responsible and put him away before Adam even had a clue. He would never have to know.

She sat up and pulled her knees to her chest as Adam returned from the kitchen with a plate of grilled cheese sandwiches, crisp and golden and cut into triangles. Dropping in next to her, he pulled her legs across his lap in their customary lounging position. He handed her a sandwich and she devoured it in seconds. He handed her another.

"What happens now?" Adam asked gently.

"Well…first, I have to call his father. Tonight. And then his body will be flown back to France to be with his family." She swallowed hard and roughly shook her head to clear it. "I'm closing La Croix temporarily. Out of respect for Peter. It would seem so wrong to have it open and serving customers without Peter there. He had become the backbone of that place. All of the staff will be mourning and it's just not right for them to feel they have to work in that state. We'll do a small get-together to honor him and then I'll give them all a paid vacation for a couple weeks."

"And then?"

"And then I'll find a new head chef and reopen. There are several viable prospects that are already working in that kitchen. Peter and I trained them ourselves. Promoting from within would be what Peter would have wanted."

"Well, this may sound selfish, but I'm glad you're not considering going back to running the kitchen full-time. I like having you around." He smiled and reached over and stroked her cheek with the backs of his fingers. "And our little one will like having you around also." His hand slowly dropped to come to rest on her abdomen.

"You don't have a selfish bone in your body, Adam Callahan." She covered his hand with hers. "And I like being around too."

"Good." He slid out from under her legs and stood. After a kiss on her forehead, he carried the empty plate out of the room. He stopped just before turning the corner. "Let me know when you're ready to make that phone call. You'll feel better if you do it soon and don't wait on it. I'm here if you need me."

She smiled as he disappeared into the kitchen. She didn't deserve him. And he didn't deserve a life as messed up as hers. She should have let him go back when she first met him. Back when she first misled him about who she was and what she had been through. But she couldn't. It hadn't taken long for her to become utterly addicted to Adam Callahan and the light that shone within him. Since pulling him in, her own light had begun to shine through. But now the darkness was knocking at her door, demanding to be let back in.

She would open that door, but only for a moment. Only long enough to do what needed to be done. And then she would be happy spending the rest of her life making it up to him…without him ever knowing what she was making up for, of course.

Rebecca stood and plucked her phone out of her purse. She opened the front door and stepped out into the warm spring air and into the front seat of her car. She wasn't going anywhere. She just needed privacy. She couldn't risk Adam hearing what she had to say to Peter's father. It would change everything.

Chapter 9

It was 9am on Monday morning and Rebecca and Spencer were back in Dr. Adler's office. Spencer had since talked to his captain and successfully secured Rebecca a spot on the investigative team as an official consultant, complete with an official temporary ID badge.

Captain Vance had wanted her under witness protection, but Spencer went to bat for her and convinced him that, if she was working the case with him then she could be under his protection. Vance couldn't deny that she could be of some help to the investigation.

At the moment, the three of them were elbow-deep in paperwork. Dr. Adler rifled through the autopsy details of both murder scenes, Spencer scoured the police reports, and Rebecca sorted through pages of witness statements.

Dr. Adler began the discussion with the results of the second, most recent crime scene, since that was the autopsy that she had performed herself. "A single partial print and several hairs containing root tags were found embedded in the hardened wax of the male victim," she said.

"Neither the print nor the DNA from the hair root was found in any of our databases," Spencer added. "However, those samples will be compared to a suspect, when one arises."

Dr. Adler flipped to the next page of the lab report and donned the purple reading glasses hanging around her neck. "The wax coating that covered the hands, neck, and face area…as well as the sternum, lower legs, and feet of the female victim, was paraffin."

"Candle wax," Rebecca said. "A hobbyist could easily get it from any craft store. Or they could just melt down existing candles."

The doctor nodded. "I'm actually quite surprised that it held up as well as it did for the purpose it was used. Paraffin is a hard wax that is brittle and cracks easily if it's applied as a thin coating, such as was done here. Yes, there were several layers built up to create thickness, but it wasn't nearly as thick as I thought it would need to be to stay intact while the bodies were moved."

"Well, if I remember correctly, it did shatter like glass as soon as those bodies hit the floor." Spencer glanced up and caught Rebecca's eye. He lowered his head apologetically. "But none of that is really important anyway."

Rebecca was trying to remain professional, but she couldn't get it out of her head that Peter was one of the *bodies* they were referring to. Although, she needed to detach herself emotionally from that fact. Spencer would throw her off the case just as fast as he had put her on it if she let her personal feelings get in the way. She straightened her shoulders and lifted her head. "Was the same type of wax used in the first crime scene?"

Dr. Adler flipped open a folder and pulled out the lab report that she had received from DC that morning. "The first *scene*—I'll just refer to it as that—was created just short of one month ago. There were no prints, hair, DNA, or any trace evidence found that would have shed any light on who killed them, where, and why."

"Well, I think we know the why," Spencer interjected.

"We'll get to that." Dr. Adler peered over her glasses at him. "The wax used in this first scene was different than that used in the second. It had been altered and mixed with vegetable shortening."

"Why?" Spencer asked.

Rebecca perked up. "I bet it softened the wax and made it easier to work with." If there was one thing a great chef knew, it was her cooking oils. "The shortening would have made the wax smoother and more pliable. Less cracking around the joints." She paused and waited for an interruption. When none came, she continued on. "The mixture would have provided a little bit of "give" so if the bodies moved slightly, the wax wouldn't crumble into pieces. It could be spread over the skin like icing. And, it would slow the drying time just enough so that prints and hairs wouldn't get stuck in the wax while it was hardening. I'm sure that's what went wrong at the second scene. It just dried too fast and caught him off-guard. Ripped the hair right out of his head."

Dr. Adler looked impressed and gave Rebecca an approving nod.

"Then why change it?" Spencer asked. "If it worked so well the first time, why change it? If you have a formula that works, stick with it."

"But it didn't work so well the first time." Rebecca skimmed through her pile of witness statements. "Apparently, they started melting in the sun. Candle wax on its own has a melting point of over 100 degrees Fahrenheit. Probably closer to 120 or so. Mixing in some shortening or oil will soften the wax, but it'll also lower the melting point. This first scene occurred in the middle of April. It was an unusually warm sunny day, but not hot. Although, it was warm enough that once the 'scene display' lost its shade and the direct sunlight hit…it didn't stand a chance."

"But the house was temperature-controlled," Spencer said. "Melting wouldn't have been a problem."

"Does it really matter though?" Rebecca asked. "Why he used this wax or that wax? The point is that he killed these people and waxed them up to put on some kind of sick show. Why does it matter that he altered it a little the second time?"

"It matters because we need to know if the same person created both of these scenes."

Rebecca straightened. "You think two separate people did this?"

"Has to be," Spencer said. "Or a team, at least. It would be extremely difficult for one person to pose and rig the bodies alone. There had to have been at least two people working together."

At that moment, Dr. Adler stepped in and offered her two cents. "The first scene on the sidewalk was forensically blank with no trace evidence. The atmosphere at the house was significantly more accommodating, although the scene was far sloppier with regards to the trace left behind and the sub-par waxing process. It's as though the hallway scene was the first attempt and then they got smarter and did the Tussauds scene. But we know that is not the order in which it occurred."

"How about a teacher/student kind of thing?" Spencer offered up his new theory. "Teacher does the first one and student messes up the second one. Then the only major change in method is the harder wax and we can just base that on them not wanting to risk another melting fiasco."

"Very plausible. And for the sake of moving on, let's accept, for now, that both of these crime scenes were created by one team consisting of at least two people," Dr. Adler said.

The three of them spent the next hour searching through all of the documents while trying to compare and organize them into something comprehensible. They shot theories back and forth to each other, but it seemed like they were simply moving in circles.

"Let's shift gears for a moment and focus solely on the first staged scene," Dr. Adler said as she leaned back in her chair and removed her glasses. They dangled from the thin chain around her neck. "Location. Was it a forensic countermeasure to cross state lines with the murders? Both of the inspiring events happened at the Donovan house. I understand that only one would have been possible to stage there due to the fact that it would instantly become a crime scene and compromise any future break-ins, but to jump all the way over to DC…did they want to officially say hello through the museum itself?"

Rebecca nodded. "It definitely added an effect. How many people walked by thinking they were a display set up by the museum? How many tourists took photos of it on their phones? How many posed with the bodies, not knowing that they were actually rotting corpses underneath?" She shuddered. "And then to have them all start moving and crumbling to the ground at the same time? I'd say that's pretty dramatic."

"You think they were watching?" asked Spencer. "Sounds like it might have been pretty entertaining to a couple of psychopaths. Pop some popcorn and do a little tailgating out of the back of their truck?"

"They would have had a truck," said Dr. Adler. "Or van or some kind of large vehicle to transport three bodies and the furniture used for the display."

Spencer looked back down at the police reports in his lap. "What about cameras? Did any security or traffic cams catch them setting up? It had to have taken a while. Did any camera catch a large vehicle approaching or leaving that area that morning or the night before?" He flipped back and forth through the pages. "Damn. Never mind. The cameras in front of the museum and across the street were vandalized two days prior and had not been replaced yet. The other cams don't have a line of sight because of the angle." He turned another page and continued. "Traffic cams showed numerous big box trucks and delivery vans coming and going in that area beginning around 4am, which would be normal because the food businesses get their deliveries then."

Meanwhile, Rebecca had been scouring her own pile of reports. "It says here that several witnesses saw a big blue tarp or tent set up outside of the museum. The type of barrier you'd put up if there was construction or painting going on. So, early morning people were walking by while the scene was being put together behind the tarp."

"How long does it take rigor mortis to set in?" Spencer directed his question to Dr. Adler. "Could they have transferred limp bodies, set up the tarp, and then pose them and wait for them to harden?"

"Rigor starts to set in approximately two to four hours after death. It begins with the facial muscles. That is usually the indicator that it's starting."

"And how long does it last? Is it normal for them all to come out of it at the same time?"

"I don't think that was part of the plan. It likely wasn't their intent to have them all come out of rigor that quickly. After all, it ruined the display and ended the show. And that kind of timing is not something one could predict to that degree, especially between three different subjects. Yes, it's possible for rigor to only last a few hours, but it can also last an entire day." Dr. Adler raised her eyebrows and shook her head. "It's quite amazing actually, that the timing was so perfect. Perhaps the heat had something to do with them all coming out of it at the same time. But beyond that..."

"So, they killed three people, drove them to the museum, set up the tarp, transferred them covered up somehow, and then posed them and waxed them all within a couple hours?" Rebecca asked. "Wow. That's impressive."

"And organized," Spencer added. "And also, rather incredible that this was the first time these guys used this MO, but I searched through databases nationwide, and nothing even remotely similar to corpses posed as statues has come up. Anywhere. If this was their first murder, they did one hell of a job with it."

"How about the wax?" Dr. Adler asked. "They used a good amount of it and it likely came from one source given that there were no variations in color or tint. Caucasian-flesh-colored across the board, regarding both scenes."

"Boom." Spencer reached across the doctor's desk and dropped a printed receipt. "Michael's Arts and Crafts in Rockville filled an order for three buckets of Georgia Peach paraffin wax on April 9th. Twenty pounds each and the 9th puts the pick-up around a week before the first murders. Unfortunately, it was picked up in person and not delivered to an address. And paid for online with a Michael's gift card, so no name either. Organized."

"Sixty pounds? That sounds like a lot of wax. Is it though?" Rebecca tried to picture the amount in her head.

"Hmm…" Dr. Adler did so as well. "For the second scene that was found at the Donovan house, I removed eight pounds of it from the male victim and eleven pounds from the female victim. There would surely be enough in the other forty-one pounds to work over the three victims from the first scene, even allowing for spillage and mistakes." Her eyes scanned the documents in front of her. "Twenty-three total pounds removed from the DC victims. And that batch was cut with shortening so less of the purchased wax was actually used."

"Okay, so only the exposed areas of the face, neck, and hands were waxed," Spencer said. "When did they do it? Before they posed them? After? During?"

"And how and where did they melt and mix twenty-plus pounds of wax and shortening?" Rebecca added her questions.

"The wax could have been applied earlier, soon after death," Dr. Adler said. "It didn't cover any large joints other than the neck so they could have posed them after the waxing as long as the heads didn't move too much."

"Or have a big pot cooking over sterno or a portable stove while they were waiting for the rigor to set," said Rebecca. "And then just paint it on, pack up, and leave. It wouldn't take long at all to dry and set." She let out a low groan. "It's pretty sick any way you look at it."

After several hours of going back and forth between the mountains of reports from both crime scenes, they finally had a better understanding of the method itself, but were still no closer to any leads on the team's identity or whereabouts. They were at an official Dead End, pun intended.

Rebecca exhaled forcefully. "Now, can I go see Tyler?"

Chapter 10

An enormous corrections officer, with a bald head and a face to match, walked Rebecca down the long empty hallway that led to Tyler Maddox's cell. She smoothed out the white, silk, dress shirt that hung loosely over her athletically curved frame as she trailed a step behind the CO.

Her outfit choice had been an endless deliberation with herself. She had not looked Tyler in the eyes since his sentencing in court and it upset her that she had to make a strategic decision on her attire at all. But she needed something from him. Information…a confession…even an accidental slip-up would do just fine. Therefore, she had to play the game, and the first step was to direct the blood away from his brain and into those neglected areas that tended to cloud his judgement.

Tyler had always been perceptive. He would have known exactly what she was up to had she shown up with her bosom spilling out of a low-cut crop top. Thus, she opted for the unbuttoned collar that showed off her neckline and the faded blue jeans that showed off her ass. She remembered what his weaknesses were.

The hallway was quiet. Not what she had expected at all from a prison full of the most hardened criminals in the state. Although, she was not getting an accurate representation of what the rest of the prison was actually like.

Tyler had worked his magic while negotiating his price for that exclusive True Crime interview. It was to air live on primetime television and the network was willing to pay to make it happen. The cost—a cushy corner cell in a segregated wing reserved primarily for celebrities, politicians, and the super-rich. The wing had been dubbed *Park Avenue* and residing there kept him out of general population and out of harm's way. As pretty as Tyler was, he would have been passed around the block at every opportunity had he not made that deal. His inability to physically fight back wouldn't have helped his situation either.

The corridor was missing the blinding white fluorescent lights that illuminated the rest of the prison. Instead, a soft warm glow lit up the area as if the walls were adorned with fiery lanterns. They weren't, of course, but it was the feeling she got. It was just another soothing perk that accompanied money and fame.

There were only cells along one side. The other side was a concrete wall, but painted a pale yellow, for comfort of course.

It probably had a name like *Pineapple Delight*, or something like that. Rebecca rolled her eyes. *They call this prison?*

She slowed, glancing inside each of the cells as she passed by them. Several were empty and slightly darkened, while others appeared lived-in although their occupants weren't home. She turned her wrist and peeked at her watch. Almost noon. At lunch, perhaps? She was happy to not have to deal with curious ears during her visit with Tyler. She had no idea how the conversation would go, but she did know that it would require discretion.

"You have a visitor, Mr. Maddox," the CO said as he reached the end of the hall and stopped in front of the last cell. He then grabbed a folding chair from the corner and set it up in the middle of the hall, facing the wall of iron bars that made up Tyler's front door.

As Rebecca strode the last few feet, the inside of Tyler's cell slowly came into view. A corner lamp projected a shaft of light that stretched beyond the cell wall and illuminated the empty chair like a spotlight. Being that it was a corner cell, two of the walls housed windows that let in the day's natural light as well.

It was a large room and not at all what she had expected. A twin bed with a colorful bedspread sat in a back corner. Definitely not standard prison-issued linens. A tall privacy shade hid what likely was a toilet and sink in the other corner.

Penciled sketches and acrylic paintings, likely art therapy projects, adorned nearly every inch of exposed wall. Some depicted trees, birds, and landscapes. Others were of a girl with long blonde hair and emerald green eyes. She recognized herself immediately. He was still in love with her. Or he stared at her face while he fantasized about gutting her. Probably a little of both.

The decor rounded out with a bookshelf desk along the wall nearest the cell door. Dozens of opened letters on assorted stationary lay scattered across the surface.

In the center of the cell was a generous, open space. And inside it, a metal wheelchair containing the man that had killed Peter. Indirectly or not, he was responsible. She was certain of it.

It took a moment for her presence to fully register to him, but it was clear once it did. His eyes widened, his posture straightened, and a disturbing smile crept slowly across his face.

She met his eyes and held them as she walked toward the empty chair and stood assuredly in front of it. Her blood boiled inside her, yet her face wore no expression.

"You need me to stay?" the guard asked.

"No, thank you." Her eyes remained locked on the crippled man in front of her. "I can take it from here."

"Okay. I'll be right down the hall. Just holler if you need anything."

"Thank you, sir."

He gave her a nod and was on his way.

Rebecca remained standing while they sized each other up, neither addressing the other just yet. Aside from the wheelchair, he still showed small signs of the stroke, but they were minimal. A slight droop to his left eyelid. His left arm was at an odd angle, lying in his lap as if he didn't use it much. The guard informed her that he was unable to walk on his own, but could stand for short periods if he had something to hold on to.

"I can't believe you're here," he said.

She sat down in the chair and cross her legs. "Believe me, I can't either."

"You look amazing! Glowing, even."

She shifted in her seat and crossed her forearms across her abdomen, not sure if his last comment was perceptive or coincidence.

His eyes scanned her from head to toe. "Although, you could do without that planet-sized rock on your finger." His face scrunched into a scowl, but then quickly released. "Is that why you haven't come to see me until now? Is Loverboy boring you? You need a little taste of the dark side?"

She rolled her eyes and huffed at him.

He laughed. "Seriously, though. You know you're the only thing that keeps me sane in here. Just look around." He waved his arm at the drawings of her that papered the walls of his cell. "I've missed you so much. I think of you every day and of what we had together."

She had let him ramble on just to see where his head was at. She noticed a very slight slur, especially when he began talking fast. A sign leftover from the stroke.

"What on earth are you talking about? What we had together? You tried to kill me, Tyler!"

"No." He shook his head. "That's not true and you know it. I just needed to subdue you temporarily until I tied up another loose end."

"You mean *kill* that other loose end. Harmon."

"Let's not get off-track here, Rebecca. The point I'm making is that I could never hurt you."

"Oh, really? My concussion said otherwise."

"Well, I'd say you did far more damage to me." He gestured at his wheelchair.

"You got off easy."

He smiled and folded his hands in his lap. "We're quite a pair, aren't we?"

"Let's cut the shit, Tyler. I know it's you." She glared at him. "I know you're responsible for the murders that are happening."

A hearty laugh broke out from deep within his throat. "You've got to be kidding me. Look at me. How could I possibly be out killing people while I'm strapped to a wheelchair inside a prison?"

"So, you *do* know what murders I'm referring to."

"It's been all over the Washington Post news feeds. Gimme a break, I'm not entirely out of touch with the outside world."

"Oh, I don't think you're out of touch at all. In fact, I think you're the one that's pulling the strings."

"How do you figure?"

"I've seen the photos. I recognize those scenes. And you and I are the only people alive that were there and know the details."

"Do you have the photos with you? They haven't released them to the press so it's a little difficult to know exactly what you're going on about."

"Boy, that would serve as some serious fantasy material for you, wouldn't it?"

"Maybe you're the one responsible. After all, you are the *only* other person that has the details. And you're currently *not* in a prison cell. Perhaps you set this all up just to have an excuse to come in here and raise hell." His smile hung smug and arrogant on his lips. "Admit it. You miss me."

Heat rushed through her cheeks as her hands balled into fists. They stared into each other's eyes with completely contrasting expressions. It was a stand-off.

A rattle of metal from down the hall finally drew her attention away. A young woman in a white apron, obviously a contracted kitchen worker, pushed a wheeled cafeteria cart in Rebecca's direction. The woman parked it against the wall a couple cells down and grasped the lone steel tray. She carried it the rest of the way to Tyler's cell, giving Rebecca an absent-minded nod without actually looking at her.

She slid the tray into the food slot of the cell door and left it balancing on the slot shelf. Naturally, Rebecca was interested in what culinary masterpieces the prison chef cooked up for his

V.I.P. Park Avenue inmate. After one peek at the mounds of mashed food that filled the separate tray compartments, Rebecca grew nauseous. Delayed morning sickness? Or disgust at what was intended to be a human diet?

Although he hid it well, passing off his crooked smile as a sly smirk, some of Tyler's facial muscles had never regained full function. It had led to severe chewing difficulties and choking hazards on more than a few occasions and resulted in him being fed like a baby. *An insult to babies everywhere*, Rebecca thought as she subconsciously rubbed her abdomen.

A pile of orange, a pile of white, and a pile of gray. Carrots, banana, and chicken in gravy, perhaps? And a tall cup of possibly cranberry juice to wash it all down. The smell of warm salted meat rose in the air and drifted toward her. Her stomach turned over as the nausea kicked up a notch.

"Bon appétit, Mr. Maddox," the kitchen woman said.

Tyler turned his head and winked his right eye at her.

She responded with a shy smile before sauntering back down the hall toward her cart.

Rebecca was surprised, but not overly so. Tyler had always had a flirtatious way about him. She never should have underestimated him. Even in a place like this and in his debilitated condition, he still had the women swooning. It made her even sicker just thinking about it.

Tyler rolled himself over to the slot and awkwardly pulled the tray through with one hand. He set it on his lap and held it steady with his other arm.

"I know you want to blame me for all of this," he said as he loaded up his spoon with gray matter. "And it's possible that I could be just a teeny bit responsible. But the truth is..." He waved his spoon at the pile of open letters strewn about his desk. "...I can't stop those that are willing to kill in my honor...just as you were never able to stop me from killing for you."

Rebecca shot up from her chair, toppling it over in the process. She took two quick strides until her face stood just inches from the wall of iron bars. "Oh, but I *did* stop you, Tyler."

"Did you really though?" His eyes bore into hers. They became dark and sinister right in front of her. It was the same look he had back when he had squeezed her throat in his hands and repeatedly slammed her head into the hospital floor.

An icy chill traveled up her spine as the horrific memories from that day flooded back. He was right. She didn't stop him. He was still killing and he was doing it while hiding in plain sight. Her worst nightmare was starting all over again.

She knew he saw the fear in her eyes. His smirky smile proved that. She should have listened to Spencer and stayed away. Instead, there she was, giving Tyler exactly what he wanted—her presence, her attention, her terror.

Without another word, she spun on her heel and scampered down the hall with her tail between her legs.

"See you soon," he called out after her. "I'll wait for you."

Chapter 11

"You can use this conference room to look over all of Tyler Maddox's correspondence files," Warden Wayne said as he fumbled with his keys outside of the locked door.

Rebecca's heart still raced as she stood impatiently behind him at the conference room door. The disturbing meeting she just had with Tyler still had her shaken up.

The warden finally opened the door and Rebecca and Spencer followed him inside.

In the center, a long rectangular table stood surrounded by painful-looking metal chairs. Two school-style desks with computers lined up against the far wall.

"Each letter to and from Mr. Maddox is opened, scanned into a digital file, and uploaded," the warden said. "Emails are also in there. You can access it all through the database." He leaned over one of the computers and began pecking at the keyboard. "There you go. You're all set and logged in." He then jotted down the user ID and password on a Post-It note and stuck it onto the desk in between the two monitors.

"How many letters do you think there are?" Spencer asked.

"Thousands. He's a busy guy and five years is a long time in here." The warden gave them a nod and headed for the door. "Have fun."

Spencer and Rebecca stared at each other for a moment before they each sat down at their individual computers.

"This is where we're going to find them," Rebecca said, her voice laced with optimism. "They have to be in here somewhere."

As their monitors lit up, they both dove in. Their eyes tracked back and forth across the screen as they read line after line of incoming fan mail. It didn't take long for Rebecca to become utterly disgusted with what she had come across. Countless letters of praise and idolization had made their way into Tyler's hands. There was also a fair share of hate and those screaming for his head on a spike, but Rebecca was certain that those only served to amuse him.

She thought back to the media blitz that had surrounded the case in its early days. *Forensic Files* had dedicated an episode, *True Crime* had their exclusive, and *Lifetime* put out a television movie in record time. Tyler Maddox had become a celebrity overnight and he had fans. Sick fans. And that was where he was finding his pool of psychopaths.

However, for his fans to know the details of his life pre-Gut Wrencher, they would have required personal contact with him. And that contact could have only gone through the prison-approved communications and, therefore, *had* to be somewhere within the computer box she was staring into. She would accept no other alternative.

The hours ticked by as Rebecca and Spencer searched. Some of the scanned letters had been typed, some handwritten. An abundant supply of adoring women had made themselves known, along with a string of marriage proposals. It was absolutely repulsive.

"Here's something." Spencer finally broke the silence with his discovery. "Did you know there's a Gut Wrencher Fan Club?"

"Well, I'm not surprised after reading all of these disgusting love letters," Rebecca replied.

"Listen to this one." Spencer leaned forward into his monitor and strained to read the barely legible cursive on the page.

"Dear Tyler,

I would like to thank you for making me finally feel normal. For as long as I can remember, I have suffered from an obsessive disorder. I need to put things where they don't belong. Especially inside my body or someone else's. I don't know why I need to do this, but inserting foreign objects into my body is insanely gratifying. And by the way, this is not a sexual thing.

I'm not talking about putting fruit up my butt or swallowing doll heads. I actually cut open my skin and slide marbles inside.

I always thought that I was the only one that did things like that. But then I saw your story and what you did. You took it to another level. It was art. It was exquisite. It was masterful. I think we are very similar in many ways and I have been greatly inspired by your work.

I hope I can meet you someday and we can talk more."

"What the fuck?" Spencer's mouth hung open after he read the letter aloud.

"Normal?" Rebecca added. "How could either of them be even remotely considered normal?"

"That's just the thing. Two wrongs make a right in a psycho's head."

"Well, if you think that was bad, how about this?"

"I wish I could have been one of your women. I would have been great. I have always wanted to experience the feeling of being pregnant, but I don't want the baby that comes with it. I would let you fill my stomach with whatever you wanted, whenever you wanted to. I would have been your favorite.

P.S. You're so hot!"

"Uh, does this genius not realize that you don't survive having your insides ripped out and replaced with whatever he decides to put in there?" Rebecca shook her head in disgust.

"At least he's hot though," Spencer snickered.

"I just can't believe the people that are out there. I mean, are they serious with this shit?"

"I'm afraid so. This world is filled with sickos. And currently, Tyler seems to be their president." Spencer reached into his front pocket and took out his phone. "We're gonna need some help."

Chapter 12

The following morning, the cavalry arrived in the form of three police academy recruits. They were young and eager and entered the conference room in a single file with their laptops tucked under their arms. Like a choreographed dance, they each simultaneously pulled a chair up to the center table, popped open their computers, and began typing away.

Rebecca and Spencer shot approving glances at one another before settling back into their own searches. They searched meticulously, keeping a careful eye out for odd language that could contain hidden clues or codes. If all of Tyler's communication was monitored and had ceased to raise any red flags, then they had to expect it wasn't going to present itself so easily.

Every now and then one of them would read off a particularly disturbing letter and the group would cringe in unison. However, throughout all of the sick and twisted praise that Tyler had been showered with, nothing had stood out yet as being an actual lead.

Spencer pushed back in his chair and stretched his arms over his head. Rebecca knew his body language. It was break time. She stood and walked over to the coffee pot in the corner and filled five mugs. After delivering three to the recruits, who were apparently super-human and didn't need breaks, she settled back into her chair and handed Spencer his steaming cup.

"So where does Adam think you are now that the restaurant is closed?" he asked. "I take it you still haven't told him about all of this, correct?"

Rebecca sighed. "Correct. He still doesn't know the whole story."

"Or any of the story, it seems."

"He thinks I'm visiting my brother, Marcus, in Pittsburgh. I'm grieving and I need some sibling time. Adam's busy teaching an online summer course anyway so he didn't even ask to come along."

"Seriously? So you're going full out with the lies. Where are you even staying at night? You can't go home."

"I've got a room at the motel in town. And I don't need you lecturing me about Adam." She glared at him. "This is how I protect him. By putting in the work and catching these sons of bitches. And I wouldn't be able to do that if my husband was all over me with a thousand questions."

Spencer sat up straight. "Wait, you're at a motel? In the middle of nowhere? That's not safe. For God's sake Rebecca, take this seriously. It would be open season on you if any of Tyler's sick fucks found out you were sitting in some run-down motel all alone. What are you thinking?"

"I'm thinking that I need to focus one hundred percent on this case and I can't do that if I'm running back and forth and trying to keep my story straight. And if I'm next on Tyler's list, then I say *bring it on*. I'm not afraid of them."

"Really? You should be." Spencer scooted his chair back up to his computer. "That chip-on-your-shoulder-bravado act is what's going to get you killed." He looked at her long and hard. "And just so you know, I'll be booking a room at that motel as well."

Rebecca rolled her eyes to seem annoyed, but in truth, she was thankful for the company.

"I think I found something." Sonya, one of the young recruits, drew her long auburn hair into a quick ponytail and zoomed in on her screen. "In this letter from Tyler, he's talking about a fond memory he had in the hallway of the Donovan house. He describes it in total detail, even talking about the white robe and how he was leaning against the wall."

Rebecca jumped up from her seat and raced over to peer over Sonya's shoulder.

"The rest of the letter is vague with weird sayings," Sonya added. "He talks about 'working with *Determination*'...capitalized. The letter is addressed to *Strength*.

He also says that '*Strength* and *Determination* can accomplish anything.' Again, capitalized."

"Sounds like names." Rebecca's voice was excited. "Tyler teamed two people up together to commit that murder scene." Her heart pounded in her chest. They finally had a lead. This was the letter that instructed the second murders.

Spencer had joined Rebecca behind Sonya, reading over her shoulder. "What about the corresponding envelope? What's the address?"

Sonya pulled up the next file. "It's addressed to the Gut Wrencher Fan Club. PO box 77 in Rockville."

Spencer pulled out his phone and logged into his own police database. He tapped at the screen and pulled up the name on the account. "Well, what do you know…the renter's name is Tyler Donovan. How fitting."

Chapter 13

Spencer pulled into the parking lot of a long strip mall. The Rockville Post Office sat at one end and a Capital One Bank sat at the other. In between, an array of various businesses ranging from dry cleaners and Chinese take-out to pizza and an Italian deli.

He parked his car and checked the time. It was nearly 5pm and the post office would be closing soon. He jumped out and scurried across the lot.

Inside, he was met by the postmaster—an older man in his sixties, thick and gruff, with a full gray beard and forearms like tree trunks. He appeared better fit to be chopping down oaks than stamping packages.

"Hello there," Spencer chimed as he approached the counter. He pulled out his badge and flashed it at the man. "I need some information on a PO box that's registered here. Specifically, the identification of the renter."

"Then you better show me a warrant." The man leaned forward and spread his large hands on the counter. "I don't care what kind of badge you've got. This is a federal facility and I don't go around just handing personal information out to anyone who wants it."

Spencer took a step back. He hadn't expected the postmaster to be an obstacle. He had just assumed they were both on the same team and would work together. The naivete of a twenty-four-year-old detective was apparent. He wasn't used to his badge not getting him the assistance he needed.

Still, he was confused as to why the man, a fellow government employee, was being so uncooperative. Or, more specifically…why was he being such an asshole?

"I already know the renter's name," Spencer told him. "I'd just like to know if you're familiar with him. Have you ever seen him? Can you give me a description?" He took one last stab. "Can you open the box for me?"

The man laughed. It was an unnerving laugh. One that made your bones rattle, if that made any sense.

Spencer took a deep breath. Admittedly, he came in rather aggressive and authoritative at the start and that obviously was the root of the problems he was having now. He moved on to a calmer approach.

"I understand, sir, that you are just doing your job and I commend you for that. But what you don't realize is that many innocent people have been ruthlessly murdered." He kept his voice calm and respectful. "And we're quite certain that the renter of this PO box has information that could help us. I'm not here to arrest anyone," he lied. "I'm just hoping I can get in touch with the person that uses that box so he can answer some questions."

"Yeah, that all sounds great," the man said with gravel in his voice. "Come back with a warrant and I'll give you whatever you need."

"Fine, I'll go get one. Be right back."

Spencer stomped out through the door and returned to his car. He slid into the seat and sat, staring out through the windshield at the man he had just left. He could see him clearly through the large glass front of the post office, sitting back behind the counter as if nothing had happened.

"Dammit!" He banged his fist on the steering wheel. A federal warrant would take time. A lot of time that he didn't have. He wouldn't even get one with what little they had. So far, all Tyler did was write to his fan club and describe a personal scene from his life. A scene that resulted in a double homicide, but even so, he needed more.

There was a small part of Spencer that thought the postmaster might be working with whoever was using the box. Hell, maybe the postmaster was Tyler Donovan himself. He doubted the man would go that far and shit where he worked, but Spencer still couldn't understand why the man was being so difficult. Was he being paid off? Was he being paid to warn the so-called Tyler Donovan if any cops came around asking for him? Or was he just simply an asshole?

In a way, Spencer almost hoped that the postmaster did try to alert someone. If he thought the warrant was coming soon and he tipped off the box user, maybe that person would then rush down, empty the box, and wipe it clean, and he could nab him then. Although, it would be easier to just have the postmaster clean out the box, but that would make him an accessory. The risk of prison time was a big favor to ask of someone, even if a little cash was involved.

He continued to surveil the post office through the glass front until he spotted a woman he hadn't noticed earlier. She approached the counter from the back. Reaching high above her, she grabbed the lever of a rolling metal door and pulled it down behind the counter, sealing off the area. Closing time.

A few minutes later, the woman and the asshole appeared in the section off to the side where the wall of PO boxes stood. They exited through the side door and separated in the parking lot with a slight wave. That side door would remain unlocked throughout the night and it was Spencer's only chance to find out who Tyler Maddox was talking to.

In the meantime, his best bet was just to sit there and wait. He would wait and watch and run up on anyone that showed up to open that box. If they were guilty, they'd likely be aggressive. Spencer could then find a legal way to arrest them, take them in, and compare their prints and DNA to what Dr. Adler had found. *Then* he would get his federal warrant and seize every single letter that ever passed between The Gut Wrencher and his fan club. Spencer leaned back in his seat and smiled. *Oh, how neat and tidy that would be.*

Chapter 14

Franklin "Frankie" Lewis weaved in and out of the crowd as he made his way to the front of the room. A mountainous black man of Caribbean descent, his bald head nearly grazed the air duct that ran along the ceiling.

The basement was dim, yet cozy. Dark wood paneling covered the walls and tan plush carpeting lay over the floor. A pinball machine rested unplugged in the back corner. The room felt small and claustrophobic due to the low ceiling, but at the same time, open and spacious. Twenty-five folding chairs stood lined up in rows in the center of the room.

Frankie reached the front and turned to face the crowd. His audience was diverse, to say the least. From young college kids to gray-haired grandpas. White, Black, Asian, Latino…it seemed everyone had a horse in the race. "Please take a seat," he said, a slight accent to go with his slight beard.

Two dozen mingling bodies scurried about and filled the seats, leaving one unoccupied in the front row for their superior.

"As always, I'd like to welcome all of you to the Gut Wrencher Fan Club Senior Assembly. I can see everyone is here so let's get started." A wide grin spread across his face. "Tonight is very exciting because we will be welcoming a new member." Frankie extended his hand to the front row. A teenaged boy stood and joined him up front.

A round of applause broke out within the room.

"This young man was lost and was desperately seeking an association where he could be himself. He has found that here with us. He has passed his tests and will now be welcomed into our arms and our souls." Frankie draped his arm across the boy's shoulders. "Tell them about yourself, son."

The boy's eyes lowered to the floor. His nerves were evident as his head sunk into his shoulders and he shoved his hands into his front pockets.

"You can do it." Frankie urged him on. "We're all here to support you."

"I've never felt like I belonged anywhere," the boy said, his voice low and soft. "Ever since the sixth grade, I've had these violent thoughts that I can't get out of my head. I've always felt guilty about it." He took a deep breath and exhaled it slowly. "When Tyler Maddox killed those women…my friends and parents and teachers were all talking about how sick it was. But I didn't feel that way." He raised his head and looked out among his audience. "I never told anyone…but I was obsessed with the Gut Wrencher." His voice grew louder and stronger. "He didn't just kill them…he created art. He sent a message. His killings spoke. And he was just a normal guy, just like me. He didn't look or sound deranged or psychotic. He was just a man in love who was expressing his love in his own unique way. A way that no one understood. But I understood."

Another round of applause erupted.

"I started writing to Tyler a couple years ago. I couldn't believe it when he wrote back. It was the greatest day of my life. It felt so good having someone I could talk to. I wanted to tell him everything…everything that was going on inside of my head, but I knew I couldn't. I knew they were watching and probably reading his mail. And that's how I met Frankie." The boy smiled and glanced at the man still standing at his side. "Tyler hooked us up so I could have someone to talk honestly with. Someone who I didn't have to censor my thoughts with. He became my sponsor and we met every week to talk. And now, I'm so excited to be a part of this club with all of you."

More applause.

Frankie grasped the boy's hand and raised it above his head. "Your new name…*Awakened.*"

This time, a standing ovation.

The boy's smile stretched ear to ear as he hugged the large man and returned to his seat.

"Would anyone else like to share?" Frankie asked as the crowd settled.

A man from the second row stood and walked up to the front. He was lean and wiry with a gaunt face hiding beneath a blue Yankees cap. Frankie shook his hand before giving the man the floor and taking the empty seat beside the boy.

"I was at the dry cleaner last week to pick up my wife's clothes. The line is always so long and it takes forever. I hate doing it, but she needs her clothes for work." He removed his cap and wrung it tight in his hands. "There was a woman there in front of me. I've never seen her there before, but something about her...I was attracted to her so fiercely. She tossed her hair over her shoulder and it hit me. She literally hit me with her hair. And I could smell it...I could smell her. She drove me crazy." He put the cap back on his head. "After she got her clothes, I got out of line and followed her out to the parking lot. I didn't even pick up my wife's clothes." He snorted a little as he laughed. "I watched her get into her car. I wanted to talk to her, but there was no way I could do that. She was way too pretty for me to talk to. She drove away and I haven't seen her since." He swayed back and forth as he stood. Then he removed his cap again, crushing it in his fist. "But I've been thinking about her non-stop. I've been thinking about hurting her and how good it would feel to wrap my hands around her pretty little throat and squeeze the life out of her. I know my stories aren't as interesting or creative as some of the other members, but it's all I wanna do. Strangle. Squeeze."

Applause.

The man talked a few minutes longer, and after him, several others took the stage. Each of them told a story, each more horrifying than the last, until there was nothing left to say. Then, each member stood and drifted toward the refreshment table, spending the next half hour standing in small circles and sipping on plastic cups or bottles of beer.

Frankie reached into his shoulder bag and pulled out a handful of white envelopes. He snaked through the crowd, delivering envelopes to those that were lucky enough to get one. Each one was received with a wide smile and pats on the back.

With one final envelope in his hand, Frankie walked toward a lone man in the back of the room. He was middle-aged and sturdy, with a silver high-and-tight military haircut. The man accepted the letter and gave Frankie a nod before turning and tucking himself into an empty corner.

Frankie continued to watch him as he opened the letter and read its contents. An expression of pride swept over his face. He nodded his head repeatedly to himself as he searched through each of the bodies that stood around the large room. He found who he was looking for and headed toward a young man in his late teens. He showed him the letter, eliciting a similar prideful response. They then shook each other's hands and headed off together, exchanging enthusiastic words.

Frankie smiled as he watched the next phase take form.

Chapter 15

Spencer's stomach rumbled as he sat, parked in his car outside of the post office. Other than plenty of crappy coffee at the prison, he hadn't consumed anything since early that morning. He checked the clock on the dashboard—9:34. No wonder he was starving.

He scanned the various businesses lined up within the strip mall. His eyes came to rest on the deli at the far end of the strip next to the bank, its neon Michelob sign still lit up in the front window. Saliva began to collect in his cheeks when he thought of how delicious an Italian hoagie would be. Without a second thought, he hopped out of his car and headed across the lot.

As he stepped up onto the curb in front of the post office, he paused for a moment. He patted along the bottom hem of his shirt. Then he checked his sleeves and pulled his collar out away from his neck. Not finding what he was looking for, he returned to the bottom hem and raised it to his mouth, biting into the fabric and tugging until he formed a sizable rip. After that, finding a loose fiber was easy. He grasped a loose end and gently pulled out a seven-inch segment of gray thread.

Strand in hand, he walked around to the side door of the post office that led to the PO boxes. Once inside, he laid the barely visible filament across the divot that formed part of the handle of the box. He tucked it in enough to prevent it from falling out on its own. Satisfied, he headed back out of the side door and jogged down the strip toward the deli.

It took less than ten minutes for him to get his sub and soda and return to the post office door. However, he knew it would only take one minute for someone to slip inside, empty the box, and slip back out again. Spencer was fairly certain that he hadn't missed anything with his little meal run, but his pulse still raced as he ducked inside the side door and sidled over to Box 77. The thread still laid across the handle, just as he had left it. No surprise there.

With nothing more to do at the moment but wait, Spencer returned to his car and proceeded to devour his sandwich. He watched as, one by one, the businesses began closing down for the night. As the time approached 10pm, each neon light flickered off, until the entire strip was wrapped in darkness.

Cars and trucks parked in the rows in front him turned on their engines and drove away. It wasn't long before Spencer's car was the only one left on that front side of the parking lot.

He felt visible and exposed as the overhead streetlamp shone a spotlight down on his vehicle.

He glanced around the parking lot and spotted three cars spread out along the farthest side of the lot. They hadn't budged in hours and he detected zero movement coming from inside. He noticed the high-rise apartment complex further down the street and theorized that the cars likely belonged to the tenants there. It was a short walk over a curb and through a few trees to get from the back of the strip mall lot to the apartment lot. It looked like a good spot to blend in and sit unnoticed.

Spencer started his car and drove it over to the side lot. He reversed into a spot just outside of the beam of light descending from the streetlamp on that side. Switching off the engine, he reclined his seat and settled in for a lonely post office stakeout.

From his new position, he had a direct view to the wall of windows and the unlocked door on the side of the post office. The door that led to PO box 77. The inside was brightly lit and Spencer could even see the individual boxes from his spot at the back of the lot.

His mind went over what he would do if someone suddenly pulled up, yanked that door open, and went inside. And what would he do if that person made a beeline straight for Box 77.

He would have to jump out of his car and head straight for the door as soon as he saw someone enter. It would only take a minute to unlock the box and empty its contents. Would that be enough time for Spencer to cross the parking lot, get to the door, and see which box they were unlocking? It would have to be.

And if they were accessing Box 77, he'd simply walk in behind them. Anyone would be nervous in that situation late at night, and even more so if they were hiding something. Spencer was sure he would be able to provoke them into acting suspiciously...or even aggressively. It was the only way he could bypass a warrant and bring the suspect in. It would work. It had to, because he was sure the renter of Box 77 was involved with killing five people and putting two of them in his house.

It was personal.

♦ ♦ ♦

Rebecca and her team of recruits had been working tirelessly throughout the night. They had run out of coffee around 4am and had since been running on fumes.

She hadn't realized just how difficult it would be sifting through thousands of scanned letters. They weren't able to have the computer search for specific keywords. The prison software was not that up to date and could not recognize words on scanned documents. Therefore, they had to look at each one old school, and that took time.

When 6am rolled around, two of the recruits had fallen asleep on their keyboards and Rebecca was not far behind. It was the loud shriek from Sonya that woke them all up.

Sonya was a workhorse. Rebecca was sure she wasn't even human. And she just broke the case wide open.

Chapter 16

A car door slammed. Spencer jolted awake, still feeling the slam reverberating in his teeth. He rubbed his eyes as he looked around. He was still in the driver's seat of his car. Through the windshield he saw the sun just beginning to peek out between distant buildings. After blinking several times, his eyes focused on the dashboard clock—6:17.

Instantly, he was upright and alert. His heart pounded fast as he threw open the car door and crossed the parking lot at a breakneck sprint. Yanking open the side door to the PO box room, he dashed inside. Within three long strides, he stood in front of Box 77.

His eyes fell to his feet and to the lonely gray thread that lay there.

"Fuck!"

His foot struck the wall several times before he would accept the situation. He messed up. He had one job…wait and watch and see who opened the box. One chance and now that chance was gone.

He wondered if his secret box renter knew he was there. Did he see him asleep in his car? Did he wait for him to fall asleep before making his run?

Spencer did his best to justify his mistake. He convinced himself that, had he remained awake, the suspect never would have gone in to empty the box. It was a stretch, but it was the best he could do. There was nothing he could do about it anyway. Time to move on.

Just then, his cell phone rang in his pocket. He saw it was Rebecca and prayed she had better luck than he did. "Please tell me you have something," he begged of her.

"I know who killed Peter!"

♦♦♦

Rebecca placed her phone in the middle of the conference table and switched it to speaker. Sonya spread out onto the table the six letters that she had just gotten from the printer in the warden's office.

"Spence, you still there?"

"Yeah, I'm here." Spencer's voice rang out from the phone.

"Sonya found a huge lead. Remember the letter we found from Tyler that described in detail that hallway scene? And remember how it was addressed to *Strength*, and we figured that was a code name? Well, we still think it's a code name."

"Okay, but how is that a lead? We already knew that?"

"If you'll let me finish…Sonya found a letter from *Strength* to Tyler, thanking him for the promotion within the fan club. That letter, and the earlier one we found describing the actual scene, both used the address of the fan club PO box, which apparently you've already run into a roadblock with."

"Go on, I'm listening."

"The letter from *Strength* to Tyler was typed and printed from a computer, but the scanned copy of the printed letter shows a smudge on the edge of the paper."

"A smudge? Seriously?"

Rebecca ignored his interruption and continued. "We were lucky that the entire piece of paper the letter was printed on was scanned because the smudge was right on the edge. It's an ink smudge from the printer itself, like a printer fingerprint. And we're lucky that Sonya has such an eagle eye," she said as she flashed a smile at the beaming recruit standing next to her. "Because she noticed other scanned letters that had identical smudges, meaning they also were printed from the same computer. And those other letters were dated earlier and didn't use the name, *Strength*."

"What name did they use?" She heard the anticipation in Spencer's voice.

"Vinh Lỳ," she answered. "They were generic fan letters to Tyler going on and on about how much respect the guy had for him. And then he stopped using his real name, started going by *Strength*, and thanked Tyler for the promotion."

"He was a fan first and then became one of Tyler's minions."

"Yes. Vinh Lỳ is *Strength* and *Strength* killed Peter. Vinh Lỳ killed Peter!"

"Please tell me there's an address."

"Yep, and it's not a PO box either."

Chapter 17

Spencer pulled up in front of Champion Home Security. The company had several locations in the tri-state area, but its Silver Spring branch was the home base. He had just come from Vinh Lỳ's empty apartment and was beyond frustrated. They had a name and an address. Why couldn't he have been there and made it easy for them? Instead, the only thing Spencer left with was hope that Vinh would show up for work.

He opened the front door and a bell signaled his presence. A small, older, neurotic-looking man with slick black hair instantly popped out from a back room and took his place behind the counter.

"Can I help you? Are you looking for a security system? Have you ever owned a security system before?" The man rattled off his questions.

"Easy now. I'm not a customer." Spencer approached the counter and took out his badge. He glanced at the small brass nameplate pinned to the old man's shirt. *Joe DePalma – Manager.* "Mr. DePalma, I'm looking for Vinh Lỳ. I understand he works here."

The manager's eyes widened, resembling ping pong balls stuck in his face. "Is he in trouble?"

"He has information I need."

"His shift doesn't start until two. I can call him. He doesn't have a cell phone, only a landline. But I can call him at home for you."

Now why couldn't the postmaster be this accommodating? "Yeah, could you do that for me?" Spencer didn't expect much. He had just come from his home, but there was always the chance Vinh had just run out for breakfast or coffee or something. Perhaps he was back and ready to answer a call from his boss.

The man scurried around the counter while he dialed the phone. He stopped directly beside Spencer and leaned into him, positioning the phone between their ears so Spencer could hear it as well.

Spencer took a step back to create some distance. Vinh's boss seemed a little *too* eager. Or maybe he was just excited to be in the middle of a police investigation. Either way, he made Spencer quite uncomfortable.

"What should I say if he answers?" the man whispered, his eyes growing even wider than Spencer thought possible.

"Just ask him if he can come into work early. Tell him you have an installation that needs to be done and no one else is available."

"Okay, okay, got it."

Spencer laughed to himself. Boss-man was excited, but harmless. And mildly amusing. Unfortunately, it was apparent that Vinh Lỳ still wasn't home to answer his phone and Spencer watched the enthusiasm drain from the manager's face as he hung up.

"Don't worry about it. I still need your help."

The man's face lit up again. "What do you need me to do?"

"I'll be back here at 2:00. When Mr. Lỳ shows up, do not tip him off in any way. Just act natural and we'll come in and get him. And if you hear from him before then or if he shows up early..." Spencer leaned in and locked serious eyes with the man. "...text me on this number." He scribbled his cell number on a scrap piece of paper and handed it to him. "Can you do that for me?"

"Absolutely."

"Great. Then I'll see you around 2:00 if I don't hear from you earlier."

"Is he dangerous?" the man asked.

"To you, probably not. But I'll have a plain-clothed officer watching from outside so don't worry about it. You'll be fine."

"Okay, but I'll be ready just in case." The man reached underneath the counter and pulled out a shotgun. He pumped the barrel and an empty shell ejected and bounced onto the floor.

"Holy hell, man! Put that thing away before you kill someone." Spencer stepped around the counter and took the gun from the man's hands. He picked the shell up from the floor. "When did you shoot this?"

"Don't worry, it wasn't here. I take it camping and practice shooting it there."

"Well, put it back anyway. And don't bring it out again. Mr. Lỳ is not dangerous to you, but if you pull a gun on him…" Spencer placed the gun back in its cradle underneath the counter. "Just text me if you see or hear from him early, okay?"

The man lowered his eyes and nodded, disheartened that his role didn't call for a little more action.

Spencer left him and made a stop at the blue sedan outside containing the undercover officers. "Keep a watchful eye on the place. The boss is enthusiastic and might have a bit of an itchy trigger finger."

◆◆◆

Spencer pulled back into Champion Home Security at 1:30. He rolled up alongside the blue sedan and asked for an update.

"All quiet. There's nothing going on in there," the officer said.

Suddenly, a loud shot rang out and the glass front of the security store shattered. Multiple alarms began ringing out from inside.

Spencer leaped from his car and sprinted toward the building, pulling his pistol from its holster. Broken glass crunched beneath his feet as he slowed and cautiously stepped through the now glassless window. He was met with Mr. DePalma, shotgun in hand, yelling at a man crouched behind a display of security lights.

"I got him!" he yelled at Spencer. "He's right there!"

"Put the gun down, DePalma! I told you before to put it away and leave it there!" Spencer crouched behind a display himself. He clutched his pistol tight in his hand, hoping he didn't have to give the manager a leg shot to bring him down.

"But he was gonna run. He saw me about to call you. He knew we were onto him."

"Put the gun down. You did good. You caught him. Now, put the gun down."

The old man did as he was told and gently place the shotgun on the floor at his feet. As soon as he did, the crouching man jumped up and ran toward the open front side of the store.

Spencer stood and intercepted him at the broken window. He holstered his gun and grabbed the man's arm as it flailed around. He pinned it to his back as the man's other arm swung and struck him in the jaw. It stunned him for a second, just until he felt the man turn to face him, reach for his gun, and pull it from its holster. He squeezed the trigger and Spencer felt the bullet rip across his ribcage.

Spencer gasped as searing pain spread along his side. Chest to chest, he grabbed the man's hand and reached to pin it to his back before he could fire again. Holding him face to face with both arms restrained behind him, Spencer slammed his forehead into his opponent's nose. The man swayed and then crumbled to the floor, blood trickling from each nostril and across each cheek.

Spencer stood over him, watching for signs of consciousness. Satisfied that he was out cold, he lifted his shirt to inspect his first-ever gunshot wound. "Son of a bitch," he said as he wiped the blood away with the back of his hand. The bullet had only grazed him, but hurt liked hell.

He turned toward the store's manager. "What the fuck, DePalma! I said to *not* pull a gun on him."

The man lowered his head, dejected, but Spencer didn't care. He was a loose cannon with a gun and was surely at least half-crazy. And, now they had to arrest him for discharging the damn thing. One of the plain-clothed officers appeared from the back of the store and behind the old man. DePalma didn't resist as the officer cuffed his hands.

Spencer knelt down beside the man on the floor and rolled him over onto his stomach. He pulled both arms behind his back and secured them with zip-cuffs. "Well, at least you gave me something to actually arrest you for," he said to the man still sleeping off his head-butt. "Grabbing an officer's gun and shooting him with it? You're mine for the foreseeable future, so thank you for that."

The man's eye fluttered open and his body wriggled like a snake on the floor. Spencer rolled him back over onto his back and locked eyes with him. "Vinh Lỳ, I presume? You have the right to remain silent."

Chapter 18

Spencer stared through the one-way glass into Interrogation Room #2. He watched Vinh Lỳ fidget and pace back and forth, wall to wall. He looked scared, which bode well for what Spencer needed from him. The more afraid his suspect was, the more likely he'd give up the whole operation, including his partner, just to save his own ass.

"Did you find anything out on his fingerprints, Baker?" Spencer asked the officer approaching him.

"At first glance, the suspect's fingerprints appear to match the partial found on the male victim from the hallway scene. He wouldn't volunteer DNA, no surprise there, but the warrant you submitted for will take care of that."

"And we've got all night. There's no way this piece of shit is walking out of here any time soon," Spencer said.

"It seems that you getting shot was the best-case scenario," Officer Baker said, giving Spencer a slap on the back. "No judge is going to grant bail to someone who just shot a cop. And with his own gun."

"Yeah, can you *not* keep reminding me of that." Spencer shot an angry look at the officer. "I messed up and that mistake could've gotten everyone in that room killed. Learn from that, but don't ever mention it to me again."

"Yes, sir." The officer gestured the zipping of his lips. "You ready to go in?"

"Yep, let's do this."

The two men entered the room and closed the door behind them. Their suspect sat at an empty table with his cuffed hands in his lap. Sweat beaded and dripped from his forehead as he glared at them. Spencer and Baker took their seats in the two empty chairs that stood on the opposite side of the table.

Spencer placed his elbows on the table and looked deep into the eyes of Vinh Lỳ. "You're in a bit trouble, my man. You fucking shot me."

The man immediately began spewing an earful of angry Vietnamese. Spit flew from his lips as he gritted his teeth and hissed his words at them.

Spencer leaned back in his chair. "Oh, I get it. You don't speak English. How convenient." Spencer stood and casually walked around to the side of the table. He towered over the man as he sat on the edge and glared down at him. "Do you even know why I came to your work this morning? I mean, I know you know why. You might not know how…but I know you know why."

Once again, the man responded in his native language, shouting and slamming his cuffed fists on the table.

"Let's cut the bullshit," Spencer roared and slammed his own hand on the table. "I know you speak and write perfect English! Hell, your English might even be better than mine, so I'm not falling for this language barrier shit!"

The man straightened and puffed his chest. His eyes stared straight ahead, defiant as he looked right past both men and focused on a blank spot on the wall.

"That's okay. I don't need you to talk right now. You can just listen." Spencer forcibly grabbed the man's chin and turned his face toward him. The man's eyes closed, unwilling to give Spencer the satisfaction of eye contact. "Forget grabbing a police officer's gun. Forget shooting said police officer with said gun. You're in here for first degree murder. Five counts of it. You killed five people and we have the evidence to prove it."

The man's eyebrows twitched and he slowly shook his head, although his eyes remained closed.

"That's right. And for the record, you do some pretty sloppy work, leaving your fingerprints and DNA all over the damn place." Spencer exaggerated slightly, but his suspect didn't know that. He released the man's face and walked back around to his side of the table. He placed both hands on the surface and leaned into them. "I know you're not working alone. I know you've got a partner. If you cooperate, we might be able to work something out. If not…well then you can just go down for all five murders all by yourself. How does that sound?"

Still nothing. No response, not a single tic that time.

At that point, frustration overwhelmed Spencer and he tagged Baker in to take over and keep their suspect occupied. Spencer left the room for a cup of coffee and checked in with the district attorney about his warrants, both of them. The judge had long since left for the day, therefore, Spencer's DNA collection would have to wait until morning.

His PO box search warrant was much more complicated. It was federal and they simply needed more evidence. Spencer hoped that with Vinh Lỳ in custody, he wouldn't need to bother with the box. However, he hated loose ends and really wanted closure on that front. Whether he would get it or not remained to be seen.

His next call went to Rebecca and she wasn't happy either. She was still at the prison, neck-deep in Tyler's letters and not pleased with the lack of communication with their only suspect. He promised some information soon and was told not to show his face until he had some. She wasn't being literal, but then again…she probably was. He grabbed his coffee and one for Baker and headed back to the interrogation room.

Hours had passed and it was nearing 9pm. Spencer and Baker had each gone a few more one-sided rounds with their suspect to no avail. It was clear to Spencer that Vinh Lỳ had suddenly fallen mute and had no issue with wasting everyone's time.

In the morning he'd have his warrant and the ball would start rolling.

Chapter 19

Spencer's phone rang loudly from his nightstand. The clock read 5:35am and he awoke exhausted and disoriented. By the fourth ring he was able to rub his eyes open, find the source of the noise, and answer the phone.

"Sorry to wake you, buddy," the voice on the line said. "But we've got another mannequin murder."

His room was still dark and he hoped that he was still asleep, the phone call being nothing more than the beginning of a bad dream. Reaching, he switched on the bedside lamp and glanced around the room. No luck. Nothing out of order and no oddities to imply that the call wasn't happening in real life and real time.

"You still there?"

"Yeah, I'm here. How many victims?" He sat upright and tossed the blanket off of his legs.

"Two, but no ID yet."

"Send the address to my phone. I'll be right there."

Soon after, Spencer pulled his car into a Dunkin Donuts/Baskin Robbins combo store just ten minutes from his house. He found the first officer on the scene and approached her.

"An employee showed up for work at his usual 4:30am. He found them and called the police with no idea what was going on. He reported it as a break-in and vandalism because of the statues that were left. Poor guy had no idea they were dead bodies until we told him." She pointed to her squad car, equipped with a trembling teenager sitting in the front seat. "He's over there having a nervous breakdown if you want to talk to him."

"I'll get to him later. First, I need to see the scene."

She led him to the front door, decorated with a large hole and a pile of broken glass.

"Looks like he broke the glass, reached in and unlocked the deadbolt, and brought the bodies straight in through the front door. That's pretty bold," he said as he surveyed the area. "But is it any bolder than spending hours setting up an entire scene behind a tarp in the middle of downtown DC while a hundred people walked by?"

The officer carefully pulled open the door with a gloved hand and Spencer stepped inside. The café was somewhat divided. The Dunkin Donuts section was on the right and the Baskin Robbins ice cream section filled the entire left side.

There were a handful of tables scattered about, but he was only interested in the table in the far corner of the ice cream section. There were two figures and no mistake about who they were supposed to be. One blond male and one blonde female. They each had a wax-covered hand wrapped around, what appeared to be, a melted milkshake.

Spencer moved in for a closer look. It was the same MO. Wax-dipped bodies. Faces expressionless, staring at each other with glossed-over eyes. No wigs.

He stood behind the male victim. Immediately, he spotted matted blood surrounding a large puncture wound at the base of the skull. Circling around the table to the female, he donned a pair of latex. He gently parted the back of her hair and saw the same matted blood and puncture.

This time, the killer had found victims that almost perfectly matched Tyler and Rebecca—no wigs needed. Was it luck or did he search them out? Spencer made a mental note to ask Rebecca if she and Tyler, at any point within the past six years, had met up for milkshakes. He knew one hundred percent what her answer would be.

"Dammit!" He was upset, and rightfully so. He had thought they would at least have a little breather with Vinh Lỳ in custody. Was this done by his accomplice? Spencer leaned in for a close look at the wax itself. Was Vinh Lỳ the teacher or the student? It was *his* print that they had found at the last scene. Mr. Lỳ must be the sloppy student.

He raised his hand and brushed the woman's hair back and off of her neck. Hoping to find embedded fingerprints or ripped-out hair, he was, of course, disappointed. The wax coating was smooth and flawless. *Yes, this was the work of the teacher.*

"Hey Spence, lay off my crime scene." A CSU tech stepped through the door and approached.

Spencer raised his palms in a hands-off gesture and took a few steps back, allowing the young man to take his place. He watched the tech work for several minutes, while at the same time, trying to organize the questions that were running through his head. *Was the accomplice trying to shake up their case by staging another scene while his partner was in custody? Did he assume they would just release Vinh Lỳ thinking he was innocent since another murder happened while he was in holding?*

No, it was more likely the accomplice was toying with them. He was letting them know that Mr. Lỳ was just a small player and not necessary. He was telling them that he was still out there and they couldn't stop him. Spencer's hands balled into fists. He was itching to get Vinh Lỳ back into that interrogation room and badger the hell out of him. And to top it off, the judge would be in soon and he'd have his DNA warrant.

Spencer took one last look at the two corpses sitting upright at the corner table. It was so unbelievably sick. As he turned away, a loud clatter behind him brought his attention right back. The woman's face had smashed into the table's surface. Shattered pieces of hardened wax lay scattered around her forehead.

Spencer knew what was happening. He also knew what came next and wanted no part of it. He turned back toward the front door and headed that way, moving quickly to escape the horrifying rhythm of falling bodies behind him.

Chapter 20

It was 7:06am when Spencer strolled into the precinct. The knot in his stomach was a mix of disgust and anger. And although he didn't want to admit it, there was a touch of fear in there as well. He was afraid of showing up to the next crime scene and finding Rebecca underneath an inch of wax. Not a look-alike either…the real deal. It was only a matter of time and that thought scared him to death.

"Baker!" he called out to his friend at the end of the hall.

Officer Baker turned and headed his way. "I just heard," he said as the two men met in the middle. "You thinking it was his partner?"

"Had to be," Spencer answered. "And I need Vinh Lỳ in an interrogation room immediately. I'm done fucking around. He's gonna tell me who he was working with, so help me God."

"Man, we went at him for like eight hours yesterday and he didn't say a word...not in English anyway. What makes you think you can get him to talk now?"

"I don't know, but we don't have any other options. This guy is our only link at the moment. We still can't get into the PO box so, as of right now, Lỳ is it." Spencer began walking as Officer Baker followed. "We already have a matching print tying him to the second murder scene and I'm sure I'll have my DNA warrant within the hour. It'll take time to get results, but we can at least threaten him with it. He knows it'll be a match. He knows it's his hair and that he screwed up. And most importantly, he knows he's on the block for five counts." Spencer smiled as he turned the corner toward the wing of holding cells. "He'll make a deal."

"I sure as hell hope you're right."

The two men walked through a double door and came to a plexiglass partition with a uniformed officer sitting behind it.

"Is he up yet?" Spencer asked, referring to the wing's only overnight occupant.

"Nope. Haven't heard a peep from him all night...well, not since I moved him to the end of the hall. He made quite a racket up until then." The officer stood and came out from behind the partition with a jingling key ring. "But after that, not a sound." Spencer and Baker followed the officer down the corridor of holding cells. "I wish all of my visitors were that easy."

They came to the last cell and Spencer looked inside. He saw his suspect curled up on the cot with his back to them.

"Rise and shine," the night officer said.

There was no movement from the man on the bed.

"He's very good with ignoring us," Baker said.

The officer reached for the nightstick on his hip and dragged it across the cell's bars, resulting in a string of deafening clangs. "Get up, I said."

Still, not even a twitch.

The officer thumbed through his keyring and unlocked the cell door. He walked inside with Spencer right behind him. With his nightstick still in his hand, he nudged the man with it several times. Nothing.

Spencer elbowed his way past the officer and grabbed Vinh Lỳ's arm. He pulled on it until he rolled over onto his back. The sight he was met with took his breath away. Blood…and lots of it.

"What the hell!" The officer grabbed the radio clipped to his shoulder and yelled into it. "Jim, this is Leonard down in Holding. Get Medical down here! Now!"

Spencer bent over the man, shaking his head. "Son of a bitch." He reached and place two fingers on the side of the man's neck, knowing he would come up empty. Because Mr. Lỳ was empty. He had bled out all over the bed, and the flannel blanket he clutched in his arms had soaked it all up.

"You wish they were all as easy as him, huh?" Spencer glared at the officer. "Maybe he was so easy because he was so dead. Did you check on him at all before now?"

Officer Leonard's voice trembled. "I didn't want to disturb him. He had been so riled up for hours before I moved him. I thought he was just sleeping because he was so exhausted."

"No, not sleeping." Spencer's eyes scanned the body. Lỳ's left arm lay outstretched across the mattress. The inside of his wrist was mangled and shredded and smothered in blood. From what he could see without touching him more than he already had, the right wrist had suffered the same fate. Spencer's eyes then lingered on the blood smeared across his mouth and chin. "Mr. Lỳ wasn't sleeping all night. He was wide awake…and busy chewing through both of his radial arteries."

A stampede of running footsteps echoed through the hall and Spencer stepped out of the cell to give the medical team their space. There was nothing more for him to do there anyway. He headed back up the hallway and Baker followed him until they exited back through the double doors. Once clear of the holding area, he leaned up against the wall and let out a long exhale.

Baker joined him and they both stood in silence for several minutes. It wasn't even 8am and his day had already turned to shit. The lab would get Vinh Lỳ's DNA and it would match, but it wouldn't matter. His prints already matched and they already knew he was one of the killers. But he wasn't the master. The double murder that happened while he was in custody proved that he wasn't even needed. He was obviously expendable and therefore, of no use to Spencer if he wasn't talking…and absolutely no use to him as a dead man.

"There's got to be more," Spencer finally said. "This has to be more than just a two-man team. Lỳ wasn't just covering for his partner. He was covering something much bigger. Something big enough to kill himself over."

"How did this morning look?" Baker asked. "Could it have been pulled off by one person?"

Spencer grimaced and tilted his head back and forth. "I don't know…maybe. They were sitting so that would be easier. Hoisting them with fishing line into a standing position like the scene at my house…that definitely needed at least two people. But this morning…I just don't know."

"What if it was more than just a team of two all along? Lỳ gets nabbed, but they still have two or more people left to get the job done."

"If that's the case then we're really dealing with something big. Serial killers aren't as common as the general public thinks. And they often work alone because of how uncommon they are." Spencer lowered his eyes and shook his head. "Just to find one partner is tough. But to find two…or a group?"

"Or a cult…with their Manson sitting in a cell at Savage River."

Chapter 21

Rebecca sat in her usual spot in the prison conference room as she finished up her lunch. Over the past two hours, Sonya and the other two recruits had not looked up from their laptops even once. She envied their limitless energy and how they worked non-stop like machines. Once upon a time, she had been accused of the same. Nowadays, she still had the determination and drive, but needed a little help from caffeine and food.

She balled up the empty deli paper from her sub and tossed it into the trash bin. Swiveling her chair, she turned back toward her computer monitor and continued the tedious work of manually looking through all of Tyler Maddox's correspondences. The four of them had already singled out a couple more "letters of interest," but had yet to come across another identification or location lead. She rested her cheek on her fist as she slowly scrolled through pages and pages of scanned handwritten letters.

Her focus was interrupted as the door opened and Spencer walked in. Without saying a word, he shambled over to an empty chair at the conference table and collapsed into it. Rebecca spun her chair around to face him. His eyelids stood at half-mast and the beginnings of a dark beard had spread across his chin.

"You look like hell," Rebecca informed him.

"Well, thank you. That's the greeting I was hoping for."

"No problem. It's my job to keep you grounded." She flashed him a smug smile. "What happened with that suspect you picked up yesterday...*Strength*? Did you get the warrant? Does the DNA match?"

"Got the warrant. Got the DNA. It'll be a few days for results, but it doesn't really matter because he's dead."

"What? How?"

"Suicide. In Holding. Son of a bitch actually chewed through his radial arteries and bled out in the middle of the night without anyone even knowing."

"You can't be serious." Rebecca's eyes were wide and unbelieving. "Were you able to get anything out of him before that? Anything at all about his partner?"

"Nope. Nothing." Spencer placed his elbows on the table and began massaging circles into his temples. "And he absolutely has a partner because I was at another wax-covered crime scene this morning...while our suspect was bleeding out in his cell."

"Was it ice cream or movie stars?" Rebecca asked him.

Spencer jolted upright and stared at her. "Ice cream." His eyebrows furrowed in confusion. "But how—"

Rebecca rifled through a pile of printed letters and pulled one out. She stood and walked over to the table and placed the letter in front of him.

Spencer looked at it, his eyes darting back and forth across the page as he read. "Holy shit! This is it. This is the exact scene I was at this morning...down to the last detail."

"They're not done. Whoever they are," Rebecca said.

"So, you also think this is more than just a team of two."

"And then some." She pulled another letter out of the pile and placed it in front of him. "There'll be another one, at least."

Spencer read the second letter even faster than the first. His mouth fell open as he looked up at her. "The next one will be three?"

"We don't know if that's the next scene or if it's four scenes from now. The dates on the letters are not in chronological order of when the murders occurred. It's as if Tyler sent the instructions and then someone else shuffled them and pulled the next scene out of a hat. Until we get through all of these correspondences, we won't know how many are planned."

"Christ," Spencer said under his breath as he read the letter again.

"There's something else." Rebecca pulled her chair over to sit next to him. "So far, we've found four scene letters written by Tyler and addressed to the fan club PO box. In each of those letters, a scene is described in detail and two code names are used—one as the addressee and the other appears to be the partner."

"Yeah, *Strength* and *Determination*."

Rebecca shook her head from side to side. "Spencer, there are more than just two names in these letters."

He swiped up both of the letters and read them again. "*Strength* and *Determination* are not even mentioned in these at all…anywhere." He held up one of the letters. "This one is addressed to *Force*. Who the fuck is *Force*?"

"Exactly. And who the fuck is *Intensity*?" She pointed to the other letter. "And we didn't even notice it because we saw it before realizing the code name thing, but that first scene…the one in DC…*Power*."

Spencer's eyes locked with hers and she watched his face as it all began to make sense to him.

"Dr. Adler said there was a difference in skill between the first scene and the second. We assumed two psychos were taking turns on the lead, but according to these letters…each murder is done by a different team. Catching one didn't even slow them down. If anything, it sped them up." She crossed her arms across her chest. "He really does have a pool of psychopaths working for him."

"Or a cult of psychopaths."

Chapter 22

The next morning, Rebecca found herself in the passenger seat of Adam's truck crossing the Chesapeake Bay Bridge and heading for the coast. The sun was high and reflected off of the choppy ripples of water, sparkling like diamonds as the rays hit. She lowered her window slightly to breathe in the hint of saltiness in the air. It wasn't as beachy-smelling as where they were headed, but it was enough to whet her appetite for white sand, blue crabs, and the lack of wax-themed conversations.

The findings from the day before had taken a bit of time to sink in, but when it finally did, the severity of the situation slapped her in the face. She had been in that spot before. More than once she had ignored the red flags and continued on her Catch-A-Killer quest with no regard for her own safety or those around her. And people had been hurt because of it.

She thought back to the night when Tyler had murdered Michael Moretti in the parking lot of her townhouse. Michael had no idea he was even in danger. He had no idea she had a psychotic stalker killing for her. He had no idea because she had never told him. She didn't want to scare him off. Instead, he died less than fifty yards from her front door.

She remembered what the detective on the case had said to her: *You put Mr. Moretti's life in danger by keeping him in the dark. His actions and level of alertness would've been much different had he known.* It was absolutely true. Michael was clueless about what was going on in her life and it cost him his.

Rebecca glanced over to the man behind the steering wheel. She never in a million years thought she'd find herself in this predicament again. She should have learned the first time, but she still couldn't bring herself to tell Adam the truth. Instead, she told herself how this time would be different. She may not have told him about the cult of psychos that were recreating her life via *Corpse Art*, but she *was* taking action. She was taking him away…far away from all of it. He wouldn't be the next target because they wouldn't even be able to find him.

Adam must have felt her gaze on him because he turned his head and flashed her a smile before giving her thigh a playful squeeze. No, she wouldn't allow him to become the next victim…the next Michael…the next Peter.

She turned her head and stared out of the side window at the boats below, slicing through the water with effortless grace. The evening before, she had returned home from the prison paranoid and shaken. She had kept up her story of visiting her brother, Marcus, and Adam accepted it wholeheartedly.

When she crawled into bed that night, however, everything got so much worse. She hadn't slept a wink, jumping at every sound, every car driving by, every headlight that flashed across their bedroom window. She had spent the night sitting upright, her knees pulled to her chest, watching Adam slumber away in his innocent dreamland.

And when the sun rose that morning, Rebecca had made up her mind. She wasn't going to spend any more sleepless nights waiting for *them* to come for her…or him. They were getting the hell out of there. She was still confident that Spencer would find the evidence to bring that killer cult crashing down into a pile of deranged insanity. Then, Adam and her could continue their blissfully ignorant marriage in peace.

That morning, she had convinced Adam that they needed to get away for the weekend. With La Croix still closed, it seemed as good a time as any. Her mother owned a vacation home in North Ocean City and it was empty at the moment, just waiting for some visitors to come and show it some love. It was almost June and, as far as Adam knew, she needed to get down there and clean up the landscaping before her mother moved in for the summer season. And, she absolutely needed Adam there to take care of a few handyman repairs, or so he thought. She could easily snag her fingernail on the porch screen and secretly rip a hole the size of a basketball. Or ram her suitcase through the hallway drywall while he was outside unpacking the rest of the truck. The possibilities were endless.

Rebecca turned her attention back to her husband. He was deep into a story, full of animated gesturing and laughs out loud. She was bummed that she had been so busy running around in her own head that she missed the beginning of his tale. Adam truly was the human equivalent of a Golden Retriever sometimes. He was inches away from rolling down his window and sticking his head out, she was sure of it.

The smile on his face convinced Rebecca even more that she was doing the right thing. Adam's light burned so bright and it was her responsibility to keep it that way. There was simply no room in their lives for her tidal wave of drama and terror.

Chapter 23

It was almost midnight and Rebecca sat inside the screen porch, staring out into the narrow neighborhood road. She had spent the last fifteen minutes watching a trio of teenaged girls pout and pose for dozens of Instagram-worthy photos. They had gathered under a streetlamp and showed no signs of continuing on their way. The house across the street had a monstrous rose bush in the front yard and the girls couldn't resist it as a backdrop to their informal modeling careers.

The street was lit fairly well, but Rebecca's porch remained dark. It was long-past awkward. The girls didn't even know she was there and it was too late to announce her presence without it being super-creepy.

When they had first turned onto the street, giggling and stumbling, drunk or simply acting like it…Rebecca had assumed they would just pass on by within a minute or two. She remained sitting quietly in the dark so as not to alarm them. However, the flowering tower caught their eyes and they had decided to hang around for much too long.

Her eyes scanned the screen that enclosed the small porch. When she and Adam had arrived, he was the first to notice the handful of roof shingles laying in the driveway, followed by two strips of siding that had also come loose. Winter and spring brought strong winds that affected most of Ocean City's structures in some way or another. Homeowners that spent the off-season inland were accustomed to starting off the summer with a list of needed repairs.

The good news was that the shingles and siding would occupy Adam enough that she might not need to stab a hole into the screen to keep him busy. But just in case he worked too fast, she had spent a few minutes surveying the intact screen and deciding where she would do her damage if the need arose.

The girls continued to giggle and snap photos, sending blinding camera flashes out into the night sky. Rebecca gently rocked back and forth in the porch chair, stealing a glance at her silent companion. Ed Harmon occupied the chair beside her and it was clear he was feeling the awkwardness as well. Rebecca had called him as soon as she and Adam had arrived. He had been living about fifty miles from Ocean City on Chincoteague Island since he hung up his homicide detective hat and retired a few years back.

Rebecca had run down the street to the seafood market and picked up a dozen jumbo crabs and the three of them had spent several hours feasting and catching up. It had felt so good to feel normal again, even if it was fake and only for a short time.

Adam unfortunately had brought up the topic of "that crazy case with the wax-covered people" and Rebecca's stomach had knotted up immediately. He knew a little about the mannequin murders from what he had read online, but he had no idea that she, Spencer, or Peter were involved in any way. Peter's name hadn't been released and even Spencer, the lead detective on the case, had managed to keep himself off the press record.

Her husband had asked her once if Spencer was working on it, considering he was a Montgomery County detective and the second murder scene was found there, but she threw out a quick lie and that was the end of it…or so she thought. She nearly choked on a crab claw when he had brought it up again to Harmon.

Harmon responded by saying he had read something about it also, but the sideways look he gave Rebecca told her that he knew more than he was letting on. Of course he did. He still had a lot of friends at MoCo PD. Hell, Spencer had likely put out a call to him himself.

With that single look, it was obvious to Rebecca that Harmon knew the details of the case, and that he was aware that Adam did not. His expression had displayed such disappointment in her that Rebecca had contemplated retreating inside for a refill and never returning. She didn't though. She wouldn't dare leave Harmon alone with Adam. Instead, she just spent the next half hour picking her crabs and sipping her club soda.

After their feast, Rebecca had put on her bartender hat and fed Adam several, quite strong, beachy cocktails. And now, he slept comfortably in the back bedroom and Harmon and Rebecca were finally alone to talk...if you didn't count the teenaged models that still hadn't left their outdoor studio.

Rebecca swiveled toward Adam's empty chair and propped her feet up on it. The discomfort between her and Harmon was palpable. After Adam had gone to bed, Rebecca had only gotten a sentence or two of explanation out before the young intruders had shown up and silenced her. Now the two of them had been stuck sitting in the dark in quiet stillness until they left.

"Alright, that's enough of this," Harmon finally said. "Move along, ladies," he called out. "You've got plenty of pictures."

All three of the girls startled and stared, mouth agape, at the dark porch across from them. Then, all at once, without a single word between them, they took off at a sprint, bare feet slapping the pavement and echoing throughout the street. They were alone at last and Rebecca braced herself for the onslaught of fatherly preaching.

"Go ahead. Lay it on me," she said.

"Do you really think it was fair to practically drug him to sleep?"

"I needed to talk to you alone. Adam doesn't need to be involved." She lifted her feet off of the empty chair and swiveled to face him. "Harmon, I'm gonna be honest with you...I'm a little scared. Actually, I'm a lot scared."

"Why haven't you told Adam that the mannequin murders are about you?"

Rebecca heaved a heavy sigh. "He doesn't know about my past. Andrew...Tyler...he doesn't know about any of it."

A look of surprise spread across his face. "How many years have you two been together and you still can't be honest with him?"

"I'm plenty honest with him. Just not about my past."

"Or your present apparently."

"It would change the way he feels about me if he knew the things I've done. I'm a different person now. My past is just that...in the past."

"And yet, here we are again...now." Harmon shook his head slowly in the most disheartened manner. "The truth will catch up. It always does and it's never pretty. He'll find out at some point, but it'll go over a whole lot easier if it comes from you...instead of me."

"You wouldn't. Would you?"

"If you don't tell him what he's in the middle of, then I will."

"Okay, okay. Just let me find the right time."

"Tonight would have been a pretty good time. Especially with me here. I could've backed you up. I could've explained that you did what needed to be done to save lives."

"Do you really believe that?" she asked, her question laced with hope. "Do you believe I had no choice?"

"I do. I was right there in it with you, remember?"

A slight smile spread across her face as she nodded. She hadn't realized how much she missed Harmon until right then. She had forgotten what it felt like to have someone in her corner. Someone to watch her back. Someone who knew of her demons and accepted them. Yes, Spencer was a great friend and ally to have also, but Harmon truly understood her. He didn't always agree with her methods, but he saw her motivations as pure.

"But...I need to put my two cents into your current situation," he continued. "Stay out of it. The case, I mean. I realize you have a difficult time keeping blood off your hands, but you need to try...for Adam's sake and your own. Follow procedure and allow the justice system to work." He turned his chair to face her directly. "Do you think you can do that?"

Rebecca remained silent for a moment. She knew what he was asking and she wanted so badly to follow his advice. She even *planned* on following his advice. But she also knew that what she plans and what actually ends up happening are two totally different things.

"Don't answer that." It was as if he read her mind. "I know you too well. Just promise me something." He took both her hands in his and squeezed them. "When the time comes and you're faced with that dilemma that you know all too well…let me help you. You and I both know that I'll wholeheartedly disagree with you when you get to that point, but that doesn't mean I want you to go at it alone. Remember, I have friends everywhere within the system that owe me favors. Use me. I have a lot less to lose than you."

"I really don't want it to come to that, Harmon. I swear I don't."

"I know. But we both know that eventually it will."

"Not this time. I don't want anything to do with this cult of psychos. Did you hear what I said? Cult. Psychos. Lots of them." Her head dropped, hiding the tears welling up behind her eyelids. "I just want them to leave me alone. I just want out of this recurring nightmare."

"I know. And you will. You'll get out for good and live happily ever after. And you'll need my help to do it, so make sure you take it."

They sat in silent darkness for the next hour. There was no need for words. They both knew each other well enough to know exactly what the other was thinking. Harmon knew she was mapping out how she was going to kill Tyler…and she knew that Harmon was thinking if he should stop her.

Chapter 24

A gloved hand brandished a small pocketknife and opened the blade. The man owning the hand took a casual glance around him before sliding the knife through the porch screen. He drew the blade upward, resulting in a four-inch slit adjacent to the locked handle. Long fingers slid inside and flipped the door's flimsy lock. The dark figure slid inside and onto the porch with nary a sound.

The air was motionless and deathly silent. It was nearing 4am and not a soul could be seen or heard along the quiet street. Even the usually constant squawking of seagulls had ceased for his noiseless entry. It was if they knew who was in charge…and they were right.

He crossed the small porch, his dilated pupils allowing him to easily dodge the array of scattered metal furniture. He reached the sliding glass door that led inside the house and gently tugged on the handle. It was locked as he had expected. Lifting his shirt, he reached into the waistband of his jeans and pulled out a thin strip of spring steel—his Slim Jim lockout tool. With speed and expertise, he slid the thin metal into the door jamb and pulled upward until he felt that familiar click.

Holding his breath, he once again tugged on the handle. The door glided open, smooth and silent. He opened it only as far as needed to slip his tall lanky frame inside. He looked down at the floor and the cut broom handle that lay next to a pair of flip-flops. Had it been positioned inside the door track where it was supposed to be, he wouldn't have been able to enter the home so easily.

"Tsk, tsk, tsk," he whispered to himself, shaking his head.

Drunk people were often too lazy or too dizzy to bend over and pop the stick into the track. He scanned the dimly lit dining and kitchen area and spotted several empty beer bottles in the trash bin. *Yep, drunk people.*

He quietly slid the door closed behind him and took a few steps, testing the creakiness of the fake wood floors. Not a sound. The neoprene water shoes he had bought at the souvenir shop earlier was clearly a good investment. He quietly glided through the kitchen and down the carpeted hallway as if his feet didn't even touch the floor.

Several rooms passed on either side of him. He paused at each door, stilling his own breath and listening for others. He then came to the end of the hall and a bedroom door that stood slightly ajar. He turned his ear and held his breath. Immediately, he heard the whirr of a ceiling fan interspersed with two separate tones of deep slow breathing.

He pushed the door open just a little more and slipped inside the dark bedroom. Moonlight filtered into the room through sheer curtains and cast a dim glow across the two slumbering bodies.

He chuckled to himself. The duo in front of him dozed away as if they hadn't a care in the world. A barely locked door. The white noise of a ceiling fan. Sheer window treatments that offered no privacy at all. Not a care in the world.

His chuckle quickly turned to disdain. He stared at the woman stretched out on the bed. There was no reason for her to be sleeping so peacefully. She should be barricaded behind dressers and armoires and cowering in the corner, a pile of sobbing fear. Definitely not dreaming away with her arm slung across her husband's chest. *How insulting.*

He took a few deep breaths to settle the hostility growing inside of him. Emotion was the root of all failures. He had spent years learning to turn his emotions off. Learning to do his job with robotic calculated precision, unable to be shaken or stirred.

Still…there was something about her, wasn't there? He reached out and lightly stroked a lock of hair off of her cheek. She twitched and her hand shot up to aggressively swat the side of her face.

He stepped back onto his heels and froze, motionless. Her eyes remained closed, but he feared they could open at any moment. He held his breath, not daring to make a sound that might alert her to his presence.

He could handle her if she woke up. He could handle the both of them easily. He just didn't want to. It wasn't her time yet. He hadn't yet had the chance to show her his skills...his expert craftsmanship.

She swiped at her cheek again, softer this time. Then her hand tucked itself under the blanket and pulled it up to her ear, nestling herself deep into the luxurious fleece.

He let out his breath slowly and quietly. How exhilarating. He might actually understand the obsession others had for this woman. He couldn't pinpoint the exact cause, but there was something. Quiet arrogance maybe? Hidden strength? That was more likely. He knew what she had done and what she was capable of. He had heard the stories.

He took a step closer, hovering over her bedside. She looked so weak and innocent. Sleep did that to people, but he wouldn't allow himself to be fooled. She was dangerous...even deadly. She would make a worthy prize and he hoped he'd be the one chosen when her time came.

He had been waiting to prove himself. Most of the jackasses that came before him were complete idiots. It was a wonder that *Strength* was the only one caught. They weren't all bad though. *Force* was definitely one to be reckoned with. He pulled off quite a great scene just the other day. Kudos to him. *But he's still not me.*

I am Power.

He brushed his fingertips across her face one last time before gliding around to the other side of the bed. He sneered down at the sleeping man, breathing deep and slow. *Pathetic.* Lifting the pocketknife he still held in his hand, he leaned in. The blade hovered just inches above the sleeping man's right eye. He waited for movement, even wanted it this time. Any excuse to bury the knife deep within Adam's eye socket, forcing Rebecca to awaken next to a corpse rotting away in a pool of blood. She wouldn't sleep so peacefully then, would she?

However, his excuse never came. The man slumbered on, completely unaware of how close he was to death. *What kind of man are you? You have no idea what you're doing and who you're doing it with, do you?*

A light tapping came from the window behind him. He turned and saw the dark silhouette of a thin figure. *Idiots…all of them.* He parted the sheers and directed the figure away from the window with irate hand gestures.

He despised working with partners. It was necessary for the job, he knew, but that didn't make it any easier. Hopefully, he'd prove himself and be able to work on his own shortly.

He turned away from the window and glanced back down at Adam. "Your time will come sooner or later," he whispered softly. "I'm thinking sooner."

Chapter 25

Spencer spun around in the swiveling office chair a few times while waiting for Dr. Adler to get settled. It had been a few days since he had been called to the ice cream shop for the third murder scene. It had also been a few days since their only suspect in custody committed suicide inside the precinct and right under their noses. All three cases were jumbled up in his head with conflicting MOs and little to no trace evidence, other than Vinh Lỳ's prints and DNA. However, that evidence was of no use to them now that he was dead. What a mess.

"Oh, how I love when you drag me in here on my days off," Dr. Adler said as she sank into the chair behind her desk.

"At least I waited until the afternoon so you could sleep in," Spencer replied. "That was nice of me, wasn't it?"

"No, actually it's not. I've got a house full of people eating my queso and drinking my beer." She slapped a file on the desk and flipped it open with obvious annoyance. "The Ravens are about to kick off and I'm stuck in here with you. You're going to owe me big time for this."

"I'll give you anything you want if you can shed some more light on this case. I'm going crazy waiting for the judge to give me a search warrant for the mailbox and I just need to feel like I'm doing something to move this thing along."

"Well, you're going to be waiting a long time for that warrant. Federal warrants take forever. You'd be better off catching these killers without the mailbox," Dr. Adler said.

"Which is why we're here together on this beautiful Sunday afternoon." Spencer smiled.

The doctor leaned back in her chair and clasped her hands across her stomach. "As much as I truly do enjoy our brainstorming sessions, don't you have a partner you're supposed to be doing this with?"

"No, I don't. Baker is the closest thing I have to a partner and he's great for bouncing ideas off of, but he doesn't know the inner workings of this case, nor does he have the experience." Spencer leaned forward and propped his elbows on her desk. "I wish you were my partner, Doc."

"Are you flirting with me, young man?" she asked jokingly while adjusting her reading glasses.

"Always," he said with a smile.

"Alright, alright. Let's see what we can make of this mess." Dr. Adler pulled out several sheets of autopsy reports and spread them out across the desk. "We have the first scene that was discovered in DC, the second scene from your house, and the third scene from Thursday morning at Baskin Robbins." She glanced up at him. "Are you going to take notes? You heard me say this is a mess, correct?"

Spencer jerked himself up off the desk and reached into his jacket, pulling out a small electronic tablet. He powered it on and began poking at buttons on the screen. Dr. Adler continued to peer at him over her glasses.

"Any minute now," Spencer said. "It just needs a minute to start up."

The doctor reached into her desk drawer and tossed a large yellow legal pad at him. She followed it up with a blue pen. "The old school way will be just fine for now. You can transfer your notes to your pocket computer later. Honestly, how does your generation get anything done when you constantly have to wait for things to power on and boot up and download and find a Wi-Fi connection? And don't get me started on when a cold autopsy room makes a battery suddenly die right in the middle of my report."

"Yes, ma'am. It won't happen again. Pen and paper for me from here on out."

She gave a curt nod and half a smile and began laying out her findings. "Let's start with the obvious. The unique signature in all three of these is, of course, the wax. Have you gotten any hits on who might have purchased that much wax?"

"Actually," Spencer tapped a button on his tablet and the screen lit up. He stole a peek at Adler as he pecked at the screen as fast as he could, sensing her irritation at the hold up. "I found another local art supply store that had a bulk order placed for peach-colored candle wax," he said, reading from his notes file. "But just like the first one, the customer placed the order in person and prepaid with a gift card. Untraceable. The order was shipped to the store a few days later and held there until the customer picked it up. There was no phone number or ID attached to the order because it was prepaid."

"How about a name?"

"Sure. Tyler Donovan was the name given. And, of course there are no surveillance cameras in these little art shops."

"Okay, so no ID on the purchaser of the wax. Let's move on to how the wax was handled, shall we?"

"The first and second were slightly different. How was the third?" Spencer asked.

"We had already found that the wax from the first scene had been mixed with shortening before application. We deduced that this was to make it more pliable. However, that also resulted in the wax melting off of the bodies prematurely due to the lower melting point of the shortening."

Spencer nodded. "And the second scene didn't contain the shortening mixture even though the bodies would be temperature controlled in air conditioning and not at risk of melting. Why didn't they mix it? Instead, it caused the wax to dry too fast, which was good for us because they left prints and hair behind."

"Well, we already know there's more than one killer," Dr. Adler said.

"But it's more than that. Rebecca found several different code names in letters that Tyler wrote to his fans. They involved specific descriptions of the scenes dated before any of them happened." Spencer leaned in across the desk for emphasis. "Two people did the DC scene. Then, a different set of two, one of them being Lỳ, set up the second scene. And if the letters are accurate, the third scene was set up by two other people, not present at the first or second. Yet, the wax between the third and first are the same so they must at least be talking to each other. It's as if they're following a manual on how to kill these victims and set these displays up. And Lỳ was just a weak link that did it wrong."

Dr. Adler nodded slowly while she gathered up the papers spread across her desk and stuffed them back into the file. She flipped through a few more pages, pulled out three more, and laid them out. "If they are following a manual or talking to each other, they're also being given some creative liberty," she said. "Cause of death—different MOs with each group of victims."

"None of them were killed the same way?" Spencer asked.

"That's right. All three victims of the dinner table scene involved blunt force trauma to the head followed by strangulation. The causes of death in the hallway scene were blunt force on one and strangulation on the other. And, last but not least, the victims from the ice cream parlor were both stabbed in the head with a large blade strong enough to puncture the skull."

"The head-stabbing appears pretty quick and efficient," Spencer said. "And the most competent, wouldn't you say?"

"I would," the doctor agreed.

"Ugh." Spencer leaned back in his chair and rubbed his face hard with his hands. "You're right, Doc. This is a mess." He dropped his hands and exhaled forcefully, bringing his focus back to the woman sitting across from him. "Rebecca believes that Tyler Maddox is the leader of a pack of psychopaths."

Dr. Adler stared deep into Spencer's eyes. "I believe that Rebecca is correct."

Chapter 26

Rebecca stretched out her legs and dug her toes underneath the sand. It was cooler and grittier the deeper she went. A distinct contrast to the warm soft grains that covered the surface. She adjusted the incline on the back of her beach chair and stretched out even further.

Adam occupied the spot next to her, his chair fully reclined to lie flat six inches above the sand. He hadn't made a peep in almost an hour and Rebecca was certain he had fallen asleep. She couldn't blame him for that though. It was a glorious Sunday afternoon. The temperature sat in the mid-seventies with a slight breeze. Not quite warm enough to swim, but perfect for lounging in the sand and watching the ocean waves crash along the shore. It created a soothing white noise that blended seamlessly with the squawking seagulls that soared overhead. Occasionally, the ambient beach sounds would be interrupted by a sudden rush of screams riding the breeze from the nearby rollercoaster.

They didn't usually hit the beach this far south, often opting for the quieter less-crowded beaches on the north side of Ocean City. Rebecca, however, needed the distractions that the chaotic boardwalk and pier provided. The crashing waves alone worked wonders on her anxiety, but they still left too much room in her own head. Room for her to consistently rehash the previous week in all its terrifying glory.

A low grumble came from her stomach. It was well into the afternoon and she still hadn't eaten anything. She had spent the entire weekend thinking about her conversation with Harmon and trying to decide when the right time would be to come clean to Adam. If it was solely up to her, *never* would be the answer. But it wasn't. Harmon had made it clear that if she didn't fill Adam in, he would.

She was running out of time. They had made dinner plans with Harmon for tomorrow. If Adam still displayed his naïve cluelessness by then, it would be Game Over for her. The stress of that deadline was eating her up inside and effectively killing her appetite. But the salty air perfectly complimented the scent of Thrasher's Fries that drifted through the air and suddenly, food was all she could think about.

Glancing over at Adam, she watched him stir slightly before shifting to his other hip. She hated to wake him, but knew that if she didn't get him his own food, he would just end up eating hers. She had officially raised her hunger level to "starving" so sharing was not an option.

"Hey, babe," she said quietly. "Are you awake?" No response. She leaned toward him, her head blocking the sun and forming a dark shadow that engulfed his face. "Adam," she said slightly louder.

His face contorted and his eyes squinted open, and then shut again. "Are we leaving?" he muttered.

"No, I'm just going to get food. Bull on the Beach. You want a pork sandwich?" She knew better than to give him too many options in his sleep-induced stupor. Yes or no questions was all he needed.

"Yeah, okay." He rolled completely onto his side and adjusted the towel pillow he had stuffed under his head. "And fries."

"Of course." It would be a crime to visit the boardwalk and not walk away with a hot and salty bucket of Thrasher's fries. It had been Ocean City tradition as long as she could remember. "Be right back."

Rebecca hopped up and slipped a tank top and shorts over her swimsuit. She didn't even know why she had worn it in the first place. She wasn't there to swim or work on her tan. Maybe, in the back of her mind, she thought her bikini-clad body could scramble Adam's brain just enough that when she eventually enlightened him with the truth, he wouldn't even care that she had been lying to him.

Today was just not her day though. He was out cold and snoozing away, which was mostly her fault. He had already fulfilled her half a dozen times since yesterday morning. He was exhausted and she owed him a break. Tomorrow then. Tomorrow she'd tell him.

With flip-flops in one hand and her wallet in the other, she made her way across the warm sand. By the time she got to the small set of steps leading up to the paved sidewalk, her calf muscles were burning from the difficult trek. She dropped her flip-flops onto the concrete, stepped into them, and zig-zagged her way through the crowded boardwalk.

The crowd thickened the closer she got to the pier, but she managed to snake her way through without too much jostling. When she reached the video arcade she crossed to the other side of the boardwalk. Her ears rang at the sound of dart-stabbed balloons popping and blaring sirens signaling a winner. A man with a megaphone speaker singled her out and challenged her to attempt his setup of various carnival games.

"It's easy," he said. "Just knock all three blocks off of the table with a softball and win a prize. Three balls for only ten dollars."

She wondered how anyone would fall for that. It was obvious the blocks were weighted. But people did fall for it. As soon as she shook her head at him, he turned his attention elsewhere and immediately got a bite. Three young boys with blue cotton candy-stained faces, jumped up and down and dragged their exhausted parents along behind them. The mother fished some cash out of her purse, gave it to the oldest boy, and stepped to the side to collapse on a nearby bench.

Rebecca had watched this exact scene happen over and over for years. She had always felt so sorry for the parents, using every last drop of their energy to ensure their kids had a fun and memorable vacation. But this time it packed a little more of a punch. Her and Adam would be parents before the end of the year. In a couple more years that would be her groaning and half asleep on that bench. She shuddered a little at the thought and pivoted to continue on her way.

The moment she turned she bumped shoulders with a man trying to get past her. He stopped in his tracks and locked eyes with her.

"I'm so sorry," she said. "I wasn't watching where I was going."

The man said nothing. He continued to stare into her eyes, standing only a foot away. He appeared to be not much older than her. Black hair, black eyes, and a face as white and blank as a crisp sheet of paper. His expression was emotionless. No anger, no irritation, no exasperation. Also, no joy, no forgiveness, no accepting of her apology. Just nothing.

Rebecca was frozen. She wanted to apologize again because maybe he had a hearing difficulty and didn't hear her the first time. She wanted to turn and walk away. She wanted to do anything but stand there and stare into the man's black emotionless eyes. But his eerie stare held her there instead.

A group of rowdy teenagers passed by on her left and their hoots and hollers snapped them both out of their trances. The man finally broke eye contact and turned and walked away.

Rebecca let out a deep breath that she didn't even know she was holding. Her whole body shook as she tried to wrap her head around the strange encounter she just had. "Don't do drugs, kids," she mumbled, convinced that the man was obviously high on something.

She reached the other side of the boardwalk and stepped up to Bull on the Beach's ordering window. An older woman's head popped out and asked her for her order. Rebecca fumbled with her wallet and fumbled with her words and could not for the life of her remember what she was there to get. Even though she easily explained away the strange man's behavior, he still had done a number on her nerves.

"Sweetie, are you ready to order?" the old woman asked.

"Yes, I…uh…"

"How about if you take a minute to look at the menu and I'll help the gentleman behind you while you figure it out."

Rebecca stepped to the side without thinking. Why was she so shaken up? She's had countless run-ins with weirdos like that, especially there on the boardwalk. Why did that guy jumble her brain so much? She turned her head and looked off into the direction where she had bumped into him.

He was there. That same man. Standing there and staring at her just like before. A gasp caught in Rebecca's throat. It didn't even seem real. He didn't seem real. He just stood there in a sea of people, and they all moved around him like a river flowing around a rock.

His eyes locked with hers again. A wide grin spread across his face. It continued to grow wider and wider until the man was swallowed up by two dozen people exiting a nearby ride. The group dispersed and the man was gone.

Chapter 27

It was late, nearly midnight, and the Fenwick RV campground was dark and quiet. A lean black-haired man stepped out of the beaten-up Winnebago. He jumped from the last step and landed without a sound onto the packed sand. Behind him, a younger man, maybe nineteen or twenty years old, mimicked the other man's actions. He jumped off of the step and landed with a thud and crackling of broken twigs. The sound was small, but boomed like a cannon due to the silence and stillness of the forested area.

"Idiot," the older man mumbled to himself.

The black-haired man and his "apprentice," for lack of a better word, had spent the day lurking and watching a small group of young twenty-somethings drinking and partying at their campsite. There were five of them in total, but only three that he was interested in. It had taken two days and three different campgrounds, but the effort was well worth it. These three were perfect.

The man crept silently along a narrow path through the tree line that bordered his campsite. His lead-footed shadow followed close behind. They both came out of the trees on the other side and stood for a moment, surveying the scene.

A roaring campfire illuminated the face of a petite blonde girl with long flowing hair sitting in a folding canvas chair. She was looking into her phone screen, tilting her head and pouting her lips, and shooting an endless stream of selfies. Next to her sat a young man in a straw cowboy hat. His hand clutched a half-empty beer bottle. He was nearly passed out, but his head continued to jerk and nod, fighting for consciousness.

The silver and black RV parked behind the fire was massive. These were rich kids with wealthy parents, no doubt. Not a single light shone from the windows and not a sound emitted from inside. The group's other three members were likely inside sleeping off the booze.

The older man made a motion with his hand and the two of them split and started off in opposite directions like two velociraptors stalking their prey. They met back up directly behind the couple. *Power* rose up behind the girl and watched himself come into focus on her phone's camera screen. The girl gasped and jerked her head around to look at him. He slapped his hand over her mouth and pulled her backward into his chest. *Promise*, the young apprentice, mimicked his mentor's actions and subdued the drunk cowboy.

The two men both brandished large hunting knives and held them to the temple of their victims. They threw a glance toward one another. The blades gleamed and shimmered with the campfire's light. *Power* gave a signaling nod and simultaneously, they both drove their knives deep into the temples of the couple. The blades met resistance as they hit the skull, but with a little extra pressure, they broke through and slid smoothly into their victims' brains. Quick, clean, and efficient.

They then pulled the camp chairs closer together and propped the lifeless bodies up against each other. To any unknowing passerby it would appear the couple was just passed out drunk or sleeping. They would only be left alone for a couple minutes though. Just long enough for the murderous duo to retrieve their third body.

Power snatched the cowboy hat off of the dead man's head and set it atop his own. Then, he took the man's beer from his hand and poured it over the fire, dousing the flames. A long hissing sound accompanied the cloud of white steam that billowed into the air.

With his apprentice in tow, *Power* headed toward the RV. He adjusted the hat and, knowing he could easily be mistaken for the group's cowboy friend, opened the door and stepped up inside the mammoth vehicle. It was even darker than it had appeared from the outside. The dim glow from the digital clock on the kitchen's microwave was his only source of light. He let his eyes adjust for a moment.

In the meantime, he listened.

Deep breathing. Slight snoring.

Easy.

He recalled from his earlier recon of the group that, aside from the couple out by the fire, the RV should contain two more males and one female. He turned an ear toward the open space and listened for the location of his next target. A deep exhale came from the wall across from him. As his pupils dilated further, he was able to just barely make out the outline of the sofa against the far wall.

Behind him, *Promise* entered the RV, but was abruptly stopped in his tracks by *Power*'s halting hand in his sternum. He turned and signaled him to stay put. The younger man obeyed.

Power took several steps and approached the sofa. A hulking figure lay sleeping on top of it. Firmly, he placed his gloved hand across the man's mouth. Eyes opened and immediately grew wide with terror. The danger that engulfed the man was unmistakable, even in his half-drunk, half-sleeping state. *Power* positioned his knife along the side of the man's head and slid it into his brain like he had previously done outside.

Taking a small flashlight from his pocket, he shone it on the man's face. It wasn't the one he needed. He needed the blond one that he had seen earlier. Unfortunately, the other occupants of that RV were going to have to suffer the same fate. There was just no way around it.

Hearing the low masculine snoring coming from the rear of the vehicle, *Power* knew that was his next destination. He walked down a narrow hallway and came to a door, slightly ajar. He pushed it open slowly and could see it was a bedroom containing a large queen-sized bed. A sleeping couple laid across it.

A blanket laid in a heap on the floor along with various items of discarded clothing. The man's jeans were around his knees and the woman was topless. The scene displayed sexual intention, yet without achievement, likely due to the copious amounts of alcohol the two had been consuming all day. They had tried, but "whiskey dick" was no joke.

He walked around to the man's side of the bed and recreated the kill he had just performed out front. On the other side of the bed, he did the same. Taking out his flashlight again, he shone it on the couple. There he was, his prize, the blond with the cropped tousled spikes.

Stashing his flashlight, he walked back around to the man. He lifted a heavy arm around his neck, hoisted the body onto his shoulder, and headed out of the bedroom. Quietly as ever, even though there was no one left alive to hear him, he glided down the hallway to the front where *Promise* obediently waited for him. The younger man exited the vehicle and *Power* followed.

As they approached the smoking firepit outside, young *Promise* veered off toward the two bodies still slumped over in their chairs. He stepped up to the cowboy and lifted his arm around his neck. He bent his legs and grunted and groaned as he attempted to lift the body onto his shoulder. Instead, it crumbled back into the chair with a series of thuds and cracks.

He stole a glance at the older man who simply shook his head and nodded toward the petite blonde in the other chair. *Power* knew his young student was just trying to pull his weight, but his stature was small and he simply didn't have the strength to handle the men.

With disappointed eyes and slumped shoulders, *Promise* stepped over in front of the girl and easily picked her up and threw her onto his shoulder. He followed the older man into the tree line and along the sandy path that led to their small RV. They carried the lifeless bodies up the steps and into the back of the vehicle.

Once inside, *Promise* dropped the girl's body onto the empty metal floor with an echoing thud. Power turned and glared at him.

"You certainly are not living up to your name. I expected more from you," the older man said with a frustrated tone.

"I'm sorry." The boy's voice trembled. "I didn't think it would be so loud."

"It's not about the noise. It's about the lack of respect." *Power* hoisted the blond man off of his shoulder and gently laid him on the floor next to the girl. "Come tomorrow, these two will be stars. Celebrities along with their friend out there. Please don't damage them before they get on stage."

"Yes, sir."

Satisfied with his short lecture, *Power* then exited the RV and returned a couple minutes later with the cowboy. He closed the door behind him and, like the man before him, gently laid the body down. He tossed the man's hat from his head and wiped the sweat from his brow.

The inside of the small RV had been gutted, leaving only a stovetop, a refrigerator, and a small counter with cabinets underneath. The rest of the space was void of any furniture except for a couple of folding chairs and a pile of clear plexiglass pieces of varying sizes and shapes piled up in the back corner. There were no beds, which suited them just fine. They wouldn't be sleeping that night anyway. There was work to be done.

Power slid into the driver's seat and started the engine. Without even waiting for his companion to take the seat beside him, he maneuvered the large vehicle out of the campsite and headed down the gravel road toward the campground's exit.

♦♦♦

A couple miles down the road, the RV pulled into the parking lot of a Motel 6. *Power* steered the vehicle toward the back of the lot. The rear space was reserved for oversized vehicles and he felt lucky that they weren't the only vehicle there. Two eighteen-wheelers and another RV were also parked.

He pulled in between the two big-rigs. It was great camouflage. They didn't stand out being the only vehicle and the two trucks blocked their view from the motel windows and the road behind them. He shifted into park, cut the engine, and strode to the back of the RV.

Promise was already back there waiting for him. Apparently, his earlier lecture was taken to heart. The young man pulled out two large pairs of scissors and handed one over. The two worked quickly cutting the clothes from the bodies and discarding them into a large trash bag.

When all three victims were stripped to their undergarments, *Power* opened the cabinet under the counter and pulled out a large duffel bag. From inside, he pulled out a long yellow spandex jumpsuit. He tossed it at his partner who laid it neatly beside the girl's body. He did the same for the men's costumes. When all of the outfits had been distributed, *Promise* took his time assembling them fully on the floor next to the corresponding corpse.

He laid the coiled whip and brown fedora next to the blond man. The thigh-strapped holster and toy laser blaster went to the cowboy. The three-foot Katana sword belonged to the girl. When he was done, he stood and took in the whole picture, ensuring each costume was complete. Success. They were perfectly authentic with perfect accessories.

Meanwhile, *Power* walked over to the pile of plastic in the corner. He brought back several long plexiglass rods, as well as a two-foot rectangular piece. Each of the pieces had nylon straps attached at several points.

He knelt down next to the blond man and began working on him first. *Promise* crawled over next to him to assist. Working together, they attached the two poles to the back of each leg, from the top of the hamstring to the back of the heel. The nylon straps were fastened and pulled tight, making them snug and secure. Then, Promise maneuvered the legs while *Power* slid a pair of khaki pants onto them and pulled the pants up over the sturdy rods.

The legs were stiff and stable and the joints immobilized.

Next, *Promise* rolled the body onto its side so *Power* could attach the rectangular segment to the back. He cinched the straps tight around the waist and chest. At the bottom end of the torso segment were two small rods with a hinge in the middle. He slid the bottom of the rods into the top of each leg piece and snapped them into place. He then adjusted the angle of the hinge to keep the hips, legs, and torso straight and in line. Shorter rods with hinged middles attached to the posterior surface of each arm, the hinges aligned with the elbows. The arms were then fed into the sleeves of a dirty khaki shirt, pulled together at the front and buttoned only half-way.

When all of the plexiglass supports were in place, they hoisted the body up and stood him upright. Power held him up as his partner slid a platform underneath the feet and snapped the leg rods into it.

The older man's preparation and attention to detail had surely paid off. He had been working on the pieces for weeks. He didn't want to resort to *Strength*'s fishing line method of standing them up. It was sloppy and unpredictable. And, up until yesterday, he hadn't known exactly where he was going to place them and therefore, didn't know if running fishing line through the ceiling was even an option.

Therefore, he had gotten to work designing his plexiglass stands. They were beautiful, functional, and failsafe, as well as a far superior method for posing and articulation. These bodies stood independently and that was magnificent. He stepped back and admired the dead man, standing there seemingly on its own.

The torso piece only reached as high as the top of the shoulders, thus causing the head to droop forward. He hadn't wanted the supports to show through the clothes and was careful not to extend them beyond the sleeve cuffs and shirt collars. But he was a master of preparation and had planned accordingly. He reached down and picked up the last piece remaining from the pile.

It was a tiny piece that held a six-inch ice pick on one end and two small dowels on the other. He walked around to back of the standing corpse and positioned the pick at the base of the man's skull. Forcefully, he shoved it upward and snapped the lower dowels into the top of the torso support.

Only an inch or two of metal was visible on the back of the neck. He fluffed the collar to cover as much of it as possible. For the final touch, the young apprentice walked over and slung a brown leather satchel over the man's head and diagonally across his chest. His mentor gave him an approving nod.

They repeated the process with the other two bodies.

When all three were standing, perfectly posed and upright, *Promise* went to the cabinet beneath the stovetop and pulled out a large white bucket. He popped open the top and inspected the peach-colored candle wax inside. He returned to the cabinet for a large cooking pot and placed it on the largest burner. Grabbing a metal ice cream scooper from a drawer, he began shoveling the wax into the pot.

He then turned on the burner and watched it grow red as it warmed up. Within a minute, the big scoops of wax began softening and turning to liquid. Reaching under the cabinet again, he pulled out a second container of Crisco. He threw a couple large scoops of the shortening into the pot. Not too much though. Power had been specific about the ratio between wax and shortening. He wanted the softness, but did not, under any circumstances, want the melting fiasco that had occurred at Madame Tussauds.

While *Promise* was busy stirring the wax mixture with a wooden spoon, *Power* was behind him adjusting elbow and hip hinges and posing the bodies exactly how he wanted them. He then locked the joints into place. The Crisco actually wasn't even necessary. The supports were flawless and his bodies were in a perfect position, unable to move even an inch in any direction. But the softened wax looked nicer and smoother and would give an overall better finished look.

When all of the wax was liquified, the two men worked together to hoist the huge pot and carefully fill two smaller containers with the warm liquid. After a few minutes of patience, the wax had cooled enough to reach the consistency of warm batter. They each donned latex gloves and began spreading the waxy butter across the flesh surfaces with rubber spatulas.

They worked quietly. *Power*, in the zone and engulfed in his own concentration. Promise, emulating his idol and smoothing every wayward drip to create a finished product that was up to his master's standards.

When they finished, every exposed surface of skin had been covered with a thick coat of the flesh-colored wax. *Power* walked to the front of the RV and turned up the air conditioning to the rear of the vehicle. It wouldn't be long before the wax hardened to its final state allowing the finishing touches to be done.

While he waited, *Power* pulled over a folding chair and set it up directly in front of the three statues. His eyes scanned each of them and an approving smile crossed his lips. They were not finished, but they were coming along very nicely. The surfaces still contained small ridges and smears from the spatula, but they would be taken care of. For the moment, he just wanted to sit and rest and marvel in his own genius.

The plexiglass frame supports he had made for the bodies worked even better than he had imagined. The figures were posed so naturally, they could even be mistaken for live human beings. That level of positioning could have never been accomplished with something as elementary as fishing line. He scoffed as he thought of his incompetent colleague.

When the wax had solidified as much as it was going to, *Power* took a metal file out of his pocket and approached the standing figures. He went to work filing down the raised edges, spatula marks, and the occasional wayward drip. He then lit a small candle of his own. It was a fitting method for his project. He waved the dancing flame across each of the areas he had just filed down and watched as the wax softened and smoothed.

Afterward, the surfaces resembled glossy porcelain. He stepped back and took in the sight. It was as if he was on the red carpet hanging out with three of his celebrity friends. That was how alive they looked, standing there in front of him. Except for one small important detail he had almost forgotten.

He went back into his duffel bag and unzipped a small pocket. He took out three contact lens cases and a bottle of saline solution.

"After all, the eyes are the windows to the soul, right?" he said as he carefully parted each eyelid with his fingers and lightly touched the lens to the corneal surface, sucking it off of his finger. He repeated the process until all three were looking at him with lively curiosity, as if they were silently asking him what he would like them to do next. He had really outdone himself this time.

"That looks really good," *Promise* said as he stepped up next to him.

"Of course it does." *Power* glanced down at the watch around his wrist. "Rigor mortis should be setting in within a few hours." Although, with his corpse stands, he didn't actually need the rigor. But it was more fun when they were nice and stiff.

They had plenty of time to get the bodies into position and set up the scene. And he knew exactly where he was going to put them. It would be perfect.

Chapter 28

"Okay, show me," Detective Roberts said as he and Detective Reid were led into Ripley's Believe It Not by a young officer with a nauseous-looking face.

Ripley's was one of Ocean City's most popular boardwalk attractions. It was a museum that involved outlandish stories that just seemed too crazy or weird or impossible to be true. And that was the question that was posed right there in the name—do you believe it...or not?

The two detectives followed the officer deeper into the first room, passing by a "real" shrunken head, the skeleton from a two-headed child, and countless other oddities and freak show attractions. On the way to the next room they walked through a wide-open hallway with framed newspaper clippings on the walls and strange sculptures on the sides.

The next room was large, open, and spacious, probably to give the crowds a little bit of a breather before entering the next hallway. Roberts scanned the open space. Like the hallway, a lot of "historical" framed photos and newspaper clippings adorned the walls. In the center of the room was a wooden park bench. And sitting on it was a wax figure of a man in a 1940's looking business suit. There was an empty spot next to him on the bench, presumably so tourists could pose for their own photos with the statue.

"It's over here."

The detective turned toward the officer's voice. He had missed it when he first walked in, but in the back corner of the room was a few more wax friends. Ones that he knew well. There was a high bar table with a rounded tabletop. Three wax celebrities stood around the table apparently having a few drinks and chatting away with each other.

"Well, that's a scene that would never happen in real life," Roberts said as he started toward it.

"Really? Why not?" the young officer asked.

"Seriously? How young are you?" The officer continued to stare at him, dumbfounded. "You are serious, aren't you? That's Han Solo," Roberts said, pointing to the dark-haired figure, standing with a wax hand on his thigh-holstered laser blaster.

"I know that," the officer said, offended.

"And that's Indiana Jones standing across from him." He then pointed to the blond figure with his hand on his hip grasping the coiled whip that hung there.

"Okay."

The detective paused for a moment, not sure if that "okay" meant he understood or didn't. He didn't. "Both of those characters are played by the same actor. Harrison Ford. You know who he is, right?"

"Oh yeah. Duh," the officer said, playing off how embarrassed he was at that moment. And rightfully so.

Detective Reid had been relatively quiet for the most part. He stepped out from behind his partner and walked a slow circle around the three figures. "The table is from outside. Across the boards at Alaska Stand. He unbolted one of the outside high tables and brought it in here." He continued his lap and began another. "These are just like the ones from DC." He paused several times and leaned in until his face was mere inches away from the thick waxy layer. "Are there really bodies under there?"

"Apparently so," Roberts replied. "Hard to believe, isn't it?" He walked around to where his partner stood and leaned in close just as he had. Raising a latex-covered hand, he pressed gently into the cheek of the famed archeologist. "Amazing." He then walked back around to the front of the scene and took several steps back to take in the full view. "But, why? You kill three people. Okay, I get that. There are serial killers out there. But, why cover the bodies with wax and dress them up like movie characters? Shock value? Is that it? Did those other cases come up with a motive to this particular MO? This wax fetish?"

"Not sure," the young officer said. "I think there's a point to it though. A reason they're dressed and posed like that."

Roberts waited for the officer to continue. He didn't. "Care to enlighten us with your knowledge of this case? What's the point? What's the reason?"

"I don't know exactly. There's just been talk about it. Rumors."

Roberts huffed his disappointment and turned away from the officer, unwilling to spend any more attention on him.

"I know of someone who does know though," the officer piped in. "Right after I saw them, I put a call into Washington and they redirected me to a detective in Montgomery County. They've had two more wax murder scenes there. Detective Donovan is the lead. He's on his way here. He'll probably be here in about two hours."

"Well, alright then. Now we're getting somewhere." Roberts placed his hands on his hips and nodded his head. "Congratulations, Officer. You just earned a spot at the big boy table."

The young cop smiled and stepped forward to eagerly join Detective Roberts in his examination.

"Don't push it though, Junior. Step back."

He immediately retreated back to his former distance.

"Reid. What do you see over there?" Roberts asked his tight-lipped partner.

Detective Reid scanned the bodies up and down. Crouching, he lifted the pant leg of the yellow jumpsuit. He then stood back up and rapped his knuckles in the middle of the female figure's back. A hard knock sounded out as if the woman's spine was on the outside of her body. "These plastic stands. Very well-crafted." He swept the woman's blonde hair off of her shoulder. "And that's how the head is staying up," he said, pointing at the metal spike that disappeared into the back of the woman's neck.

Another officer poked his head through the doorway from the hallway. "The press is outside and want a statement. What should I tell them?"

"I don't give a rat's ass what they want. Tell 'em to piss off." Detective Roberts despised the press. They rarely got the story right and always managed to cause more problems for him. And a case like this didn't need any more problems than it already had.

He turned his attention back to the first officer. "Those other bodies, the ones from DC…they weren't standing up like this, were they?"

"No, sir. They were sitting around a table."

"Without any plastic stands or attachments like these?"

"That's right. They started falling all over the place because they didn't have anything to support them."

"But they were covered with wax like these."

"Yep, just like these."

"What's your name, kid?" Roberts asked the young cop.

"Rico, sir. Vasquez."

"Alright, Vasquez, this is what I need you to do. I need you to get on the horn to DC and have them send over everything they've got on that wax museum bit. And I mean everything. Autopsies, witness statements, everything. And then…" He paused and cocked his head. "Why aren't you writing any of this down?"

Vasquez pulled out a small notebook and began furiously writing.

Roberts continued. "And then, I want you to get back on with Montgomery County and have them send over everything they have on their cases. I know they got a guy on the way, but I want to prepare myself before he gets here so I don't look like a jackass. Do a state-wide search to see if any similar cases occurred in any other Maryland county. Then check the surrounding states. Delaware, Virginia, West Virginia, Pennsylvania. Go back two years. I wanna know if this guy did this to anyone else outside of those we already know."

"You think he did more? Earlier?" Vasquez outwardly shuddered.

"He had to start somewhere. Sickness like this doesn't just pop up out of nowhere. He learned it. Either by trial and error or someone else turned him on to it. But this…" He waved his arm at the high table scene. "…this is just not right. Not even for your average SFP."

"SFP?" Vasquez questioned.

"Sick Fuckin' Psycho."

Chapter 29

Rebecca stood inside the screened porch sipping her coffee. She watched two boys ride past on BMX bikes, looking to be about twelve or so. They each dragged a boogie board by the wrist tether while steering with the other hand. She wondered how far they'd get before one of the boards blew into the spokes and sent both boy and bike into an X-Games worthy front flip. The way the boards were blowing in the wind and bouncing off each other, she figured, at the very least, the tethers would tangle and rip both boys from their bikes. She wondered if it would happen within the next hundred feet so she could witness it.

She took another sip and stared intently, waiting for the catastrophe. It was mean to think that way, she knew, but these were the same boys that kept cannonballing at the pool the day before and soaked her Kindle, which was now fried and dead. They could use some karma.

She watched as they reached the end of the street and turned the corner out of her sight. Shrugging, she accepted that it would be another boring day. She wasn't sure if she wanted boring or not. She did when she first got there. When she grabbed Adam and high-tailed it three hours away to the coast, she hadn't wanted anything but mundane, mind-numbing days. But that was three days ago and now she was, well, bored.

She gulped down the rest of her coffee and turned to go inside. She stopped when movement caught the corner of her eye. The screen on the porch door had ripped away from the frame and flapped in the late morning breeze.

She remembered how she had originally planned to tear up the screen a little to give Adam a job to do and a reason to stay longer. But she hadn't actually done it. Or had she? She was sure the tear had not been there when they arrived. She had specifically surveyed the porch screen, deciding on where she would do her own damage. Without a doubt, she would have noticed if it was already ripped up.

She stepped closer and examined the tear, just to find that it wasn't a tear at all. It was a cut. A precise slit in the screen done with a sharp blade, leaving no fraying edges. It was at the top of the door adjacent to the metal hook that latched and locked the door from the inside. She reached out and touched it, poked her fingers through, and found she was able to put her entire hand through the opening. Her pulse picked up a few paces as the realization began to hit her.

She removed her hand and ran her fingers down the length of screen alongside the door frame. When she reached the door's handle, her fingers slid through the screen again. Another slit, right where the second lock on the door handle was. It was a smaller cut, but it was also a smaller lock that only required a flip of a small switch to unlock the door.

She officially entered panic mode. Did someone break into her house? And when? The longer she stood there staring at the mauled screen, the more confident she became that it was not like that when they had arrived on Friday afternoon. She was even sure that it wasn't like that when her and Harmon sat out there talking. It had to have been done at some time over the weekend while they were there. Did they steal something? She and Adam had only left to go grocery shopping and to the beach and she hadn't noticed anything out of place or missing when they had returned.

A wave of nausea suddenly washed over her and she felt the color drain from her face. Her body began to sway and she stepped away from the screen and steadied herself on the rocker behind her. It wasn't morning sickness. She had gotten over that hump last month. No, the reason for this bout of nausea was so much worse.

They never locked the porch door when they ventured out for the day. Each day when they left to go to the beach or to the store, they locked the door going into the house, but the porch door always remained unlocked.

It was a pain in the ass to lock because the metal hook was thick and corroded from the humid salty air. It took a lot of jiggling and tugging and often even a broken nail or two to get the hook to slide into the locked position. It was so annoying and sometimes painful that she only messed with it twice a day—once in the evening when she locked it for the night and once in the morning to unlock it.

Her heart thumped hard in her chest. Her eyes darted back and forth between the upper slit near the hook and the lower slit near the handle. The screen wouldn't have needed to be cut if it was unlocked. Surely a burglar would've checked that first, wouldn't he? He would. Which meant the screen door was locked when whoever let himself in. And it was only locked at night when both her and Adam were asleep in the bedroom. Another wave crashed throughout her body.

But the stick. She always put the stick in the track of the door so that even if someone did pick the lock, they wouldn't have been able to open the door. At least, not without breaking the glass and reaching in to remove it. She always put the stick in the door before she went to bed. But…did she? Always?

"Babe, c'mere!" She heard Adam calling her from inside and it was the most reassuring sound she had ever heard. She threw open the sliding glass door and rushed inside to tell him about the break-in.

He stood there in board shorts, a tank top, and bare feet, halfway between the carpeted living room area and the parquay floor of the kitchen. His eyes were glued to the flat-screen tv mounted on the wall.

Rebecca sidled up to him and hooked her arm in his. His sturdy size and warm skin immediately made her feel safe and comforted.

The local news was on. It was a live feed and a woman reporter stood on the boardwalk in front of the Ripley's Believe It or Not museum. The wind whipped her hair across her face and families passing behind her hollered and waved, knowing they were on camera.

She ignored the distraction as she spoke of the triple murder that had occurred early that morning and the horrifying way in which the bodies had been found. She warned the viewers that what she was about to describe was disturbing and graphic and those that were squeamish should tune out for the remainder of the program.

She spoke of how the bodies were found covered in wax. Rebecca felt the weakness in her knees and tightened her grip on Adam's arm. She spoke of how they were posed and mistaken for sculptures at first by the museum's staff. Rebecca's skin broke out in a cold sweat as the reporter's words punched her right in the throat. She spoke of how they were dressed as movie characters. Han Solo. Indiana Jones. Uma Thurman's character from *Kill Bill*. Why did no one ever know that character's actual name? That was her last thought as the room grayed and she began to slip out of Adam's arm.

Suddenly, her body rose, weightless. She floated across the room and landed gently on the sofa. Warm fingers brushed hair off of her forehead. She heard his voice. It sounded far away. Under water. Little by little, his voice grew louder. Clearer. The gray dissipated and she saw his face hovering over hers.

"Beatrix Kiddo," she said, with all the breath her lungs would allow.

"Say what?"

"Beatrix Kiddo. That's the name of Uma Thurman's character."

"Okay…don't know how you know that…didn't know you were into pulp kung-fu movies…that's super hot…but whoa, did you hear what that reporter said? Three wax bodies found here in Ocean City. Right inside Ripley's. We were just there yesterday." Adam's eyes were popping out of his head, he was in such shock. "It's the Mannequin Murderer. He's here. That's crazy, isn't it?" His eyebrows furrowed as he cautiously looked around. "It's almost as if he's following us. Now, *that* would be crazy."

Adam stood and walked into the kitchen, returning with a bottle of water and her gel eye mask from the freezer. He dropped to his knees and propped her head up with the pillow. Then, he opened the bottle for her and held the ice pack on her forehead while she drank.

He picked up the remote and switched off the television. "I don't think we should go to the beach today." He moved the ice pack along her cheek to rest on the side of her neck. "I think we need to stay right here where it's safe."

"We can't stay here," Rebecca said as she scooted herself into a more upright position. "We need to go." She grasped his hand, squeezed it tight, brought it to her lips, and planted a kiss across his knuckles. She then swung her legs off the sofa and stood. The weakness remained and she swayed for a few seconds before finding her bearings. "Not to the beach, but we need to go."

"Where?"

"To the police station," she said, looking down into his confusion. "That Mannequin Murderer? He *did* follow us here."

Chapter 30

It was a quiet, yet thankfully short drive to the police station on 65th Street. Adam had begun pummeling her with questions as soon as they got into the car. Finally, he gave up when she said, for the millionth time, that she'd explain it all when they got there. He wasn't happy, but at least he had stopped asking.

The dread was heavy in her belly, like a boulder just sitting there, ready to roll out of her and rip her apart at any moment. It hurt. A dull ache that radiated outward throughout her body. She had come to terms with the murders that had occurred there that morning. Of course the killers followed her when she ran. Of course they were now taunting her with their reach and abilities. Given her past, why would she expect anything different? But Adam…Adam was a situation she had never dealt with before. That was what the boulder was made of.

Adam's opinion of her was about to sink to the bottom of the deepest sea.

They reached the station and Rebecca pulled into a shaded spot. Adam followed behind her as she rushed across the parking lot. She felt his suspicious eyes on her back. It had already begun. He had begun looking at her differently, cautiously. She was involved in something bad, but that was all he knew.

She could have softened the blow by giving him the Cliff Note explanation on the way. Maybe. Maybe that would have made things even worse. The truth was, she was procrastinating. She didn't want to be alone with him when he found out. She didn't want to hear the disappointed tone of his voice or the names he might call her. Perhaps he would go easy on her if there were other people in the room. Perhaps.

They entered through the glass doors at the front of the station and were immediately met by Harmon lounging on a waiting room bench.

"Oh, thank God." Rebecca rushed over to him. She didn't even allow him to fully stand before wrapping her arms around him and squeezing as tight as she could.

He returned the hug and added some comforting pats on her upper back. "I've been trying to call you for two hours."

"My ringer has been off since last night." She released him and sank onto the bench. "What are you doing here? How did you get here so fast?"

"Not that fast. Spencer called me a couple hours ago. He's on his way." Harmon, still standing, extended a hand out to a dumbfounded Adam. Adam shook it, but remained silent. He turned back to Rebecca. "I'll go let them know you're here with some more information. The detectives on the scene are on their way back. We'll get a conference room and be ready when they get here."

Several painfully awkward minutes later, the three of them were led to a private room in the back of the station. There was a long rectangular table in the center with chairs all the way around. Rebecca collapsed into the first one she came to and buried her face in her hands.

"They followed me here. They killed again here in Ocean City just to prove I can't hide from them, that they can get to me anywhere." Her voice was shaky and nearly muffled as her hands still covered her face.

"They're much more sophisticated and organized than I had originally thought," Harmon said. "It's difficult to take such a complicated killing method on the road. The fact that they were able to find three victims with the 'right look,' wax them up, and pose them even better than before…and set them up inside a business. That's impressive." He pulled out the open chair next to Rebecca and sat. "Where do they prepare the bodies? And how were they able to make it mobile and do it with even more precision here in OC?"

"Excuse me? Hello?" Adam had been standing silent and patient, listening until he finally spoke up. "What the hell is going on here? Will one of you please enlighten me? What do you mean killers are following you?" He walked around to the end of the table so he could see Rebecca's face and directed his onslaught of questions at her. "Did you have a run-in with someone back home? What do you have to do with what happened this morning?"

She couldn't look at him. His eyes were burning holes right through her, she could feel it.

He placed his hands on the table and leaned down closer to her. "A half hour ago we were watching a live news report about the mannequin murders. And now we're in a police station talking about it. And you're on the verge of tears." He reached out and put his hand under her chin, turning it toward him until she had no choice but to look into his eyes. "Please, Rebecca. Show me an ounce of respect and tell me what the hell we're doing here."

She pulled her face away and hid behind her hands again.

"If you don't tell him, I will," Harmon said.

"Tell me what?"

Just then, the door opened and two detectives walked in. Rebecca didn't know if it was perfect timing or if the situation just got exponentially worse. The younger of the two closed the door and leaned against the wall next to it. The older one walked toward the table and shook their hands one by one.

"I'm Detective Roberts," he said. "And that wallflower over there is Detective Reid." He motioned to Adam, still standing. "You can go ahead and take a seat, sir."

Adam sat and Roberts did the same. Reid continued his job of holding up the wall.

"I've been getting a lot of different information coming in between DC and this Detective Donovan that's on his way here," Roberts said. "But what I really want to know is…" He leaned forward on the table and looked deep into Rebecca's eyes. "…who are you? Why are you here? And what do you have to do with any of this?"

"It's mine," she said, mustering up all the calm and composure she had in her. "The scene this morning is mine."

Roberts flipped open a file, pulled out a photo from that morning's crime scene, and slid it across the table to her.

"Yes, that's me in the *Kill Bill* jumpsuit."

Adam leaned over slightly from his seat next to her to get a closer look at the photo. His brows furrowed as he looked back and forth between her and the photo. He leaned back into his seat, saying nothing.

"It's from a Halloween party I went to five years ago. Han Solo was a guy a started dating for a short time. That was the first time I had met him."

"And Indy?" Roberts asked.

"He was a friend of mine that turned out to be an obsessive psychopath and is responsible for all of this."

"So, you're saying this psycho friend of yours is killing these people?"

"Not directly. He's in prison, but he's in control of it."

"How? You got evidence to back that up?"

"Nothing concrete, but trust me, he's responsible."

A deep throaty chuckle escaped Roberts' mouth. "No offense, ma'am, but trust you? I don't even know you, and what I'm hearing so far…is not looking good." He moved on. "Is this Han Solo boyfriend of yours someone we can talk to?"

"He's dead. Murdered by Indy not long after that scene took place."

"I'm sorry, what?" Roberts leaned back and dramatically looked at the ceiling and corners of the room. "Is there a hidden camera in here? This cannot be a real conversation that I'm having right now."

Rebecca let out a deep sigh. "Hard to believe, isn't it? As is my life. Or, at least, my past."

She glanced over at Adam to gauge how he was taking it all in. He sat silent, his eyes cast down on the photo between them. He was clearly confused, but Rebecca didn't sense anger. Not yet.

Although, he had every right to be angry. She had lied to him and hid her past for years. They were married and expecting a baby and she still lied to keep her true self from him.

Her heart broke for him. She loved him so much and had never wanted to bring him into her mess. But here he was, holding on by a thread, thinking he had heard the worst of it and completely oblivious to how bad it was about to get.

"Let me see if I got this straight," Roberts said. "You and your friend and your boyfriend dress up in costumes and have a night on the town. Then your friend kills your boyfriend, goes to prison, and is now reliving it all vicariously through the eyes of some other SFP killing other people and playing dress-up. Is that right?"

"Not exactly, but close enough."

"SFP?" Harmon chimed in.

"Never mind that." Roberts waved him off and leaned back in his chair. "Before I came in here, I had a very interesting phone conversation with Detective Donovan, who'll be here any minute. He said that everything started with his father, Andrew Donovan."

Rebecca's eyes shot up. She was surprised he went back that far, but it was accurate. Everything did start with Andrew. Every horrible moment that she can remember from her entire life began with Andrew.

Roberts shifted in his chair and flipped through more of the file's pages. "He was on trial for killing your sister, among others. Then he was acquitted, and then you started dating him out of revenge."

Her breath caught in her throat. Out of the corner of her eye she saw Harmon tense up as well. "It's a little more complicated than that," she said.

The detective took out another photo and slid it in front of her. A loud gasp came from the seat next to her where Adam sat. The photo was of Andrew's body. Exactly the way he was found, lying on his dining room table with his chest ripped open and his heart in his mouth. She didn't remember it like that. She had never seen photos of his body. Yes, she was there when he died, but she was in a different state of mind. Her eyes closed and she turned her head away.

"Is that how you got your revenge?" Roberts asked her.

"I didn't kill him." It was the truth…in a way. She didn't want to lie anymore, but she also wasn't going to incriminate herself. There was no evidence that she was even there.

She stole a quick glance at Adam. Her breath caught as she met his eyes, staring back at her with obvious disgust. She quickly looked away.

"You are a chef, correct? I mean, you are the one with the knife skills and this poor chap was cut to hell as if he was a side of beef."

"What are you implying, Detective?" Harmon slapped his palms on the table. "She's not on trial here. She was cleared five years ago."

"By you?"

Harmon leaned back without answering.

"Yeah, I thought so. What a strange relationship this is." Roberts expression was one of curiosity, intrigue, and even slight amusement. "And what about you, Slick?" He looked at Adam. "You're awfully quiet over there. Where do you fit into all this?"

Adam didn't answer. Rebecca dared another glance at him. He was staring at the photo still on the table in front of her, his lip curled into a grimace.

"I'm just trying to put the puzzle pieces together here. What does Andrew Donovan have to do with these wax killings and what role do you have in it all, ma'am?"

Harmon garnered Roberts' attention by clearing his throat. "Let me take a stab at a summary for you, Detective. Andrew Donovan was a serial murderer and Rebecca's sister was one of his victims. He was acquitted so Rebecca took it upon herself to get close to him, without him knowing who she really was, and find some evidence. It was during that time that she met Andrew's son, Spencer and Spencer's friend, Tyler, a.k.a. Indiana Jones. Tyler quite admired Andrew and took a liking to his lady friend over here." He gestured toward Rebecca, sitting there with her eyes cast downward, thankful that Harmon had taken the reins. "She ended the relationship because she sensed Andrew suspected she was keeping something from him and she didn't want him to find out who she was—the sister of one of his victims." He paused, looking at Detective Roberts. "You following me so far?"

"Hell yes. This is utterly fascinating to me."

"Anyway," Harmon continued. "Several weeks later, Andrew Donovan was found murdered on his dining room table. With the friends and families of five victims wishing he would burn in hell forever, it's a long list of who might have tied him up and tortured him the way he tortured those five girls. I should know. I was the lead investigator on the case and I talked to every single person on that long list."

Rebecca lifted her eyes slowly. She liked the way Harmon was spinning the whole thing, but when she looked over at Adam…he looked back at her in a way that told her he knew she had something to do with his death, and worst of all, his torture.

Harmon continued. "Spencer learned of the things his father had done and some time later, he and Rebecca became friends. It started out of guilt he felt for his father's sins, but soon became a true kinship. Tyler, who had always had a liking for her became somewhat obsessed. He was young and she kept it at friends, but he wasn't satisfied with that. He began killing to get her attention and murdered her new boyfriend to get him out of the way. Son of a bitch even tried to kill me…twice."

Roberts eyebrows shot up. "No shit."

"Exactly. Rebecca saved me, gave Tyler a stroke, and now he's rotting away as a cripple in Savage River Correctional Facility. These wax murders? Tyler's orchestrating them from his cell. Got a cult of psychos willing and eager to kill for him. And that's what they're doing. Recreating scenes from his and Rebecca's life together and publicly displayed as a way to torment her." Harmon leaned back in his chair and crossed his arms. He let out a deep sigh of relief. "Whew. You all caught up now, Detective?"

"Wow! What a crazy fucking story!" Roberts grinned as his eyes lit up.

Rebecca watched him. She couldn't quite read him. He was genuinely fascinated, just like he had said, but she also sensed that he thought they were all bat-shit crazy and lying through their teeth. Except for Adam who just sat there, obviously taking it all in for the first time just like the Detective was.

"Well, I guess it all revolves around you, doesn't it, ma'am?" Roberts took several more photos from the file and lined them up facing her. They were all photos of the previous wax scenes. "These were sent over from DC and from your pal, Spencer. Tell me about them."

Rebecca went down the line explaining them. She pointed to the first photo of the scene set up outside Madame Tussauds and talked of how Andrew invited her over dinner and it was the first time she had met Tyler. She pointed to the second photo of the hallway scene and talked of how Tyler cornered her in the hallway and scared her. She pointed to the scene in Baskin Robbins and talked of how her and Tyler had become friends and stopped in to get ice cream. And finally, she pointed to the photo from that morning and talked of the Halloween party where she had first met Michael.

"You've got some serious bad luck with men, don't you? Almost black widow-like," Roberts said with a sarcastic, yet serious tone. "The way I see it, of the three past men you've been involved with, two of them are dead and the third is a serial killer still pining for you from a prison cell." His gaze drifted toward Adam. "You might wanna watch your back there, Slick."

That was it. That was the straw that broke him. Adam shot one last disgusted look at Rebecca before standing and walking out of the room without another word.

Rebecca jumped up and went after him. She refused to lay down and die and give him up without a fight. She caught up to him outside as he took the station's front steps two at a time. He spun around and gave her the coldest look she had ever seen come out of those deep blue eyes.

"Who are you?" he asked her, not even expecting an answer. "Andrew Donovan was your boyfriend? Tyler Maddox is obsessed with you? Christ, Rebecca, I've watched the documentaries on both of them. *You* are the mysterious woman that put Tyler in the hospital? *You* are the female wax figure in all those scenes?" Adam turned away from her, gripping fistfuls of his hair in frustration. He turned back toward her, calm and serious. "Did you kill Andrew Donovan?"

"No."

"Don't lie to me."

"I didn't kill him."

"Were you there?"

She didn't answer, just stared at him with eyes pleading for understanding. Begging for forgiveness.

"Were you there?" he repeated.

"Yes. I cut him, but not fatally."

Adam threw his hands up and grasped at his hair again. "Jesus! Not fatally? And that's okay?" He was yelling at her now. "You can tie him down and slice him up, but as long as he doesn't die from it then it's okay? That's torture! You know that, right? That is straight up sadistic torture!"

"You don't know what it was like!" Her eyes burned as the tears started. "You don't know where my head was at! I was fighting for my life!"

"He was tied to a table!" Adam took a deep breath and lowered his voice. "Unarmed and incapacitated. I'd hardly say you were fighting for your life at that moment." His tone was calm, but it dripped with repulsion.

"I fought him," she said through gritted teeth. The tears streamed, but her words were hot and angry. "I woke up strapped to a table in his basement. You saw the documentaries. You know what he did to those women, to my sister. How he butchered them. And he had every intention of doing the same thing to me. I fought my way out of that basement." She took a deep breath and reflected his icy glare right back at him. "I. Fought. For. My. Life."

"Then how did he end up the way he did?"

"Someone helped me. Someone who was also fighting for their life."

"You could have called the police. You had a choice. You didn't have to tie him down and torture him. You did it because you wanted to." Adam stepped closer to her and lowered his voice even more. "I can't even wrap my head around how someone could do that to another person, no matter how angry they are or how much that person might deserve it. It takes a particular breed to kill another human being."

"I didn't kill him."

"No, it looks like what you did was even worse. Unnecessary torture. That was your choice. And it was a sick one."

"I pray you never have to make that choice." Rebecca straightened and held up her chin. "I pray you never have to fight for your life against a serial killer and make the choice between calling the police and hoping the justice system does its job—or ending it yourself and stopping his murder spree once and for all. I pray for you, Adam, I really do. I pray you'll never know what that feels like."

She stepped away to create some distance. She was done apologizing for doing what needed to be done. She was done apologizing for saving the innocent and punishing the guilty.

He must have sensed her finishing point because he suddenly turned and walked away. She stared at his back as he stepped off the sidewalk into the lot. The tears returned. The sad ones, not the angry ones. They had never had a fight like that before. Her heart wretched and twisted and real physical pain spread throughout her chest. She literally felt her heart breaking.

Adam stopped a few steps into the lot. Her breath caught in her throat as he turned around and headed back toward her. What was he doing? She couldn't handle him yelling at her again. Or his icy glare. If that was what he was coming back for, she wished he would just turn right back around and keep on walking. She held her breath as he approached.

"What are you going to do now?" he asked with genuine concern in his voice.

She erected a false front—stoic and unemotional. She had no idea where his head was at and refused to give him the chance to put her through the ringer again. "Spencer will be here soon. He'll meet with these detectives and we'll decide our next steps from there. I'm part of this case. I was working with him back home and I'll continue to do that until it's done."

He nodded, his eyes scanning the parking lot, avoiding hers. "You stick with Spencer," he said firmly. "Don't let yourself get out of his sight for a second. Not for a single second." His eyes locked on hers and held her there. He was still angry…and disgusted by her…and utterly repulsed by the whole situation. But she was still his wife. She still carried his baby inside of her. She still needed to be protected. "I need to be alone right now. You stick with Spencer."

He turned, and once again, she watched his back as he crossed into the parking lot. She knew he wouldn't be turning back around this time.

Harmon came up behind her. He had been standing further back, waiting for them to finish. "Don't worry, I'll look after him. Keep me updated," he said over his shoulder as he passed her and chased after Adam.

And just like that, she was alone.

Chapter 31

"We'll be there in a little over an hour," Spencer said as he moved his truck into the left lane and jockeyed for a good position. Route 50 morphed into the Chesapeake Bay Bridge, climbing gradually until the shimmering water came into view below them.

Rebecca sat in the passenger seat staring out at the white sails that speckled the vast body of water as far as she could see. She tried hard to steer her mind clear, but her efforts were futile. Automatically, her brain took her back to three days ago when she and Adam had crossed this bay in the other direction.

He had been laughing and joking and carrying on with one of his crazy stories. And now, three days later, she was leaving the coast without him, crying silently behind her sunglasses. The way he had looked at her with such disgust. She couldn't get the image out of her head. It was the exact reason why she had never told him about her past. She knew she could never bear him looking at her like that and it turned out she was right.

She should take Harmon's advice—back off and allow Spencer to work the case, follow procedure, and let the justice system work. Perhaps if she distanced herself from the case and gave Adam a day or two to calm down…and gave Harmon time to explain things to him from her corner…then maybe she could salvage their relationship.

But it was her life at stake, and possibly Adam's too. Could she even explain her way out of it? Facts were facts and she did what she did. Would the reasons behind her actions even make a difference to Adam? Likely not. If she stopped now and was still unable to make Adam understand, then it would all be for nothing.

Tyler needed to be stopped. She needed to cut off the head of the snake, otherwise she would never be able to live her life without constantly looking over her shoulder. She would never be able to rebuild a normal life with Adam, if that was even still possible.

There was a brilliant psychopath tucked away safe in his cell and if she didn't take action, he would remain safe forever. The warden could take away all of his correspondences and internet privileges, but he would still find a way to torment her. It would be his entertainment for as long as he lived. He would find another way to get at her…or Adam…or their baby.

Tyler was patient. He had waited five years until she had moved on. He waited until she was settled and starting a family and had forgotten all about him. That was when he crawled up out of his hole to drag her back into it. What would he do when this chapter was over? Wait ten years? Fifteen or twenty? Would he wait until her daughter was a beautiful unsuspecting college student, away from home for the first time? Is that when he would strike next? Is that when he would summon up more minions to kill for him? What would they do to her?

Rebecca's mind went to a deep dark place that she couldn't bear. Her imagination ran wild with thoughts of the damage and torture that Tyler Maddox could do to her future family. And he would, if ever given the chance. There was only one way to ensure that chance never came.

She had become soft working side by side with Spencer and the police. She had to remember that she was not a cop and she did things her own way. It was time to return to her roots and take care of business once and for all.

She glanced over at Spencer. He was quiet and seemingly focused on the road, but she knew the wheels were turning in his mind as well. She would let him do his thing, follow his clues, and get his warrants. But she had her own Plan B in mind and things were going to get ugly. She would apologize to him after. She would apologize to all of them…after.

Chapter 32

Rebecca pulled down the sun visor and flipped open the vanity mirror. She stared into her reflection, adjusting the shoulder-length, wavy black wig. A few blonde tresses peeked out behind her ears and she tucked them back in and out of sight.

Having Harmon as an ally had worked to her advantage once again. He had really come through for her this time. She hoped he would also come through for her with Adam.

After flipping the mirror closed, she reached into her purse and pulled out her wallet. All it contained was a twenty-dollar bill and a driver's license. No credit cards and no photos. She slid the license out of the clear plastic pocket and read the name. Amanda White. It had been six years since she had been in the skin of her alter ego. She thought she had put her to rest long ago. Amanda had done some serious damage back then and her actions had already come back to ruin her. And since she was already back in town, it was only fitting that Rebecca embrace that other side of her. She had a job to do and Amanda was the only one who could do it.

She looked closely at the picture on the license. Her hair was shorter then, but not by much. With her long blonde locks painted black and chopped into a short wavy bob, she had been a near spitting image of Marie, Andrew's estranged wife.

She didn't need the resemblance this time around. All she needed was a fake name and to match the picture on her fake ID. Although, it didn't hurt that while taking on Amanda White's physical appearance, she also took on her persona. It was the persona Rebecca had created along with Amanda. Strong. Fearless. Capable. Cunning. All of those characteristics would be useful as she fought her final battle.

Suddenly, she felt a sense of calm and peace wash over her. It was as if an old friend had hopped into the passenger seat, vowing to fight by her side to the death. It was a true *Thelma and Louise* moment as Rebecca's lungs filled with the air of rebellious courage. She stuffed the wallet back in her purse and stepped out of the car.

She scanned the storefront signs posted along the long cream-colored building strip. Kirkland Catering sat on the end next to a deserted pizza parlor. Rebecca smoothed her slacks, tugged on the hem of her dress shirt, and headed over.

The glass door stood propped open with a large brick and a train of six women in matching white polos scurried in and out of the building carrying large plastic bins. They unloaded them into the back of a white Ford Club Wagon van and then went back inside for more.

Rebecca waited for a break in the train, slid in line behind a head of brown curls, and followed her in. Once inside, the woman disappeared into the back room and Rebecca was left alone in an empty lobby. She headed over to a small office on the left and approached an older woman with a beehive auburn wig. The woman was oblivious as she tapped away at her computer.

Rebecca knocked lightly on the open office door. "Hi, can you help me please? I'm looking for Mrs. Ophelia Kirkland."

The woman looked up and peered over candy apple red reading glasses. "Then you're looking for me. Are you the cook Ed Harmon sent over?" She didn't wait for an answer. "I just lost a worker due to an uncomfortable incident at the prison." She stood and walked out from behind her desk. "One of the inmates got a little grabby during the lunch service and now I'm short-handed. Are you aware that the catering position involves cooking and serving meals at the prison up the road?"

"Yes, I am," Rebecca answered.

"And do you have any issues with that?"

"None whatsoever." Rebecca handed Mrs. Kirkland her resume.

"Great." She took the papers and tossed them on her desk. "I'll look over that later when I have time. Right now you need to head over to the prison and get breakfast started."

"Oh, okay. Right now?" Rebecca had shown up expecting an interview. It took her a moment to realize that she had just been hired.

"Can you start right now?"

"Absolutely."

"Great. Ed Harmon said you were an incredible cook and able to handle yourself around troublemaking men."

Oh, was she ever.

"I trust 'Ol Ed so I'm sure you'll work out fine." Mrs. Kirkland headed out of the office and motioned for Rebecca to follow her. "The job is full time, forty hours a week plus a one-hour break after lunch is served," she called out over her shoulder. "7:30am to 6:30pm Tuesday through Friday. You get the weekends and Mondays off for now. The schedules rotate every month."

She walked over to a stack of cardboard boxes in the corner of the lobby, reached in, and pulled out a white collared shirt. After looking at the tag, she tossed it back in, rummaged around a little more, and pulled another one out. She handed it to Rebecca along with a black apron. Both the shirt and the apron sported the Kirkland Catering logo on the upper left breast.

"Unfortunately, your break needs to be taken on-site because the transport van stays. The prison is in the middle of nowhere and you'd never be able to get anywhere, order, eat, and get back within an hour anyway. I'm sorry, but we hold you hostage during your break and it's not part of the forty hours you get paid for, but that's the way it is."

Rebecca just nodded and followed Mrs. Kirkland as she raced around the lobby and out into the front parking lot. She moved quite fast for an older woman.

"Cecelia, come here, dear," she called out to one of the women loading the van. "This is Cecelia. She's in charge and she'll show you the ropes."

A beautiful Latino woman sidled up from the other side of the van. She smiled, nodded, and then disappeared back from which she came.

"Good. Off you go." Mrs. Kirkland nudged Rebecca toward the passenger door before turning and going back inside.

"Well, alright then. Off I go."

◆◆◆

Twenty minutes later, the van pulled through the security gate and Rebecca's pulse quickened. She had changed her shirt and donned the apron on the way. Fortunately, she wasn't self-conscious. The way the other women stared at her as she stripped would have made anyone blush. Not Rebecca though. She had a job to do and that was all she would allow herself to focus on.

As the van entered the prison grounds and rolled along the service road, Rebecca took in the atmosphere. She had practically lived at the prison for several days the week before, but it looked different this time. It felt different. There was a definite air of malevolence that rolled off of the barbed wire strings and swooped down through the chain link fencing. In any other situation that sensation would have sent chills up her spine. But not in this case. She felt completely comfortable with that aura of wickedness because she knew she was the cause of it. She wasn't afraid of the malice because she *was* the malice. And although she hated to admit it, the power she felt was intoxicating.

They pulled up to the loading dock of a one-story brick building. The doors flung open and all six of the other women leaped out and began pulling the bins out of the back. One by one, they unloaded the bins and carried them in through the back door of the kitchen.

Rebecca followed their lead and jumped out as well. She walked around to the back of the van and heaved a bin onto her shoulder and carried it into the kitchen. Once inside, she placed it on the floor next to the others. She received no direction or instruction from Cecelia so she just mimicked whatever the others were doing.

Her co-workers had barely spoken to her since Mrs. Kirkland had practically thrown her into the van with them. She wasn't sure if it was rookie initiation or if they simply didn't like her. Thinking back through the past half hour, she sorted through her memories trying to find a reason for the women's disdain for her presence. She came up with nothing. They just didn't like her.

For all of half a second, her feelings were hurt by that realization. But just as soon as it popped up, it was gone. Rebecca didn't care what they thought of her. She didn't want them to get to know her. She needed to be forgettable.

She had other things to focus on as well, such as, what even was her plan for Tyler? She honestly didn't know, having not thought that far ahead yet. All she knew was that she had needed to get access inside and that she would figure out the rest later. And later had quickly become now.

She headed back out to the van with her lack of a plan sitting in the forefront of her mind. She didn't know how much time she had, but she knew she had no time to waste. Constant paranoia sets in when you assume a false identity and it was only a matter of time until that paranoia ratted her out. The faster she could accomplish her mission and quit her job, the better.

She buried the top half of herself inside the back of the van, stretching to reach the final bin.

"Uh oh, look who's here!" one of the women called out.

Rebecca straightened and peeked out from behind the van door, curious. A large black man in a navy-blue track suit turned the corner of the sidewalk. He pushed a wheelchair carrying a man, waving as if he was strolling down the red carpet.

"Watch out for that one," another woman whispered to her. "He looks harmless, but he's not." She playfully nudged Rebecca with her elbow, implying she was joking.

As the two men came closer, Rebecca gasped. She immediately turned away, ducking back behind the van's open doors. *Of course he would be here to greet me.* She prayed he hadn't seen her, or at the very least, recognized her. If he had, it would all be over. He would know she was up to something. Why else would she be in disguise and working in a prison kitchen when she had a five-star restaurant of her own? She wondered what her sentence would be if she was arrested for working at a prison under false pretenses.

Tyler's therapist followed the sidewalk as he pushed the wheelchair up the slight incline toward the van.

"You're late today," one of the women said. "You're not seeing someone else, are you?"

"You better not have any other girlfriends," another added.

Tyler just smiled as he was wheeled closer and closer to Rebecca's hiding spot. The women continued to jokingly flirt with him and he threw a few charismatic comments back. The women blushed and smiled and tossed their hair around. He had a way. He always did.

From the cat calls being thrown back and forth, Rebecca deduced that the encounter was a regular occurrence. Apparently, he got his "walk" every morning at that time and always made sure he swung by the kitchen to see his "girls."

"Who's the new girl?" he asked.

Rebecca's stomach dropped. All she had wanted was to be invisible. Forgettable. And in doing so, she had piqued Tyler's curiosity. She feared he would dig and dig until he brought everything crashing down. She sank deeper into the abscess created by the van doors. Her mind raced with what her next move would be. From her position, she couldn't see him directly, but the early morning shadow of the wheelchair and the man pushing it crept closer and closer to her.

"Come out from behind there," he said. "Don't by shy. No need to hide from me. I won't hurt you."

Rebecca wanted to jump out and scream "Liar!" into his smug face.

"Why are you being so rude?" the woman called Stassi asked. "He's not doing anything wrong. He's just trying to be nice. You could stop being a bitch and just say hi to him."

Stassi's accusations hit a nerve with Rebecca. *A bitch? Really?* That woman didn't know anything about her. What gave her the right to judge her like that? She turned and glared at the woman, her blood boiling ever so slightly. It was all she needed to change her tune.

Rebecca raised her chin, straightened her shoulders, and pulled the last bin from the back of the van. It dropped to the ground with unexpected weight. As she bent down to get another hold on it, long strands of her wig fell forward to cover her face. She used the opportunity to peek through the waves and lock her eyes onto Tyler himself.

He still approached, with his hand raised to his forehead, shielding his eyes from the low-hanging sun. Finally, something worked in Rebecca's favor. The sun beamed from behind her and cast her as a dark silhouette, and with the blinding light, one that couldn't be stared directly at for too long.

She was lucky. For the first time, she realized what a poor choice her disguise was. She hadn't expected for Tyler to see her at all until the final moments. She definitely couldn't have him see her like this. He would recognize her in a second. After all, she had first met him under the disguise of Amanda White. He had first fallen for her as Amanda White.

She was convinced that her alter ego was the worst disguise she could have gone with. But she had no choice. She needed to match her ID and it was a good one. Flawless. And it was the only way she could get a job at a prison without using her real identity. Alas, it also might have ended up being her downfall. She needed to get away from Tyler and fast.

Grunting as she lifted the heavy bin, she dipped her head and turned her shoulder toward the approaching men. She was on her way to the kitchen door and nearly in the clear when Stassi stepped in front of her, blocking her escape.

"Relax, Rookie." Stassi grabbed her upper arm and held her in place. "This is the only entertainment he gets. A couple of minutes of female conversation every morning to last him the rest of the day. Why don't you stop being so rude and hurting his feelings. He didn't do anything to you."

"You have no fucking idea," Rebecca shot back at the woman, followed by immediate regret. She was blowing her cover more and more with every word she spoke. It was simple.

Shut up and get the hell out of there. Why did she have such a hard time doing that?

Rebecca dropped the bin and yanked her arm out of Stassi's grasp, but the woman just readjusted and grabbed her harder. Another glance at the sidewalk showed the wheelchair shadow closer than ever. Another few pushes and he'd be able to reach out and grab her himself.

Her pulse raced as the panic set in. If he reached her own shadow then the sun's beams would be blocked and her shroud of mystery would be gone. He would be able to stare right into her eyes and know that she was up to something. Something that involved him, and likely, a whole helluva lot of blood. If he knew her at all, he would know that whatever she was up to…it was going to be messy.

She refused to let her one chance at justice disappear because of one idiot kitchen worker. Her arm tensed and she yanked it away again, feeling Stassi's fingernails break through her skin and tear across her bicep. She twisted and shrugged as the woman attempted to recapture her hold on her. Slapping her hand away, Rebecca blindly flailed her arms and simulated a full-blown panic attack. Stassi withdrew her hand and took a step back, obviously wanting nothing to do with the raging lunatic Rebecca had become.

Rebecca seized the moment and raced toward the kitchen doors, leaving the heavy bin on the sidewalk for the others to deal with. Once inside, she backed herself up against the wall and panted until she nearly passed out.

Without even a second to catch her breath, Cecelia stood staring at her in shock, having followed her in after the show she had put on outside. "What the hell is wrong with you?"

"I'm okay now."

"The hell you are! What was that?"

"I just had a minor panic attack, that's all. I felt a little faint and then Stassi was grabbing at me and wouldn't let me go inside. I needed to get in here before I passed out right there on the sidewalk. And her not letting me just made it worse." Rebecca took a deep breath and exhaled slowly, proving to Cecelia that her attack had indeed passed. She couldn't risk Cecelia firing her if she didn't think she could handle a simple wheelchair-bound prisoner. "I'm fine. It won't happen again. I swear."

"See that it doesn't," Cecelia warned. "You don't have to partake in the morning ritual of humoring that psycho out there, but you do have to keep your cool around here. I will not have my girls be the laughing stock of this facility. Whatever you do reflects on me. Remember that."

Rebecca nodded and watched Cecelia storm back out to the van. She took another deep breath. She was fine. But was she really? She had brought a shitload of attention to herself, especially from Tyler, the one person she needed to avoid at all costs until the time was right. And the time was definitely not right.

If his routine was to swing by and see "his girls" every morning then tomorrow would be the same fiasco. And the more she avoided him, the more interested in her he would become. Which in turn, would make everyone else interested in her as well. Her goal of being forgettable had become more and more unachievable.

She closed her eyes and let her mind go to work. Her behavior was unfortunate, but also necessary if she was to keep her identity under wraps. She was caught off-guard and paid for it. But that was in the past and out of her control. She needed to focus on what she could control.

She was there to do a job. It was unclear exactly what that job would entail, but at least she was inside. At least she now had some sort of access. Now, what should she do with that access? She didn't know, but she was creative. She'd think of something.

Chapter 33

It was her third day of working at the prison and Rebecca was fully immersed in her usual morning routine—hiding out inside the kitchen while the other women were still unloading the van. She clearly heard Tyler outside of the door talking to them.

So far, she had managed to avoid any further attention-getting encounters. Each day she jumped out of the van first and grabbed the largest bin she could reach and headed inside to unpack it. Since that first day, Tyler hadn't seen any more than the back of her head.

Although, she wasn't completely in the clear and she certainly was not forgotten. She had heard him ask about her while she hid out in the kitchen with her ear pressed firmly against the exit door. She also heard the women tell him her name—Amanda. Fortunately, they either didn't know or didn't remember her last name. If they had, her cover would surely have been blown to smithereens.

Rebecca had fed the women her backstory of recently getting out of an abusive relationship and how she didn't like being around strange men, especially those that were incarcerated. They readily bought her excuse and passed it on to Tyler without even being asked. They seemed all too happy letting him know that "he wouldn't be getting anywhere with that one."

The kitchen door had been left slightly cracked after Stassi had unloaded one of her paltry bins and Rebecca stepped closer to it. Tyler's voice drifted in loud and clear. She could hear the sly smile in his voice, and the feminine giggling that followed confirmed it. He charmed the hell out of them as only he could. If only they knew what he could do…what he had already done. The mere sound of his voice made her blood boil and Rebecca instantly became more motivated than ever to end him.

Finally, Cecelia cracked her supervisory whip and the conversation screeched to a halt. Rebecca nearly had her teeth knocked out as the steel door flew open and the women scurried inside. They placed the bins at their respective stations, ripped open the lids, and began unpacking. Rebecca stepped over to her station and mindlessly stirred the pot of oatmeal she had already started.

She looked up as a female CO leading four inmates rounded the corner and entered the kitchen from the hall. Well-behaved and non-violent inmates were rewarded with meaningful jobs to make a little extra money for their commissary purchases. Working in the kitchen was the most sought-after job and awarded the most freedom, although there was always one or two COs supervising from an empty corner.

Rebecca decided that the chance to hang out side by side with women all day also played a part in the perks of a kitchen worker. She understood that and kept her guard up, but hadn't yet run into any problems. Those four inmates were beyond respectful and well-behaved because they knew they'd be ripped out of the kitchen in a second if there were any complaints about them.

Within the span of two minutes the kitchen had become a bustling hub of bodies racing this way and that. Pots clashed and metal ladles bounced off of the floor with ear-splitting clangor. Everyone had a job to do and they sped around the room setting up for the breakfast service.

Breakfast was the easiest to make and it was nice to start each day with that. Rebecca looked over her shoulder to make sure everyone was in their usual spots. The one good thing about prison was the predictability, at least in that situation. The CO stood in the same spot every day. The women and the inmates each worked the same station every day. She never had to wonder if someone would suddenly be working in the area she needed because no one deviated from their routine. Ever. And routine proved vital if you were ever to make up a plan that hinged on every minute detail, which Rebecca did.

Eventually, she pulled over a tall wheeled tray cart and began loading it up with individual meals. Most of the inmates came to the cafeteria for their meals. However, if one was medically or behaviorally unable to be around others, or if they were in solitary confinement, then they would have their meals delivered to them in their cells.

The lower security allowed Cecelia to take on that task. Rebecca's job was to load the tray cart, but Cecelia made the deliveries. Sometimes she was escorted by a CO, but often times she wasn't. It was the only job of the day that wasn't completely predictable. Rebecca could play the odds, but it still made her uneasy knowing that one aspect could throw a wrench in her entire plan. She had no choice but to roll with it and hope fate was on her side.

Cecelia's delivery route consisted of the infirmary, solitary, and a list of individual cells. Tyler was on that list. When Rebecca and her team found his letters describing the mannequin murders, the warden stripped him of all communication privileges. He also ceased Tyler's contact with any visitors or fellow inmates. Only the prison staff was allowed anywhere near him. Thus, no cafeteria for him.

And since the stroke she gave him left him with the inability to chew, and therefore a choking risk, he was on a soft food diet. His meal differed from the others loaded onto that tray cart. It was music to Rebecca's ears when she had first learned of his food restrictions. It meant she could personally make his meal without worrying about it getting mixed up with anyone else's. That was the deciding factor in her method of execution.

Rebecca continued to load up the trays and slide them into the cart tracks. She turned back to her station and stared down at Tyler's tray. It was his usual soft breakfast meal of oatmeal with melted peanut butter, mashed banana, and a strawberry protein smoothie. It was as if she was feeding a baby. She smiled thinking of how far he had fallen.

After a subtle glance over her shoulder, she reached into the front pocket of her pants and pulled out a small vial of white powder. She knew the oatmeal bowl always came back clean and empty. *That psychopath sure does love his oatmeal.* She dumped the entire vial into the oatmeal and stirred it up. It only amounted to about a teaspoon, but it was plenty enough for her purpose.

She finished loading up the last of the meals just as Cecelia appeared beside her to take the cart. She wheeled it away and Rebecca wiped up her station and began prepping for the wave of inmates that would soon funnel into the cafeteria. It was the routine. And thankfully, the routine allowed someone else, namely Cecelia, to be her delivery system to Tyler.

It wasn't poison. It was something easier to get and less detectable. Three crushed Warfarin tablets. An odorless and tasteless blood thinner commonly prescribed after joint replacement surgery, which her mother had just gone through six months ago. He would gobble it up without a clue. However, that would only be Stage One because Warfarin didn't do any harm on its own. But when combined with a bout of internal bleeding, the results would be disastrous.

When her prep was finished, Rebecca continued on with her routine by joining Thomas, one of the kitchen inmates, to help load up trays for the incoming crowd. She kept her eye on the clock and was only with Thomas for ten minutes before leaving him to make her way to the coffee pot. She filled the water, scooped the coffee grounds, pressed the start button, and returned to the inmate's side before he had even realized she was gone.

Rebecca had spent her first days not only learning her own routine, but Cecelia's as well. After all, she was an integral part of her plan. For each meal, she would make her deliveries and return twenty-five minutes later. She would then pour herself a coffee and step outside for a cigarette. After thirty minutes, she would go back through her route to collect the empty trays. Three times a day, every day. Three cups of coffee and three cigarettes.

Rebecca had decided to use Cecelia's clockwork routine as a part of her plan and had taken it upon herself to regularly pour her coffee and have it hot and waiting for her when she returned from her deliveries. She was the boss after all and was used to her staff sucking up to her, especially "the new girl."

Breakfast and lunch were just there to reinforce the new routine. Dinner, however, was where it would really come into play. The dinner orders were more varied and complicated and took a little extra time. Cecelia didn't like the extra time cutting into her cigarette break so she was more than willing to let Rebecca tag along to speed things up. She would then revert back to her solo ways when it was time to collect the empty trays. Rebecca suspected she might do it that way so she could take her time and get out of cleaning and packing up at the end of the day. But as "the boss" she wouldn't have to do it anyway. Rebecca didn't fully understand and didn't really care to. All that mattered was the routine and how she could tailor it to work for her.

Rebecca glanced up at the clock and immediately returned to the coffee pot. She took the marbled purple mug out of the cabinet and filled it with the steaming liquid. A dash of cream and a sprinkle of sugar and Rebecca turned just in time to hand the mug to her boss.

"Not yet," Cecelia said, holding up her palm to stop Rebecca in her tracks. "I need one more choke-hazard breakfast.

Rebecca's heart skipped a beat. The routine broke. For the first time, the routine broke. But more importantly, why did Tyler need a second breakfast?

"Why? I know I put Mr. Maddox's breakfast on the cart. It was right there in his usual slot," Rebecca said.

"Yeah, well, no one told me that there was a new patient in the infirmary that just got four teeth knocked out in a fight. I had to give the soft breakfast to him and now I need another one to run down to Mr. Maddox."

Rebecca stood there, silent and stunned. Someone else had gotten the Warfarin. A variable that she had thought was nearly impossible.

"What are you waiting for? Go make up another soft breakfast. Now."

Rebecca set the coffee on the counter and hustled over to her station to make up another tray. Panic set in as she was now officially worried about who had received the drugged breakfast she had made. She took a deep breath and closed her eyes, sending a little prayer out that whoever he was, he'd be okay. It could take twelve hours before the blood thinner became effective. She hoped the inmate with the knocked-out teeth wasn't actively bleeding at the moment.

Although, now she was facing a different problem. She had only brought one dose with her that morning and didn't have any more to put into the new meal. She would give him another dose tomorrow morning, but she had wanted to do it twice just to ensure effectiveness. That, apparently, wasn't going to happen. Tomorrow was Friday, the last day of work before she was off for three days. Off for three days and never to return. She couldn't push it to the next week. It had to be done now. Tomorrow.

One dose would have to do. She would swing for the fences, but if she missed...

Chapter 34

Ed Harmon walked the length of the wooden pier, a thermos of hot coffee in each hand. It was a warm morning and the sun was just beginning to rise, which meant it was about to get a whole lot warmer. Hot coffee might not have been the best choice, but when a man is up and out before dawn, there was just no other way to go.

He reached the landing dock at the end of the pier and handed off one of the coffees to Adam before sinking into the canvas chair beside him. Harmon already felt his shins beginning to sweat underneath his jeans, but he'd rather be faced with a heat rash than a hundred mosquito bites. At that time of morning the biting bugs were relentless, especially right on the water as they were.

"You ready to catch some breakfast?" he said to his companion.

"You bet. Nothing better than an overflowing fish omelet," Adam answered.

Harmon lived about an hour south of Ocean City, on an island off the coast of Virginia. His house on Chincoteague Bay was small, but it had its own dock and privacy. Retirement had been glorious. Every day for the past several years, spring to fall, he had been out on that dock before the sun rose to catch his breakfast. He loved the solitude, but it was nice having company for a change. Adam had been nearly the perfect housemate for the past four days. Nearly. He still wouldn't budge on his new feelings for Rebecca.

The two men had bonded immensely since he'd been there. Fishing did that. Harmon had always liked Adam. He was a respectable stand-up guy and good for Rebecca. She needed someone like him to keep her grounded and out of trouble. But it seemed trouble always found her anyway. And now that trouble might have taken Adam away from her as well.

He was still angry. Harmon had tried to talk to him about it at first. He was angry that she had kept such big secrets from him. Then he was disgusted with what she had done to Andrew. Disturbed with how she had tried to kill Tyler. And now, he was back to being angry about all of it.

Harmon had tried to explain the situation and let him see it from Rebecca's viewpoint, but that just seemed to make matters worse. Adam was a pure soul, which is why Harmon liked him so much. But it was also why he would never truly understand why Rebecca felt she had no choice but to do what she did. He had never been in a situation anything like that so how could he possibly understand? He couldn't.

Harmon explained how distraught Rebecca had been over her sister's murder. He explained how Andrew was a monster that had to be stopped. In the end, justice had been served. Adam still didn't agree.

Maybe it was for the best. If he couldn't accept her for who she *was* along with who she *is*, then their relationship was already doomed from the start. It just took three years to come to the surface. Harmon decided not to waste any more time on it. Adam had made up his mind and nothing Harmon said would change it. Adam was the only one who had the power to do that.

Once Harmon accepted that, he decided to leave the subject alone. They spent the next days fishing and talking and crabbing and talking and Harmon grew to like Adam even more. It was too bad he was such a straight arrow.

The two men sat in peaceful silence, sipping their coffees and, every now and then, swirling their line in the water as if that would help them get a bite. It didn't.

"I need to go back to Rockville today," Harmon finally said. "You can stay here if you want. If you need more time."

Adam appeared to ponder the offer seriously. It wasn't a bad deal after all.

"I talked to Spencer last night," Harmon continued. "His federal warrant should be coming in today and he swears it's going give him all the evidence he needs to make an arrest. And to be completely honest, I really want to be there when he takes Tyler down. The man did try to kill me after all. Twice."

Harmon decided to leave out the phone conversation he had with Rebecca regarding her new job. If Adam wasn't onboard with the way Rebecca handled things, then the less he knew the better.

"I should probably go back too," Adam said. "I need to talk to her. Our relationship is about to get really complicated, especially because of the baby."

Harmon's heart broke. He knew exactly what Adam was saying, and although it likely was for the best, it still pained him knowing that Rebecca, once again, was about to have her life shattered.

They sat in silence for another hour or so before finally giving up on breakfast. It was as if the fish knew there was work to be done and the men needed to quit procrastinating and deal with it. They packed up their chairs, poles, and empty fish buckets and headed inside. In no time, they were both in their separate vehicles heading inland—Adam heading toward what once was a happy home, and Harmon heading toward the promise of justice.

Neither had a clue of what was truly in store for them.

Chapter 35

Nearly four hours after leaving Chincoteague, Harmon pulled his car into the lot at the Montgomery County Police precinct in Rockville. He and Adam had separated their caravan on I-495 a few miles back as they passed the Silver Spring exit. Adam flashed his lights and gave a salute as he passed into the exit lane.

Harmon wondered if he was going straight home to talk to Rebecca. He also wondered if she would even be there. She had updated him on the catering job, but then was smart enough to leave her cellphone at home so she couldn't be tracked. Her burner phone was likely in her car in Kirkland Catering's parking lot. He actually had no idea where she was at that moment, but according to his dashboard clock, prepping for the lunch service was a likely guess.

Without a clear agenda and because he simply didn't know what to do first or where to go, Harmon parked his car and headed up the precinct steps in search of Spencer. He hadn't even reached the doors when Spencer walked out of them.

"How'd you get here so fast?" Spencer asked.

"I wouldn't say fast. I've been on the road for hours."

"Doesn't matter. I got it," he said, waving a sheet of paper in his hand. "I got the warrant. This is what we needed. Let's go."

Spencer took the steps two at a time without even waiting for a response. Harmon shrugged and ambled after him. At least now there was an actual task at hand. He had been idle for too long. Retirement was great, but so was the hunt. Especially when your prey had tried to kill you.

"Over here. We'll take my car," Harmon said as he caught up to Spencer and led him to the far side of the lot. Harmon hated being a passenger and he did have seniority, but most of all, he wanted to control the situation. He had no idea when Rebecca would drop her bomb and what would be required of him when she did. Either way, he was likely going to need options and that only came with being the driver.

Spencer didn't argue and followed Harmon to his car.

"Do you know where Rebecca is? I tried calling her earlier, but it just went to voicemail," Harmon asked, strictly to find out how much Spencer knew.

"I haven't seen much of her since we got back from OC. I think she's just really freaked out that the murders followed her there and maybe she's trying to distance herself. That isn't really like her, but this one is hitting really close to home and I just want to respect her feelings on it all."

"Have you at least talked to her though?" Harmon wasn't totally worried, but there was a little part of him that agreed that she was in actual danger.

"I update her each night by phone. She's fine, just staying safe and distancing herself."

"Okay. As long as she's checking in."

"How's Adam?" Spencer asked as he slid into the passenger seat.

"Not good. He doesn't get it, but how could he? I'm definitely worried about them, but it's something they need to work out between themselves. Although, as much as it pains me to say it, I don't think it's something they *can* work out."

♦♦♦

Harmon and Spencer pulled up along the curb outside of the Rockville post office. A second vehicle carrying two CSU techs pulled up behind them. They walked inside and Spencer strode confidently up to the postmaster behind the counter. Without a word, he slapped a sheet of paper down in front of him.

The gruffly bearded postmaster glared at Spencer. Spencer glared back, or at least attempted to. His face kept breaking into a smug smile and losing all of its intimidating elements. The postmaster's eyes bored through him like lasers. Without moving his head, his eyes darted downward and scanned the paper. Then they were back up again, icier than ever. It was the most fascinating wordless exchange Harmon had witnessed in quite a while.

Finally, the postmaster accepted his defeat and begrudgingly led all four of them around the corner to Box 77. Spencer pulled on a pair of latex gloves and held out his hand. The gruff man slapped the ring of keys into his palm and walked away, retreating back behind his counter.

Harmon chuckled to himself. There were only about twenty-five or so keys on that ring and he knew Spencer would try every single one before asking his bearded nemesis for help. Stubborn pride was such a splendid show to watch when it involved someone else.

As the techs swooped in and began dusting the small square box door, Spencer studied each of the keys. He looked for clues that might narrow down the pile of metal chaos in his palm. And when the outer prints were collected and tagged, Spencer did just as Harmon had expected. He began trying each of the keys, one by one.

One of them had to be the master key that unlocked every box, but there was nothing obvious showing them which one that was. Harmon backed up against the wall, crossed his arms across his chest, and waited. It only took seventeen tries before Spencer was able to turn the key and swing open the small door.

He reached in and pulled out a stack of envelopes. They differed in size and color, but were all addressed the same way...to The Gut Wrencher Fan Club. He stepped back and allowed the techs to work their magic on the inside of the box. He thumbed through the envelopes for a minute before dropping them into an evidence bag to be processed. Spencer then headed over toward his bearded friend and Harmon pushed himself off the wall to follow.

"I'd like to see the renter information on that box—a copy of the driver's license and credit card on file."

The man once again gave Spencer the evil eye before turning away from them and opening a large standing file cabinet. He pulled out a few slips of paper and returned.

"Scanned copy of his driver's license," he said as he placed the first slip on the counter. "Receipts." He set down the remaining slips. "He pays in cash annually. No credit card."

Spencer picked up the copy of the license and turned to Harmon. "Tyler Donovan."

"Well, we knew that already. Fake name and fake license. Easy enough to get," Harmon said as he snatched the paper out of Spencer's hand. "But it's nice to have a picture of our Second in Command." The photo on the license was of a large-looking black man with a shaved head and a thin beard. Harmon stepped up to the counter and held the paper up in front of the postmaster's eyes. "Is this the same man that comes in here to empty that box? Is this the same man that pays you in cash once a year?"

The man nodded. "Yep, that's him. Comes in every Tuesday to empty it." His expression softened as he answered.

Harmon walked back over to Spencer, grinning. "Well, that wasn't so hard."

"How'd you do that? I've gotten nothing but piss and vinegar from that asshole since I first walked in here two weeks ago."

"Old-Timer's code. You don't qualify." Harmon folded up the paper and slid it into Spencer's shirt pocket. "And be glad that you don't. What I wouldn't give to be young and eager again."

He was slightly curious as to what Spencer did to piss off the postmaster so badly. He had met plenty of ornery federal workers in his day on the force, but most of them just give the local police trouble for entertainment purposes. They don't usually mean any harm by it. But in this case, the harm might have added up to several dead wax-covered bodies. The delay in getting the prints and photo ID from the PO box was long and unnecessary.

Spencer and Harmon waited for the techs to finish up before heading out to the car. They would go directly back to the precinct and make sure the prints and trace evidence from the box was processed immediately. No more time would be wasted. They couldn't afford it.

As Harmon lowered himself into the driver's seat, his phone emitted an unusual sound. A special chime set particularly for a certain untraceable burner phone. He flipped open his phone and saw a text from an "unknown number." It consisted of only a single word:

"Today."

Chapter 36

Harmon nearly choked on his crappy precinct coffee as he doubled over with laughter. Oh, how he missed the Bull Pen. He wiped away the coffee dribble running down his chin and leaned back in Spencer's desk chair. They were still waiting on the preliminary fingerprint run so Harmon took the time to catch up with some of his old friends.

Massey was there. And Jake, an old timer like himself. But his most sincere delight came from listening to his old buddy, Mario, entertain them all with embarrassing stories of when Spencer was just a rookie beat cop.

"…then he told him to step out of the car for a field sobriety test, which he did…completely naked," Mario said through howls of laughter. "And Spence looks over at me and says 'what do I do?' and I said 'give him the test, of course.' So he did and the whole time this guy had a steady stream of piss spraying two feet in front of him." Mario laughed so hard, tears began running down his cheeks. "He was standing on one foot and walking the line naked and pissing the whole time. Then he turned around real quick and pissed all over Spence's legs. Can you believe that shit!"

The crowd exploded with deep bellows and high-pitched squeals. Harmon even did a little laugh-crying of his own. But without warning, the commotion stopped in its tracks and the room fell silent. One by one, each man turned and fell away from the group until only Harmon was left. He spun the chair around to the exact sight he had expected.

"Well aren't you a buzz kill," Harmon said, downing the rest of his coffee.

"I got the results from the prints and you're not going to believe who the renter of that box is," Spencer said, his eyes brewing with excitement.

He handed Harmon an iPad with a photo of a driver's license on it. It was a face they had seen just hours earlier on a previous license. A new name and a new state, but that same shiny bald head.

Harmon squinted and used his fingers to zoom in. "Franklin Lewis. Do we know him?"

"No, but he's a physical therapist and his prints are on file because of where he works. Guess where that is."

"Don't even tell me he works at Savage River Correctional Institution."

"Yes, sir. And do you want one guess on who his top patient is?"

"Don't need it." Harmon rocked himself upright and stood. "Tyler really is running the show. He's got an inside man that he spends unsupervised hours with each and every day. And this guy is running his fan club?"

"Not just his fan club. Apparently, there's a higher level to this club, and yes, Mr. Lewis seems to have his hands in that also. And now there is absolutely no doubt in my mind that Tyler is pulling those puppet strings." He snatched the iPad back and took one more look before powering off the screen. "Ready to take a ride with me out to Western Maryland to make an arrest?"

"Only if I can drive," Harmon answered.

He followed Spencer through the precinct hallways, purposely lagging slightly behind. He took out his phone and dialed the unknown number that had texted him earlier. A sharp tone rang out followed by a recording saying the number was no longer in service.

She had destroyed it. She was at her endgame.

If he and Spencer were to show up at the prison to arrest the therapist, and possibly Tyler as well, it could really throw a wrench into whatever Rebecca had planned. He had no true knowledge of her plan. She hadn't wanted him involved any more than he already was. She had said it was to protect him, but Harmon knew her better than that. She didn't want him trying to stop her.

But now, another issue was at hand. Since he didn't know the timeline of her plan, he had no idea when it would be safe for him and Spencer to do what they needed to do. If they stormed Tyler's cell while she was in the middle of God knows what…she could end up in prison herself.

He and Spencer reached the car and Harmon slid back into the driver's seat. He paused and sat for a moment, his mind racing.

"You ready?" Spencer asked, his eyes darting back and forth between Harmon and the empty ignition slot.

"Of course."

"Well then, let's go get us a bad guy." Spencer could hardly contain his excitement as he strapped on his safety belt and gave the dashboard a loud drumming. "Let's go!"

Harmon slid the key in the ignition and started the engine. As he pulled out of the precinct parking lot, he made a list in his head of how he could buy Rebecca more time.

He had no idea exactly where Spencer stood on Rebecca's unorthodox methods of justice, and honestly, he didn't want to know. Spencer was young and at the beginning of a long career in law enforcement. Any involvement with Rebecca Black or Amanda White would end all of that in an instant.

Now Harmon's biggest dilemma was how to keep Spencer out of it. Would he get suspicious if Harmon ran the car into a tree? Not at high speed, of course. Just enough to throw off the alignment and render his vehicle useless.

Harmon took in a deep breath. Maybe he wasn't ready to get that dramatic just yet, but something would need to be done. And he only had an hour drive to figure out what that would be.

Chapter 37

From the cover of the bushes lining the back of the house, he could see directly into the back window undetected. The hedges were vital to hide him as it was only 5pm and the sun was still high. He would have been easily visible to neighbors if it weren't for the thick greenery. Still, he was dressed casually in a navy t-shirt and jeans in case he was spotted.

The backyard was private with tall hedges and thick pines lining the three sides of the rear property line. It backed up to a patch of dense woods and a public park and he was able to hug the tree line and walk right up to the house unnoticed. But from his current position, he had a straight sightline to the second story windows of the neighboring houses on either side. And if he could see them, then they could see him. Therefore, he remained within the cover of the bushes, creeping from one to the next along the back of the house.

He quickly came upon the window that gave him a visual of the kitchen and his target. He watched in silence as the large man chopped a row of carrots and threw them into a steaming pot on the stove. The man was unaware of his audience. Unaware of what his fate was.

The club hadn't received any more correspondences from Tyler, but that was to be expected. They had known that, at some point, the police would shut Tyler down and watch him like a hawk. It would all be temporary though. After all, Tyler couldn't have killed anyone. He had the best alibi out of any of them. Prison. Who could beat that?

Eventually, one of the idiots from the club would get busted and take the rap for all of the murders. That was the original plan. He had thought Vinh would be the one, but he was too sloppy and was caught way too quickly. They still had so much more to do and couldn't give it all up at that time.

There would be another one. The club was full of idiots who didn't know a thing about "leaving no trace." It wouldn't be him though. He was way too smart. Let that Donovan kid have one of the others. One of the others would take the rap.

He had to hand it to them though, the club members. They were fiercely loyal. Any one of them would have been honored to take the full blame and even take their own life like Vinh. Idiots.

Power didn't have the loyalty the others had. He did, however, have respect for Tyler Maddox and what he had accomplished during his reign of terror. That was how he had found the club in the first place. But Power was no cult follower. He was there for the fun of it. Tyler had amazing ideas and sick fantasies and Power was thoroughly entertained being a part of it.

Still, he looked out for himself, first and foremost. Yes, he would mentor a younger follower and work as a team as was required. However, he didn't agree with the method of each team rotating and only killing once for forensic countermeasures. His work at Madame Tussauds was flawless and he should have been rewarded with another scene. Instead, the next scene went to Vinh who nearly brought the whole operation crashing down. Moron.

It was time for *Power* to run the show. He didn't lose a wink of sleep when he stole the Halloween scene from *Conquer*. He deserved it. And *Promise* was none the wiser when he approached him with Tyler's letter. No one questioned why he was doing a second scene. Perhaps they did have questions but were too afraid to confront him with them. Smart. When they find *Conquer*'s body, all of their questions would be answered.

Power had needed another scene to show his expertise and how much he had evolved from Madame Tussauds. His plexiglass stands were genius. No one else would have been able to pull off that scene. And now, with Tyler likely on lockdown with no new correspondence, everyone was just sitting around playing with their dicks. Not him though. If a scene wasn't given to him by Tyler, then he just needed to create his own. And it started with this strapping chap in front of him.

He continued to watch Adam as he turned down the heat of the stove and placed a glass lid onto the pot. He then turned and left the kitchen. *Power* moved through the bushes with stealth, searching for his target. He peered into each window, came up empty, and moved on to the next.

Eventually, he came to the lighted window at the end of the house. Sheer curtains distorted his view inside, but the sound of running water was unmistakable. Adam was in the shower and would be oblivious to any activity in the house for at least the next ten minutes. *Power* seized the opportunity and crept back to his original viewing area and the backdoor next to it.

He easily jimmied the lock and stepped inside. The door opened into a tiny dining room with a round table for four. A tall glass curio cabinet nestled into one corner and a wider china cabinet stood against the adjacent wall. Following the room flow, he entered the kitchen. It was just as tiny as the dining room. Quaint and charming perhaps, but not at all what he had expected from a professional chef.

He walked through the kitchen and scanned the countertop. Grabbing the knife block, he stashed it on the floor inside the pantry. The stove burner was on low with barely a flame flickering beneath the steaming pot. He could blow out the flame, let the kitchen fill will with gas, and then blow the whole house up. But what would be the fun in that?

He turned the knob on the stove and the burner turned off. He knew Adam would return soon to check on his precious stew, and *Power* couldn't resist the irony of the chef's husband being killed in her own kitchen while cooking her dinner. So romantic.

Turning behind him, he spotted a small corner nook in front of a recessed broom closet. It was just wide enough for him to squeeze his slender frame into. He was hidden from obvious view, but from his new hideaway he had clear sight of the stove. He waited.

◆ ◆ ◆

Adam draped the wet towel over the bedpost and rifled through his dresser drawers. Grabbing the first pair of jeans he came to, he pulled them on and went to the closet for a shirt.

On his way out of the bedroom, he unplugged his phone from the nightstand charger and dialed Rebecca's number. It went straight to voicemail just as it had done every hour since he had returned home from Chincoteague. He was worried after the first few hours and called Harmon, but he assured him that she was working the case with Spencer and didn't have her phone with her.

Adam really needed to talk to her. It was going to be an impossible conversation, but one they needed to have. He didn't even know what his decision was, which was why he needed a back and forth dialogue with her.

He had learned so much about her over the past week. Mostly all of it was things he didn't want to know, but now he did and had to deal with it.

He hadn't been able to get that image out of his head—the image of Andrew Donovan tied to a table with his leg flayed and dissected and his chest ripped open. And his bloody heart stuffed into his mouth. It made the bile rise in his throat, and his wife was a part of it. She said she didn't kill him and he believed her, but there was so much more done to that man before his heart was ripped out. The fact that Rebecca didn't comment on the torture convinced him that she definitely had her hands in it.

He couldn't believe it was the same woman. The woman he immediately fell in love with, married, and was currently carrying his child. Was she even safe to be around a child? Was she a psychopath? She claimed it was self-defense, and justice, and that something simply came over her. But Andrew Donovan was tied down. How was that self-defense? She could have called the police and had them take care of it. But she didn't.

And Tyler Maddox? She had tried to kill him too…also in self-defense, or so she said. Was she just coincidentally always being attacked or was she inviting this danger into her life? Did she get some sort of sick thrill out of it? What kind of mother would she be if she walked around with a death wish?

He had so many questions. Harmon had answered some of them and tried his best to reassure him that her actions were justified. But it wasn't enough. Adam needed to look her in the eyes and talk to her about her state of mind.

The more he thought about it, the more his decision began to take form. He had been lying to himself. Telling himself that his mind wasn't made up and that if he could only talk to her, she could talk him into forgiving her and their "happy ever after" future could still be a possibility. It wasn't true though. None of it. It didn't matter what she said or what her reasons were. He couldn't spend the rest of his life with a woman who could torture and assist in killing another human being. And that realization stabbed him right in the heart.

He walked into the kitchen and picked up the wooden spoon next to the stove. Lifting the lid off of the stew, he gave it a quick stir. A cooled film sat on top of the liquid and wrapped itself around the spoon. Puzzled, he bent down and looked for a low flame. He then looked at the silver knob and saw that it had been manually turned off. He turned the burner back on and the blue flame immediately returned. His hand still rested on the knob as he tried to put two and two together. Then, a sharp pain radiated from the side of his head and the room went black.

He couldn't see. He couldn't move. But he had felt the pain as his body hit the tile floor. He felt the grip under his armpits and his body being dragged across the kitchen floor and onto the hardwood of the dining room. He struggled to open his eyes, but they wouldn't budge. The pain came and went and came again. The backs of his eyelids were white then black then white again. He heard a muffled voice as he drifted in and out of consciousness.

Finally, his eyes opened and the legs of dining room chairs came into view. He was on his side with his arms pulled tight behind him. He struggled to free them, but it was impossible. They were taped together at the elbows and his shoulders screamed as they stretched awkwardly behind him. He kicked his legs out in front of him, also tightly bound.

A cool tingle spread across the side of his head. It instantly turned to wet warmth as blood dripped down the side of his face, filled his eye, and clouded his vision. A second stream ran a similar path across his cheek, diverting as it contacted the strip of duct tape covering his mouth.

Behind him, he heard rummaging through drawers followed by heavy booted footsteps. He struggled violently, jerking his body and trying to free his arms of their constraints.

Without warning, he was flipped onto his back and staring into the blackest bottomless pits he had ever seen. The man dropped onto one knee and pressed his forearm into Adam's throat. He leaned in close until Adam could see his own reflection in his eyes.

"Do you know who I am?" the man asked with a low and raspy growl.

Adam shook his head, wincing in pain at the pressure on his trachea.

"Your wife does," he said as he leaned in closer, crushing his throat.

The pain was unbearable, but it was nothing compared to the panic that empty lungs brought. His throat screamed, his chest burned, and he watched it all on the black reflective screen of his killer's eyes. The smoky curtain dropped across his field of vision and the darkness returned.

Suddenly, the pressure on his throat was gone. He coughed and gasped and his lungs immediately filled with sweet, sweet oxygen. He breathed hard and heavy, taking in as much as his chest could hold. His vision cleared and came into focus.

The man hadn't left. He hovered above Adam, looking down at him. He shot him a quick smile before resuming his position of crushing Adam's throat. The pain returned, along with the panic and the smoky veil of near unconsciousness.

Once again, the man let up just long enough for Adam to fill his lungs before crashing back down on him. He lost track of how many cycles the man had gone through. How many times Adam had passed out and then jolted awake with a rush of air, just to have it taken away again. It was pure agony.

He couldn't speak. He could never retain enough air to form a single word. He was going to die and he couldn't even give his killer a final "fuck you" before he did. All he could do was listen. Listen as the black-eyed man rambled on and on.

"*You* are going to make the best mannequin yet. I'm not even going to use the wax. After all, I've evolved." The man released Adam's throat for just a few seconds before bearing back down on it. "Yes, in this short amount of time, I've already evolved...again. I can't hide your pretty little face behind a mask. The others, sure...but not you. You are way too important to this story."

The pressure released and Adam sucked in one deep breath before it returned.

"I want your actual rotting tissue to shine through. That would be much more effective, don't you think? I have my plastic stands in a bag right out there on your back patio. I'll pose you right here in the kitchen making dinner so that when Rebecca comes home, she'll think you're just in here cooking like a good man should."

The man wasn't even looking at Adam anymore. He gazed into nothingness, undoubtedly visualizing the entire scene. He rocked backward to allow his victim an influx of air and then rocked forward again to cut it off. Every minute or so, over and over again. All the while, fantasizing about this next scene that he created just for himself.

"She might even talk to you for a while. Maybe tell you about her day. How long would it be before she got suspicious that you were giving her the silent treatment? Maybe she'd think it was normal. It didn't look like you two left on the best of terms back in OC."

The man turned his head and looked down at Adam. "Yes, that's right. I was there." He leaned in close, timing it with the oxygen cut-off.

"How long until she storms up to you and demands you speak to her? How long before she grabs your shoulder and spins you around to face her with your cold, gray, lifeless eyes? The expression that'll be on her face will be epic. And I'll be right here to witness it. Then, I'll let your dead eyes watch while I make love to her right there in front of you. And when I'm done, I'll slit her throat and let her blood spray and cover our naked bodies with its warmth."

Adam writhed and strained, trying with all his might to break free of his bondage. He was strong and felt the tape stretch as he jerked back and forth during *Power*'s speech. But it wasn't enough and the repeated lack of oxygen had drained nearly all the strength from his body. In his head, he cussed at himself for his weakness. And when *Power* gave him a breath, he cussed at himself out loud. It was muffled by the tape across his mouth, but he understood his words perfectly.

"What's that?" His attacker appeared genuinely interested. "Are you trying to tell me something? You know, it's no use begging for your life. You're not leaving here with it."

Power hadn't yet put the pressure back on Adam's throat. It was as if Adam's muffled tantrum broke his rhythm and sent him off track. He made use of those extra breaths and turned his anger away from himself and onto the man looming over him. He shouted the most awful things behind that duct tape gag. It was unfortunate that the man couldn't make out a single word.

"You *are* begging for your life, aren't you? I'll admit, it would be fun to see a big strong guy like yourself crying and pleading like a little bitch." The man paused, thinking. "What the hell." He moved his arm away from his throat and placed both hands on Adam's broad chest. He pushed himself up and swung around to land with both knees driving into Adam's diaphragm. A whoosh of air exploded out of Adam's nose.

Power then pushed himself up again and landed in a straddle across Adam's stomach. He bounced a few times. With Adam's solid build, he had a good sixty pounds on *Power*'s lanky frame, and the smaller man needed to bounce higher and higher to achieve his desired effect.

He reached forward and ripped the tape off of Adam's mouth. He then bounced some more on Adam's stomach, each time forcing more air out and making Adam gasp and struggle for every breath. Adam's eyes were closed and his face twisted into a painful grimace. He coughed and gagged and whispered inaudible words in between.

"Still whining, my friend?"

Power leaned forward, shifting all of his weight onto Adam's upper chest. Turning an ear toward Adam's mouth, he listened intently, attempting to decipher the larger man's pleas of mercy.

Adam's mouth opened and quiet high-pitched squeaks escaped. His eyes, previously clenched shut in pain, softened and opened slightly into narrow slits. His vision cleared and focused on the man above him. His lips curled back, bearing two rows of strong healthy teeth. His head lurched forward and his teeth buried themselves within the soft flesh of *Power*'s neck.

He held tight as *Power* thrashed from side to side. His screams ripped throughout the small room, multiplying as they bounced off of each wall and returned to the source. Finally, *Power* tore free, launched himself off of Adam's chest, and crawled across the floor until he was safely out of reach. He backed himself up against a low cabinet as his hand shot up to cover the gaping wound in the side of his neck. Blood seeped out between his fingers and ran the length of his arm before cascading off his elbow into a shallow pool on the kitchen tile.

Adam, still on his back, turned his head to the side and spit out a chunk of bleeding flesh. He rolled onto his knees, his arms and ankles still bound together. The tape had loosened slightly from his violent pulling and thrashing, but not enough for him to free himself.

He scanned the room for anything within reach that he could use. The floors and tables were empty and his attacker was blocking access to any of the kitchen drawers and cabinets. His eyes traveled to the corner of the dining room and the glass curio that stood there. Without a second thought, he lunged forward and rammed his forehead into the cabinet door, shattering it and causing shards of glass to rain down onto the floor around him.

After shimmying over to the largest and sharpest piece, he rolled on top of it until his hands were able to grasp it. It took only seconds to cut through the tape at his elbows and free his arms. Less than that to then free his legs.

Power's eyes grew wide with terror as he watched Adam cut through the last of the tape and toss the shredded remnants to the side. *Power* stood, still pressing the heel of his hand against his neck. With his free hand, he grabbed the silver handle next to his hip and pulled a drawer completely out of its track. The entire contents of cooking gadgets spilled out onto the kitchen floor. He reached down and pushed the deluxe cheese grater out of the way to reveal the heavy meat tenderizer underneath. As his fingers curled around the solid wooden handle, he watched as Adam stood, free and unbound.

Adam lunged and *Power* cocked the mallet behind his head and swung with all his might. Adam raised his forearm to block it. The sound of bones cracking filled the kitchen as the contact was made. Ignoring the pain radiating through his arm, both of Adam's hands wrapped around the smaller man's neck. Effortlessly, he lifted him off the floor and threw him down onto the hard ceramic. *Power*'s body had barely hit the floor when Adam dropped down onto his chest and pummeled his face with oversized fists.

"Cold dead eyes, huh? Is that what you want?" Adam growled through gritted teeth. He pressed both of his thumbs into the man's eyes, digging into the soft tissue until vitreous fluid spurted out and covered his hands with the clear liquid.

Power's screams were deafening. Now blinded, he flailed an outstretched arm until his hand groped the familiar metal block head of the tenderizer that had slipped from his hand when his body had crashed to the floor. He gripped the handle and swung the weighted mallet upward.

Searing pain ripped through Adam's brain as the metal block smashed into his temple. Stunned, he shook his head to stop the ringing and clear his vision. He reached out and grabbed *Power*'s wrist as the man wound up for another strike. With his free hand, he ripped the mallet from his attacker's fist and swung it himself, slamming it into the man's forehead. Over and over, he pounded *Power*'s face, unable to stop, unable to regain control.

An eternity seemed to have passed when Adam finally ceased his ruthless beating. He sat, straddling the man's chest, heaving and breathless and covered with spatters of blood and teeth and brain matter.

Horrified with the sight in front of him, he dismounted from *Power*'s chest and retreated along the floor until his back pressed up against the oven door. He sat there staring at the motionless body. The face was unrecognizable, resembling a pile of ground beef instead.

He was sickened by the sight, but unable to look away. The pain, the fear, the rage…none of it rivaled the shock of what he had done. He had just murdered a man. An injured, blind, and incapacitated man. He could have stopped after that first defensive blow. He could have stood and walked to the other side of the kitchen and called the police. But he didn't. He didn't because the justice system sometimes failed. And he needed to make sure this bastard was stopped.

Adam Callahan had just murdered a man.

Chapter 38

Harmon's car inched along I-70 as he and Spencer headed west toward the Savage River Correctional Institution. Fortunately, Friday evening traffic was always horrendous westbound. They had been crawling along for the past hour and were still only halfway to the prison.

Their delay suited Harmon just fine. Whatever Rebecca was going to do, she would do it before her shift ended at 6:30. At that time, she and the other caterers would be loaded up and heading through the prison gate. If he could simply stall past 6:30, Rebecca would be in the clear and not even on site anymore.

He glanced at the dashboard clock—5:00. He needed to delay for another hour and a half. A bead of sweat dripped from his temple. The air conditioner was working fine, but his nerves weren't. His anxiety was through the roof, wondering how he was going keep him and Spencer from getting to the prison and what would be waiting for them when they eventually arrived.

A short time later, traffic began to open up and they picked up a little speed. That was the last thing he wanted. He began to think of ways he could delay them. A flat tire would be great right about now. Or, they could run out of gas. He looked at the gas gauge. *Damn.* He had filled up as soon as he had gotten into town and no amount of rush hour traffic would burn through an entire tank in that time.

A sign for their exit passed by them in a blur. A half mile until he'd be off the interstate and zipping along empty country roads. He glanced at the clock again—5:15. The prison was a half hour away once they exited. Not far enough. Another bead of sweat ran down the side of his face. His hands gripped the wheel tight and his eyes stared straight ahead. He held his lane and sailed straight past the exit for Savage River.

"Whoa, Ed! You just passed the exit," Spencer said as he turned and looked behind him, the off-ramp fading away in the distance.

"What? That wasn't it."

"Yes, it was and we just missed it."

"Sorry about that. It's been a few years since I've been up in these parts. I guess I just zoned out a bit."

Spencer sighed. "It's not a big deal. We can take the next exit and loop around."

Harmon had bought a little time with that "mistake," but he doubted it would be enough. The route off of the next exit did have more country roads and it would definitely take longer. But how much longer?

"Here, take this one," Spencer said as the next exit approached a mile later. He was not going to allow Harmon to miss that one.

Harmon veered into the right lane and followed the off-ramp. A gas station and a run-down motel sat across from each other at the first intersection, but after that, it was nothing but single-lane backcountry pavement.

With a free hand he blindly dug through the center console for his phone and checked the GPS he had activated before he left. It had rerouted, but still showed them arriving at the prison too early.

The road was empty, but narrow and winding. His shoulder pressed up against the door as he held a tight curve to the right. Speeding would surely cause them to fly off the road and into a tree at the next sharp turn. Harmon entertained the thought for a moment. No, he wasn't in the mood to spend the night in the hospital…or the morgue with Dr. Adler rifling through his insides. His foot instinctively lifted slightly off of the gas pedal as he decelerated and slowed the car down.

A mile later, he slowed down even more until his speed dropped below the posted limit. He hummed softly to himself as the car moseyed along as if it were on a relaxing Sunday drive through the country. It wasn't long before he spotted Spencer in his periphery, staring at him with suspicion.

"Why are we going so damn slow?"

"We're not going that slow. The speed limit says thirty-five around these curves."

Spencer leaned over and looked at the speedometer. "We're going thirty. And since when do you ever drive within twenty miles of the speed limit, much less below it? Dale Earnhardt on Red Bull is how they describe you at the precinct."

"Maybe I'm just getting old. Retirement will do that to you. I hardly drive at all anymore." A broad smile spread across the older man's face. "Now I just sit on my dock and fish."

"Yet, this morning you drove us through the city to the post office in world record time." Spencer eyed him skeptically. "Is there something going on that I don't know about?"

Harmon didn't answer. Instead, he sped up around the next curve and pulled into one of the dirt driveways that were scattered along the shoulder. He turned off the engine and pulled the key out of the ignition.

"So, there is something going on," Spencer said.

"I have to piss." Harmon stepped out of the car and shoved the keys deep into his front pocket. Then he walked further down the dirt path to a patch of large trees.

When he returned, Spencer was outside, leaning against the car, his arms crossed firmly across his chest. "What's going on? Why are you delaying our trip to the prison? What do you know that I don't?"

"I can't tell you that."

"Why not? Is it illegal?"

"The less you know, the better." Harmon stopped before he reached the car, keeping a good distance between him and Spencer.

"Look, Ed, you know I'm a good cop. I have to make up for my father's sins by not just being a good cop, but the *best* cop. No shady deals and no looking the other way." Spencer took his phone out of his pocket. "Whatever you're doing…I can't let you go through with it." He dropped his head and began dialing.

Harmon closed the distance between them and snatched the phone out of his hand.

"Are you kidding me right now?" Spencer said in disbelief at Harmon's bold action.

"I'm sorry, Spence. You know how much I like you, boy. You *are* a good cop…a great cop, which is why you need to stay out of this."

Spencer reached to grab his phone back.

Harmon stepped back, reached inside his jacket, and pulled his revolver. He aimed it at Spencer's chest.

Spencer stared at him in shock. Then, a glint of understanding spread across his face. He nodded and slowly backed up to resume his position against the car.

Harmon felt horrible for pulling his gun on a fellow officer, and even worse because it was Spencer. He walked around to the driver's side, opened the rear door, and tossed the phone and gun onto the back seat. Reaching into his pocket, he fumbled with the key fob and all four door locks engaged.

"This is serious, isn't it?" Spencer asked.

"Very."

"You know I can't let you do what you're trying to do."

"You don't have a choice. It's out of your hands and mine."

"Does it have something to do with Franklin Lewis? Or Tyler? Do you have a hit out on him that's going down right now?" Spencer didn't even realize how close he was to the truth. "Just give me the keys and we'll pretend this whole thing never happened."

"I can't do that."

"Dammit, Ed! Are you seriously going to risk prison time for that asshole in there?"

"No, not for him."

"For who then? Whoever it is, it's not worth it. Let the justice system work. We have evidence now. Tyler will get his punishment."

"That's what we thought five years ago. And now here we are…ten murder victims later."

"Give me the keys," Spencer said firmly, holding out his hand.

"You'll have to take them from me."

He barely got the words out before Spencer lunged at him. He sidestepped, but Spencer still got a piece as his fist collided with Harmon's jaw. He wound up to strike again, but Harmon tackled him to the ground and the breath whooshed out of his lungs. The older man planted a couple light jabs across

Spencer's mouth, splitting his lip. A stream of blood ran down Spencer's chin.

They grappled for several minutes, trading blows and moving back and forth between their feet and the ground. Harmon repeatedly won the upper hand, throwing Spencer to the ground each time, and hoping that the young man would give up and stop coming at him. However, his will was strong and he wasn't done yet.

Harmon felt like a father trying to teach his son a lesson. Or a father teaching his son how to fight. He reckoned Spencer had never been in a fist fight in his life. With a millionaire dad and expensive private schools, he was quite lacking in the street-fighter department. Add to that the fact that not many people would dare mess with the teenage child of a serial killer. How could they know if it was hereditary or not? In so many ways, Spencer was still a lost little boy trying to find his place.

Once more, Harmon knocked him to the ground and finally, Spencer stayed down.

"You're young and fast, but you don't have your full man-strength yet. Don't worry. It'll come in a few more years." Harmon chuckled and extended a hand to help Spencer up. "And I outweigh you by at least fifty pounds."

The two men staggered slightly as they walked to the car and leaned against the trunk, pressing their palms onto their bloodied faces.

"Is Rebecca involved?" Spencer asked. "Because I can't see you acting this way unless you were protecting her."

"Yes, she is."

"Then why didn't you just say so? You could have led with that and our blood would still be in our bodies. You know I'd never do anything to hurt her. After what my father did...and what my best friend did...I owe her."

"True. But I couldn't take the risk of you calling this in."

"So how long do we have to wait here? I wouldn't mind getting the hell off of this backroad and cleaning myself up a little."

Harmon glanced down at his watch. "It won't be long now."

Chapter 39

Rebecca stood at her station plating dinners for the delivery cart. She was sure to make a second soft dinner for the inmate in the infirmary. She hadn't heard any talk of a strange hemorrhaging situation there so she was confident that the man who had received Tyler's breakfast the day before was okay. The four inmates that helped out in the kitchen loved to gossip and she was certain she would have heard if someone suddenly bled to death for no reason.

She had brought a second Warfarin dose that morning for Tyler's breakfast. Another meal mix-up was unlikely since the infirmary inmate ordered eggs instead of oatmeal, but she labeled them anyway. She had wanted at least twenty-four hours for maximum effectiveness, but the morning dose would have to do.

Dinner that night was beef stew and mashed potatoes. Rebecca took two small bowls and ladled in some stew from the steaming pot on the stove. She then used two forks and began to shred the cubes of beef into small pieces that could easily be swallowed without chewing.

Cecelia had taken her earlier advice and had added chopped mushrooms to the simmering pot which worked perfectly for her camouflage. Rebecca looked over each shoulder before taking a small bag out of her apron. She had made a late-night stop at La Croix the night before and picked up a vital and dangerous ingredient. The bag contained six odd-looking red mushrooms—Fire Caps.

Aptly named due to their red color and also because they had the ability to convert to acid that burned through tissue when prepared the wrong way…or in her case…the right way. They were wild mushrooms, found only in the mountains of southern France. A delicacy with a unique nutty flavor, they were only sold to accredited restaurants because of the care needed to prepare them for consumption.

The gills on the underside of the cap contained a toxic chemical that, if mixed with strongly acidic foods, would form tribonic acid and liquefy a person's insides and burn straight through their stomach. Most French restaurants in America didn't even carry Fire Caps or serve any dish that contained them because of the risk involved if the gills weren't removed correctly.

Rebecca, however, could never resist how their fiery red hue livened up several of La Croix D'or's signature entrees. Many of her loyal customers returned time and time again specifically for her Fire Cap dishes.

The danger was very real and she did take it seriously. Only her or Peter were ever permitted to work with them. Peter. He absolutely loved Fire Caps. His memory brought all sorts of feelings flooding back and she quickly swiped a tear from her cheek before any of her co-workers noticed.

Tyler had killed Peter and now, using these mushrooms, Peter could kill him back. It wasn't exactly true, but within her own twisted logic, it made perfect sense.

She placed the mushrooms on her cutting board. With expert precision, she used the tip of a paring knife to remove the poisonous gills from the underside of the caps and then tossed them directly into the bowl of stew labeled for Tyler. Giving the stew a quick stir, she smiled as she watched the handful of gills blend seamlessly into the mushroom pieces that Cecelia had added. Undetectable. However, unable to resist as usual, she quickly diced up a few of the red caps and threw them in as well just for aesthetics. If she remembered correctly, Tyler absolutely adored mushrooms. He would certainly devour the bowl in record time.

She glanced at the order sheet on her counter that contained the full meal requests. Root beer for the infirmary patient and the usual cranberry juice-Sprite mix for Tyler. That was his drink choice every evening and Rebecca knew the acidity of the cranberry would be the perfect catalyst for her mushrooms.

She walked over to the fountain soda machine and pressed a button to fill a clear cup of ice with root beer. She did the same with the cranberry juice, although the liquid came out clear. She raised the cup to her lips and took a taste. Her face twisted into a grimace. Soda water. Her pulse quickened as the realization hit her—they were out of cranberry. She needed the acidity of the cranberry to bind with the mushrooms and form the acid. Without it, the entire plan would fail.

Taking a deep breath, she calmed herself and focused on what she could control. She looked at the other drinks available. At one point in her past, her and Tyler had become close friends and she knew him pretty well. Yes, that was five years ago, but tastes didn't change that much. At least, she hoped not. He wouldn't drink root beer or cola, but Sprite should be okay, even without the cranberry. It wasn't as acidic as the juice, but it should do the job if he drank enough of it.

She poured out the soda water, filled the cup with ice, and pressed the Sprite button. When it was done, she tasted it to make sure it wasn't also soda water. Perfect. Tyler had a serious sweet tooth and only the most sugary drinks would do.

She returned to her station with the two cups and placed them on the trays. Then she cut a few lemon slices and arranged them around Tyler's tray as a garnish. It was merely to accentuate the differences in the two meals and avoid another mistake. She admitted it was a little overkill for a prison dinner, but truth be told, it would be Tyler's last meal and she wanted to make it special. She picked up the trays and slid them into the tracks on the cart, making sure the name labels were highly visible.

"You ready?" Cecelia asked as she approached Rebecca.

"Yes. Just give me a moment to start the coffee and grab my ID badge."

Rebecca walked quickly to the coffee machine and pressed the start button. She had learned to prep the coffee grounds and fill the water ahead of time. Thus, a simple push of a button was all that was needed. The coffee was an important part of her plan as well. She couldn't risk it not getting done if Cecelia was in too much of a hurry.

She took Cecelia's purple mug from the drying rack and set it next to the coffee machine. Then she lifted her purse from a hook on the wall and began rummaging through it for her ID. She pulled it out along with a tiny glass bottle of Ipecac syrup. Expanding her shoulders to block the view from behind her, she poured a splash of the syrup into Cecelia's empty mug. Peering in, she gave an approving nod as the clear syrup clung unnoticeably to the bottom. Finally, she clipped her badge onto her apron and joined Cecelia at the kitchen door, pulling the wheeled cart along with her.

The two women spent the next twenty minutes looping through the halls, in and out of the infirmary, until they entered the east wing—Park Avenue. Rebecca's heart pounded hard in her chest. Tyler's cell sat at the very end of the hall. She sensed his presence. She physically felt his aura in the air and every hair on her body stood on end as she attempted to hide her anxiety. Not too much though. After all, it was how she had managed to keep Tyler from identifying her.

She rolled the cart down the hallway, but stopped two cells short of Tyler's door. Cecelia was used to it. She knew Rebecca was afraid of him and that was why she always avoided him when they unloaded the van in the mornings. It was also why she stopped short of his cell every evening. It was a legitimate excuse and kept her alter ego, Amanda White, from ever coming face to face with him.

Rebecca turned to the cart and grasped the tray with the lemon slices fanned out along the rim. As she handed it over to Cecelia, she saw the glint of red bobbing up and down amongst shredded strings of beef. Fortunately, she had chopped the red caps so fine that they were unnoticeable to anyone not looking for them.

Cecelia walked down to the end of the hall and placed the tray on the shelf in the slot opening of the cell door. Rebecca couldn't see him, but she heard him. The simple sound of his voice sent chills up and down her spine.

"Where's the cranberry?"

"We're all out of cranberry juice because you drink it up every single day. We'll have more when the Monday delivery comes in."

"Monday?"

"It's only a few days, Mr. Maddox. I'm sure you'll survive until then."

Rebecca smiled smugly to herself. *Don't bet on it.*

Chapter 40

Rebecca and Cecelia returned after finishing up their meal deliveries. Maneuvering the tall cart through the narrow corridor slowed Rebecca down and Cecelia walked into the kitchen ahead of her. She never broke stride as she walked a straight line directly toward the coffee pot. Rebecca's eyes widened. She gave the cart a shove toward the back wall and rushed up beside her supervisor.

"I can get your coffee for you," she said.

A loud clang rang out behind them. They both turned as the cart crashed into the wall.

"Stop being such a kiss-ass," Cecelia responded. "I can get it myself. Go take care of that cart and put it away properly."

Rebecca slowly backpedaled across the kitchen toward the cart. All the while, she kept a keen eye on the woman, hoping the Ipecac truly was invisible on the bottom of her mug.

Cecelia picked up the mug and poured the hot coffee without a second thought. Rebecca let out a sigh of relief as she watched the woman fish out a cigarette and a lighter from her purse and disappear out of the kitchen's back door.

She pulled the cart away from the wall and parked it softly next to her station. She had ten minutes before Cecelia would return from outside and maybe another ten before the Ipecac took effect. Rebecca still had pieces to put into play and every minute counted.

The dinner meals were still being served through the serving window to the inmates in the cafeteria. Rebecca took a pile of trays from a stack in the corner and began loading them up. One by one, she placed them on the sill of the window.

She returned to her station and lifted one final empty tray from the stack. She loaded it up with beef stew and began shredding it like before. After adding a scoop of mashed potatoes and a pile of mashed carrots, she crouched and slid the tray into the backside of the cart's bottom rack.

Just then, Cecelia returned and offered her assistance with the window serving. She moved slow and ineffectively, already feeling the effects of her doctored coffee. She didn't last much longer. Only a moment or two passed before she scurried out of the kitchen and around the corner.

Rebecca waited a few minutes before going to check on her. She found her exactly where she knew she would—in the women's bathroom, violently vomiting. She sounded as if she were in horrible pain and a wave of guilt washed over Rebecca.

She shook it off immediately. Cecelia was a casualty of war and there was no other way.

Rebecca cracked the bathroom door open. "Are you okay? Are you sick?" she called in. She wasn't even sure Cecelia heard her in between the loud retching echoing off the concrete walls. She waited for an opening and tried again. "It's time to collect the trays. Do you want me to just go get them? I can go get them for you if you're not feeling well."

"Oh God! Yes, please!"

Rebecca smiled and let the door fall shut. She went back to the kitchen for the cart, empty except for one untouched choke-hazard dinner on the bottom rack. She rolled it out of the kitchen and down the hall, cringing as Cecelia's painful cries filled the air.

Chapter 41

Rebecca wheeled the cart down the brightly-lit hallway. It contained a single meal on the bottom rack—a meal identical to the one Cecelia had delivered earlier, but minus the poisonous Fire Caps.

Her paced picked up as she rounded a corner and headed in the direction of the infirmary. She stuck to the usual route, picked up empty trays along the way, and tried to appear as emotionless as possible. After all, she was just doing her job—her mundane and boring routine.

Tyler's cell was last on the list. She turned the corner for the east wing and parked the cart in its usual spot, two cells up from Tyler's. The neighboring cells were empty as expected. The other inmates that resided in that wing all ate at the cafeteria. And with the post-dinner counseling sessions, it would be hours before they returned.

Her heart raced as she slowly made her way down the hall. Although she had planned for it, she was still terrified at what she would find in that last cell.

As she got closer, she saw the dinner tray sitting on the shelf in the cell door slot. The bowl was empty along with the mashed potatoes and carrots. Nothing was left but a fanned array of lemon slices. He had devoured the Fire Caps just as she had expected. Her pulse quickened even more as she passed another empty cell.

Suddenly, she stopped.

The clear plastic cup was still full. The Sprite nearly reached the rim as if he hadn't even taken a sip. She watched carbonated bubbles race up the insides of the cup walls, confirming that it was in fact the soda that he had been brought earlier. Her heart dropped into her stomach.

She crept closer until she saw him sitting in his wheelchair in the center of his cell. He faced the wall with his back to her. She stared at him, looking for any sign of movement. None. His hands weren't visible and they appeared to be resting in his lap. There was no visible blood either.

She took a step closer, trying to get a look at his face, but unable to. She didn't dare to even breathe as she watched his shoulders, waiting for them to lift and lower with his respirations. Nothing.

Was that it? Was it over? That neatly?

She gasped when his hands suddenly came out of his lap, gripped the wheels, and began turning toward her.

Without a second to think, she jumped back and scurried out of sight to the empty cell next to his. She stood with her back to the cell door, her chest heaving.

"I know you're there, Cecy," he called out. "Are you coming to get my tray or what?"

Rebecca froze, her back still glued to the bars of the cell next-door.

"Why are you hiding?" he called out again.

A hundred different thoughts ran through her head, but only a handful made any sense. He didn't drink the Sprite and therefore, the Fire Cap toxins hadn't been activated. And he wasn't going to drink it if he hadn't already.

She could abort the mission and try again when she returned to work on Tuesday. It would be easy to shimmy along the empty cells until she was further up the hall and get to the cart without him seeing her clearly.

But could she really get the plan to succeed if she tried it a second time? Everything had gone perfectly today. The stew was the ideal menu item for her mushrooms. Cecelia had gotten sick with flawless timing. Rebecca would never be able to recreate that.

After today, she wouldn't be back to work for four days. Anything could happen in that time. Tyler could be transferred. Or Spencer could crack the case and then he would have all sorts of lawyers and cops and media all around him. She would never be able to get to him as unguarded and unsuspecting as he was right now.

He would be sentenced again and a few more life sentences would be added on to what he already had. But he'd still be alive, and if she had learned one thing, it was that no one was safe as long as Tyler Maddox's heart was still beating. She had to finish this today. She had to at least try.

Rebecca took her ID badge and stuck it in her back pocket. Then, she pulled off her wig and apron and dropped them onto the floor. A quick toss of her head shook loose her honey gold waves and she stepped out into the middle of the hall. With all the swagger she could muster, she sauntered in his direction.

His eyes lit up when he saw her. She passed him by and continued on to the corner where a folded green chair stood propped up against the wall. She grabbed it with one hand, whipped it open, and placed it directly in front of him. A leery smile spread across his face as she lowered herself slowly and seductively into the chair.

"Hi, Tyler."

"Hello, beautiful." His eyes scanned her body from head to toe, lingering on the open neckline of her open collared shirt.

"Do you know why I'm here?"

He didn't respond, his focus entirely drawn to the curves of her breasts as they pressed against the white fabric.

"Tyler!" she barked. "Why am I here?"

He snapped back to attention and locked his eyes onto hers. "You want names from me. The names of those committing the mannequin murders. Or, you want to know who the next targets are. Or where. When. Am I close?"

"Would you actually give me all of that info?" she asked.

"No, of course not."

"Then why would you insult my intelligence by thinking I would come all the way here and waste my time like that? I'm not stupid and neither are you. Of course you won't give up your people...or yourself."

"Then to what do I owe this glorious honor of your beautiful presence?" he said as his eyes took another journey along the length of her body.

"I don't need information from you because the police already have enough. Your buddy, Spencer, got a warrant for the PO box and got plenty of prints to ID the president of your twisted fan club. He already knows who's organizing everything for you on the outside."

"Oh yeah? Who?"

"I wish I knew," she sighed. "Spencer won't tell me who it is. Apparently, he thinks I'm a loose cannon that would go after him and kill him myself before they got the chance to arrest him."

"And would you?"

Rebecca shrugged. "Maybe." She nonchalantly examined her manicure as she spoke. "Lord knows, I do like to take matters into my own hands."

"Yes, you do."

"Oh, and the letters that you wrote to them that described every murder scene in detail before it happened...that automatically names you as an accessory. Spencer figures that'll tack on at least another life sentence or two."

Tyler smiled. "Well aren't you smug? I already have a life sentence. What's one or two more gonna matter? I'm already never getting out of here."

"I don't think it's the time that'll matter as much as a hundred percent of your communication privileges being taken away. How will you possibly survive if you can't speak your charming bullshit to whoever will listen?"

"Ooh, you think I'm charming? I knew you still had a thing for me."

Rebecca smiled as he played right into her hand, just like she knew he would. She held up her thumb and forefinger with a small space in between. "Maybe a little. Not even that much." She closed the space slightly more. "Maybe *that* much."

His smile grew wider and his eyes twinkled like diamonds. She had never even flirted with him back when they were friends and he was actively pursuing her. *This must be blowing his mind.* And she absolutely needed his mind blown because she didn't want him thinking too hard about it. Her behavior wouldn't make any sense at all if he had all of his blood going to his brain. His belief in her was crucial.

"But then you had to go turn into a psychopath and start killing everyone," she said.

"I did it for love. I was so crazy about you that I couldn't think clearly."

"Yeah, well, it is what it is and now you're in here. I gotta admit though, I never understood women who fell for convicts in prison. Even murderers. It always baffled me. But Charles Manson…Ted Bundy…they had all sorts of women falling in love with them while they were behind bars. Didn't Manson even marry one of them while he was still locked up? I never understood it. But now…"

"Now what? Now you get it, right?"

"A little. I guess there is an inkling of sexiness with the whole bad boy image. And you can't get any badder than a murderer in prison."

"We could get married."

"I'm already married." She lifted her left hand and wiggled her fingers.

Tyler's face scrunched slightly at the sight of her ring and the reminder that she was taken. "What does Mr. Rebecca Black think of you visiting me in here?"

"He doesn't know that I've come to see you. He probably wouldn't like it, but what he doesn't know won't hurt him."

Tyler lit up again. "We could have a secret affair."

Rebecca threw her head back and laughed, tossing her hair as she did. "It's not going to be much of an affair through those bars."

"Okay, so how about just a kiss?"

Rebecca looked at him with a side eye as if she was considering it, but not quite sure if she should.

"Come on, Rebecca. Just one kiss. All that time we used to spend together and you've never kissed me." He looked to the side, into his memory. "Yes, I've kissed you without your permission and I'm sorry for that, but you've never kissed me. Just give me this one. I'm in here for life and then some. Just one kiss to keep me going. No one will ever know."

She waited a moment before standing. Then, another moment before stepping up to the cell bars. "We need this out of the way first." She picked up his dinner tray with one hand, raised the cup of Sprite with the other, and gave it one more shot. "You want to finish your drink first?"

"Nope. You are my drink of choice," he answered.

"Suit yourself." She placed the cup on the tray next to the lemon slices and turned to face the opposite wall. Crouching, she slowly placed the tray on the floor.

Behind her, Tyler gasped with excitement. He rolled himself up to the bars and locked the wheels. A string of grunts sounded as he gripped the bars and pulled himself up into a standing position.

Rebecca turned and glanced at the clock on the back wall of his cell. Making a mental note, her eyes then dropped to meet his and she sauntered toward him. The eager look on his face repulsed her and she smiled to hide her disgust. She wanted to reach in and rip his throat out, but that would only land her in prison herself. Instead, she focused on the one thing she needed to do at the moment. That one last thing.

His face mashed up against the cell door and his mouth protruded through the bars. She raised her hands up to cup his face and then pressed her lips to his. The threat of nausea radiated throughout her body. His tongue probed at her lips, trying to sneak inside, but she kept them firmly closed.

Then, it was time. She bit down into the chunks of lemon pulp she had stashed inside her cheek. Her mouth immediately filled with the sour liquid. He pressed his face harder into hers and jabbed his tongue at her closed lips even stronger. At last, she parted her lips and swooshed the juice into his mouth. He gagged and tried to pull away, but she held his head tight between her hands. She heard his muffled complaints as he continued to struggle. He spit the liquid back into her mouth, but she just sent it right back. Finally, he swallowed. She released his head and let him fall backward into his chair.

"What the hell was that?" he sputtered, wiping the juice from his chin.

"What? You didn't like that?" She sat back in the chair, puckering her lips. "I thought it was hot. Swapping juice back and forth. Haven't you ever heard The Lemon Song? Zeppelin? You're probably too young," she said with a shrug.

At first, he stared at her as if she had two heads. Then, slowly his grimace softened and a smirk took its place. "Okay, I can go with it. Whatever turns you on, sweetheart. Shall we go again?"

"Nah, I think that's enough." She spun in the chair to look at the tray laying on the floor behind her. "Besides, I'm all out of lemon."

"Okay, so when will we do it again?" His eyes danced with exhilaration.

"We won't. We can't. You'll be dead soon."

"I beg to differ. There's no death penalty in Maryland."

"Oh no, *they* are not going to kill you. I am."

She stood and folded the chair and set it back into the corner where she found it. She looked him dead in the eyes as she walked back toward him. His face wore a mask of total confusion. He was speechless, but she was not.

"Did you seriously think that was for real? Did you seriously think I would just forget those women you killed? And Michael? And how you beat me unconscious and shot Harmon? Do you not know me at all?" She walked straight up to the bars that separated them. "*I* am going to kill you, Tyler. Not them. Me."

His expression relaxed and she could see that he understood it was all a game. His arrogant smile returned as he leaned back in his wheelchair and slung one arm comfortably over the back rest.

"And how do you expect to accomplish that? I'm locked up in here for the rest of my life. Completely untouchable to you. That is, aside from sucking on your tongue a few minutes ago." He licked his lips and winked at her.

Reaching into her back pocket, she pulled out her badge. She stared at it for a moment. "After what you did to Peter...I couldn't bring myself to go back to La Croix. There were just too many memories of him there. I thought I was going to have to hang up my chef hat for good." She let out a heavy sigh, still gazing at the badge in her hand. "But then Harmon...remember him...Harmon told me of a kitchen cook position that had just opened up at the prison caterer. You have no idea how happy I was when I got the job." She reached her hand through the bars and held up her badge for him to see.

He leaned forward to get a better look and his eyes widened. "You work here?"

"I've been cooking your meals all week. But I'm sorry to say, this one was your last." She turned and picked up the empty tray. "I hope it was good," she said, returning his wink from earlier.

His eyes fell to the empty tray in her hands. "No."

"Yes." She glanced at the clock hanging on the wall over his head. "You're already dead, motherfucker."

The timing couldn't have been better. He immediately began swallowing repeatedly. Blood pooled into his eyes and streamed down his cheeks. His breaths came in short gasps as his hands rose to his throat. More blood poured from his nose and sputtered out of his mouth through clenched teeth. Then, his ears, leaving a crimson river flowing down both sides of his neck.

Rebecca stood and watched. Silent. Satisfied.

Just when it seemed there wasn't a drop left in him, blood saturated the wheelchair seat and pooled onto the floor below him.

"Every orifice. That's what Wikipedia said."

Grabbing his stomach, Tyler doubled over in agony. He screamed and pulled wildly at his shirt. The shirt ripped and his red distended abdomen was exposed. Blisters formed on his skin right before their eyes. Within seconds, the blisters began bursting, one by one, and yellow fluid oozed out and ran down into his lap.

Rebecca's face curled into a grimace. She cringed at the sight...and the smell, and took a step back.

His abdomen swelled even more before splitting down the middle. Masses of tissue peeked out of the large fissure. Tyler thrusted his hands to his belly to hold his organs inside. He looked up at her, writhing in torturous pain. The blood continued to gush down his face from his eye sockets. She simply stared back at him with cold vengeful eyes.

He let out one last primal scream before falling silent, slumped over in his chair. His hands fell to his sides and dangled off the edge of the armrests. The intestines that had been pushing against the tear in his abdomen finally broke free and landed in a bloody heap at his feet, splattering blood and bile across Rebecca's white sneakers.

It was done. Justice had been served.

Chapter 42

Rebecca closed her eyes and let out an audible sigh. She stared into the cell at the unrecognizable body slumped over in a blood-covered wheelchair. The smell of burning flesh filled the air around her and saliva began to pool in her cheeks. She turned her head and swallowed it down.

It took several minutes for her to pull herself together. However, there was no time to relax. She stood in front of a half-liquified dead body with an ID badge that didn't match her long blonde hair. She wasn't even close to being in the clear yet.

Her fingers still gripped the empty tray in her hands. She set it down on the floor and reached into her front pocket to pull out a small plastic bottle. Holding it up to the light, she examined the tiny amount of clear liquid inside. Brandishing a napkin from her other pocket, she wiped down the bottle even though the textured surface of the plastic would prevent any useable fingerprints. Holding the plastic bottle with the napkin, she unscrewed the bottle cap and flicked it through the bars and into the corner. She squatted low, stretched her arm through the bars, and proceeded to sprinkle the clear drain cleaner onto the pile of guts on the floor.

Lastly, she strategically placed the empty bottle at the edge of the gut pile. Grabbing the spork from the dinner tray, Rebecca used it to push the bottle underneath the organs to coat it with blood. She then pulled it back out again so it would be easily visible to the investigative team that would show up later. The inside of the bottle would test positive for drain cleaner. And that would cause them to stop looking any further.

She crouched and picked up the empty tray from the floor and walked it back to the cart. After putting her apron and wig back on, she resumed her identity of Amanda White. After pulling out the identical meal she had made for Tyler, she returned to his cell and placed the untouched dinner onto the door shelf. Before she turned away, she took one last look at Tyler, slumped over with his insides on the outside.

She estimated that the dinner service was just about finished in the cafeteria. The inmates would go straight to their group counseling sessions after eating. It would be hours before the rest of the east wing inmates returned to their cells.

Tyler had been removed from all contact with the other prisoners since the letters had been found. That was fortunate for her. It meant he wasn't expected anywhere at the moment. A CO would likely poke his head in to check on him at some point. Rebecca felt a twinge of pity for whoever ended up with that job. They were in for quite a mess.

Bowing her head, Rebecca gave a few moments to Peter, and to Michael, and to all of the women that suffered at the hands or mind of Tyler Maddox. Then she gave Tyler a final salute, grabbed her cart, and wheeled it away, leaving his heap of flesh melting behind her.

Chapter 43

Rebecca wheeled the cart of empty trays through the doors of the kitchen and parked it in between the sink and the garbage can. She looked around, wondering if anyone suspected why it had taken her so long to retrieve the them. No one seemed to care. That was normal and she breathed a sigh of relief.

The back door leading out to the loading dock was propped open and she heard her co-workers packing up the van. She took a few steps until she got a better view outside. Cecelia wasn't among the other women. After taking a second look around the kitchen, including the recessed nooks behind the storage area, Cecelia was still missing. Rebecca worried that she might have caused her some real internal damage.

The male inmates were busy washing the stacks of empty trays at the sink and cleaning up the stations. One of them came her way and began unloading some of the trays from the cart to toss into the soapy water.

"Is Cecelia okay?" she asked him when he returned for a second load. "She seemed so sick when she was in the bathroom earlier."

"I think so. She was in there for a while, but she came out eventually. One of the COs drove her back to her car." He dumped the pile of trays into the sink with a loud clatter. "I hope it's not some bug going around," he called out over his shoulder. "Or food poisoning. We could all get sick if it's food poisoning."

"I think you're in the clear. Cecelia always packs her meals from home so unless you steal her food when she's not looking, you'll be okay."

Rebecca slid a few trays out of the cart and scraped the leftover food into the garbage can. She paused when she came across a tray that contained six pieces of lemon peel. *May God forgive me for what I have done.*

"Don't worry, I've got this." Large masculine hands took the tray from her and dumped the lemon into the trash. "Your ride is leaving. You're going to be stuck here if you don't get a move on."

"Oh crap, thank you." She rushed over to the hook on the wall and grabbed her purse. She wasn't planning on coming back, and therefore, she definitely shouldn't leave any personal belongings behind. "Have a good weekend," she said to the inmate as she raced for the door.

"As good as I can in this shithole."

Rebecca stopped at the door, faced him, and put her hands on her hips.

He immediately corrected himself. "I'm sorry. You have a good weekend too."

She flashed him a smile and a nod and disappeared through the door, kicking away the triangular block that held it open. She hopped into the back of the van and settled into her usual seat. As the van pulled away and headed toward the front gate, she turned and watched the prison fade into the distance.

She should be happy. Her nightmare was over. Without their leader pulling their puppet strings, the killings would stop. Peter had been avenged, and Michael as well. But Rebecca couldn't find it within her to celebrate. She was a murderer herself. Was she any better than Tyler or his murderous minions? Of course she was. She was nothing like him or them.

However, she did just kill a man. And she didn't just kill him…she liquified him…while he was safe in a prison cell. She definitely wasn't the "good guy." But she did what she had to do to protect her family and friends and she would do it again. *Tyler needed to be stopped once and for all.* She spent the rest of the van ride repeating that last line in her head over and over.

♦♦♦

Twenty minutes later, the van pulled up in front of Kirkland's Catering and the women jumped out one by one.

Stassi went inside the office to return the van keys while the others scattered throughout the parking lot, digging through their purses for their own keys.

Without Cecelia there to bark orders at them, it appeared the empty bins would remain in the van until the next morning. That suited Rebecca just fine. She wanted to get out of there as quickly as she could. Falling in line with the other women, she reached her car and disappeared inside.

She didn't move, just sat there for a few minutes. The image of Tyler's disintegrating body flashed into her head and she immediately pushed it back out. She couldn't allow herself to see it, to replay those final moments. It was horrific and cruel and demented. And it was her idea. She knew what the result would be when she planned it, although it was a lot worse than she had expected. But it was done and now she wouldn't allow herself to think of it ever again.

Switching gears, she turned her thoughts to Adam. She wondered if he was still with Harmon in Chincoteague. She hadn't tried to call him. What would she say? He needed some space to think, to process all that he had learned about her. That was only her lame excuse though. The truth was, she was afraid of what he was going to say. If she didn't talk to him then he wouldn't say the words that would crush her soul. He wouldn't tell her how much she disgusted him and how he couldn't bear to even look at her. What would he think of her now…after what she had done to Tyler?

Her entire body ached when she remembered how Adam had looked at her in that Ocean City police station. He would never understand why she had to do what she did. He didn't understand what it felt like to have evil follow you and never let you go. And even when you lock that evil up, it still finds a way to destroy you.

Adam may be lost to her, but at least she was safe from Tyler's sick game. She placed both of her hands on her slightly rounded belly. Her daughter would never know the monster that is Tyler Maddox, and for that fact alone, it was worth it.

Tears streaked her cheeks and she wiped them away before anyone noticed. However, after a quick glance out of her window, she realized they had all left. She was all alone in the parking lot. Just her and her guilt-ridden conscience.

Enough.

Enough already.

Diving her hand into her purse, she pulled out her ID badge and a lighter. She held her badge to the flame and watched the photo of Amanda White distort and melt into a black splotch that quickly spread across the entire plastic surface. She then flipped the card over and melted the magnetic strip that identified the badge as hers.

The news of Tyler's death would spread quickly throughout the area. Hell, it would have the national news channels flooded by ten. She would call Ophelia Kirkland after the weekend and explain how Tyler's death was affecting her. How she simply couldn't handle being around all that danger and death. Prison work was just not the job for her. Mrs. Kirkland would understand. She would be pissed, of course. But she'd understand.

Having wallowed long enough within her guilty conscience and the rationalizing that always followed, Rebecca started her engine and pulled out of her spot. She passed a garbage can on the way out of the lot and pulled up next to it. She rolled down her window and dropped in the charred pieces of plastic to mix with the rest of the trash.

Amanda White was officially dead.

May she rest in peace.

Chapter 44

"Can we go now? Please." Spencer sounded like a five-year-old in a grocery store.

Harmon looked at his watch. It was a little after 6:30 which meant Rebecca should be leaving the prison grounds at that very moment if she hadn't already. He had no way to contact her to make sure, therefore he needed to have faith that she had accomplished whatever it was she had set out to do.

"Yep. Now we can go get your PT," Harmon told Spencer, sliding from his seat on the car's trunk.

They both got into the car and drove off without another word being spoken. Spencer hadn't asked any more questions and Harmon was thankful for that. He still was not sure what Spencer's reaction would be when he found out that Rebecca killed Tyler.

The young detective was in a tough spot—trying to uphold the law while still being loyal to his friend who was breaking the law. Harmon knew what it felt like to have to look the other way. He had felt that way when he first saw Andrew Donovan's mutilated body strapped to a dining room table. He felt that way when he saw the bruises around Amanda White's neck and knew she had something to do with it.

He knew at that moment that thirty-five years of honest, by-the-book police work was about to go out the window just sixteen months before his retirement. But he also stood by that decision and would make the same choice a hundred times over if given the chance.

However, his decision back then was much easier than the one Spencer would have to make today. Andrew Donovan had been Harmon's mortal enemy. He was the devil personified. He hadn't lost a wink of sleep knowing someone turned the tables on him. But for Spencer...Tyler had been his best friend.

Even with the horrifying things Tyler had done, Harmon knew there was still a small part deep inside of Spencer that remembered how close they had once been. A small part that also blamed himself for what Tyler had become. A thin tether pulled at Spencer's heart strings every time he thought of how much his father had influenced Tyler's actions...shaped his psychosis.

Hopefully, he could sever that tether today. He would have to.

♦ ♦ ♦

Harmon and Spencer followed a CO down an empty prison hallway. Harmon's anxiety was riding high and his nerve endings were firing on all cylinders.

It was quiet. Too quiet. Their footsteps bounced off of the walls and echoed down the concrete corridor. No alarms had sounded. No officers had knocked them to the side while sprinting toward the east wing. No announcements over the PA system. No lockdown.

He wondered if he had misunderstood Rebecca's earlier message, or if he had misunderstood her intentions entirely. She hadn't given him any details and he hadn't wanted them. However, he knew her pretty well and he was certain she had been planning his death. But Harmon saw no evidence of it and that made him even more nervous.

They walked into the warden's office and Spencer handed over the warrant for Franklin Lewis' arrest.

"Lewis? Why?" The warden was genuinely baffled.

"He works closely with Tyler Maddox, correct?" Spencer asked.

"Well, yes. Every day."

"He's also running Mr. Maddox's fan club on the outside."

"What? He's not allowed to do that. That would be a conflict of interest."

"Oh, it's more than just a conflict," Spencer said. "Franklin Lewis is responsible for organizing the wax murders we've been investigating."

"There must be a mistake." The warden gasped slightly. "Franklin has been working in our rehab sector for ten years. He's doing tremendous work and his record is spotless."

"Not anymore," Harmon piped in with a shake of his head.

"It's no mistake," Spencer said. "But he'll get a fair trial either way."

"Such a shame." The warden ran his fingers through his thinning hair and shrugged. "Follow me. I'll take you to him."

The two detectives and a CO followed the warden out of his office and toward the rehab sector and training room. Along the way, they passed a break room with the door propped open. The warden popped his head in and gestured for another CO to join them.

A short walk later, the group of five filled the training room door. Franklin Lewis was hardly visible, sitting behind a desk with his head ducked behind a laptop screen. His fingers moved furiously across the keyboard, unaware of the two officers bearing down on him.

He looked up just as the officers split and stood on either side of him. His eyes keyed in on the warden, puzzled for just a moment. Then, Spencer stepped out from behind the warden and the therapist's confusion dissipated.

"Franklin Lewis? You are under arrest as an accessory for ten counts of first-degree murder," Spencer said.

He continued with the rest of the Miranda rights as the two COs stood Franklin Lewis up and cuffed his hands behind his back.

"Where do you want him?"

"Go ahead and put him in a holding cell. We're not done here yet," Spencer said. "We need to see Tyler Maddox. He's also an accessory to the aforementioned crimes."

"Right this way," the warden said as he led Spencer and Harmon out.

Chapter 45

Harmon's heart beat wildly in his chest as he and Spencer trailed behind the warden and another officer. As they turned the corner for the east wing, he thought the organ might actually burst through his chest. He had no idea what they would find and was terrified to find out.

"He's the last one on the end," the CO said, pointing his nightstick down the hallway.

Nothing could have prepared Harmon for the sight he came upon when they reached that last cell. The pile of internal organs in a heap on the floor made him gasp out loud. The stench of steaming blood and bile burned the inside of his nose. The warden immediately turned away and vomited onto the floor, adding to the nauseating odor cocktail that surrounded them.

Harmon and Spencer looked at each other. They each had a hand covering their nose and mouth and their faces twisted into horrified grimaces.

The warden remained doubled over against the wall. "What the fuck happened here?" he yelled as he turned his head to peek into Tyler's cell. "Miller! Get on your radio and lock this place down!" He shouted the order at the CO.

The officer eagerly turned away from the gruesome scene and retreated halfway down the hall, talking into the radio clipped to his shoulder.

Harmon stepped closer to the cell door, careful not to step in the blood spatter that had extended out into the corridor. He eyed the tray still sitting on the shelf, full and untouched. "He didn't eat his dinner so it doesn't appear that he was poisoned through his food. And the kitchen worker would have said something if there was something wrong when she delivered his dinner. This had to have happened after delivery." Harmon turned toward the warden. "What time does he get dinner?"

"Hell if I know." He shrugged, spit dripping from his hanging head. "Sometime around five, I guess."

Spencer sidled up to join Harmon at the cell door. "It looks like his entire insides burned right through his stomach and onto the floor. What on earth would do something like that?"

Harmon dropped into a squat. His eyes squinted as he studied the details of the scene in front of him. "There's something in that bloody pile. Looks like a container or bottle or something." He stood back up. "My guess is, whatever was in that bottle was some serious shit. We'll get CSU to test it. I'm sure the inside of that bottle will contain trace of some sort of caustic substance."

"You think it's suicide?" Spencer asked him.

"It sure does look that way."

"But why? With this cushy cell? From the looks of it, he was living it up and having a blast. A flat screen TV, blue-ray player, stereo. Art therapy every day. Constant visits from fans. It hardly even seems like he's in prison."

"But what if all that was taken away? What if he lost this cell and lost his visitations? What if he spent the rest of his life in solitary confinement? A concrete box with no one to charm. No one to brag to. No privileges whatsoever." Harmon turned his head and looked Spencer dead in the eyes. "Because that's what he was going to get when we caught him. And he knew we were close. It was inevitable. He took the easy way out. For him, death was easier than being alone." He stepped back a few paces and took in the scene in its entirety. "But what a way to go."

"Tyler was always the dramatic one," Spencer said softly, a slight crack in his voice.

Harmon couldn't tell if Spencer was playing along or if he actually believed that Tyler had done this to himself. He had known Harmon was stalling for Rebecca to do what she needed to do, although how could anyone possibly believe she could have pulled *this* off.

It didn't matter either way because he and Spencer would never speak of it again. They would never talk about that fight they had on that dirt sideroad and what had caused it. As far as Harmon could tell, Spencer was doing a damn fine job of protecting himself and his future. A smile attempted to creep into Harmon's face, but he forced it out.

"So, we're *not* looking for a killer inside these walls?" the warden asked.

Spencer looked over his shoulder and Harmon gave him a single nod.

"No, sir. This was a suicide."

Chapter 46

Rebecca ended her call and set her phone on the hotel room desk. "Well, that's that. I just quit my job."

"Aww, honey, I'm so proud of you," Adam said jokingly as he closed the suitcase and awkwardly zipped it shut. "Is she mad?"

"Doesn't matter if she is. I told her I was very uncomfortable and afraid for my safety working there. And knowing that an inmate killed himself right after I had brought him his dinner…well, it's all just too traumatizing. And that's actually the truth…traumatizing." She turned away and cast her gaze out of the third-floor window and onto the parking lot below.

Adam came up behind her, slid his arms around her waist, and rested his chin on her shoulder. She covered his hands with hers and ran her fingers along the hard surface of the cast that engulfed half of his arm.

He had taken quite a beating. She had almost lost him for good and hadn't even known it at the time. If she had known what he was going through at the same time she was preparing Tyler's last meal…she might not have been able to control herself. She might have stormed down to his cell with a meat cleaver and hacked him to pieces through the bars.

Adam's arms tightened around her and her heart fluttered. She still felt guilty though. Adam had been beaten and choked. It was a fight to the death and he barely made it out. She wished he didn't have to go through that. If only he had stayed in Chincoteague with Harmon for just one more day.

On the other hand, he understood now. He experienced firsthand the rage that boils up inside you when someone is actively trying to take your life. You can't control it. It's primal.

Adam was a good man, a *really* good man. And even *he* lost control and took someone's life. As much as she hated what happened to him…they were on equal ground now. He understood her. And he saved all of them. He killed a murderer…and that was okay in her book.

He would hold the psychological scars from his trauma for years to come, but she'd help him through it. She had mastered that part of it—acceptance of who she was and what she could do when pushed. She just hoped she could put that part of her to sleep. And she would teach him to do the same.

Adam's hand rubbed circles over her belly. "You'll love Boston. I guarantee you won't even want to come back here to pack up and sell the house," he said, nuzzling her ear.

"Does this mean I have to become a Patriots fan?"

"Only if you want me to talk to you on Sundays," he joked. He spun her around to face him. "Don't worry about it. Nothing is set in stone right now. It's simply a job offer. I haven't accepted it yet, and I won't until we go there and spend a few weeks and you decide you want me to take it."

"Well, it can't hurt to take a look. Our house is still a crime scene so we might as well take a little New England vacation."

"That's my girl," he said, hugging her tight.

She buried her face in his chest and breathed in his lovely scent. "I actually am okay with getting away from here. There are just too many traumatic memories for me here. I can sell La Croix and open up a new place up there."

"Boston would go crazy for a snazzy new French restaurant. Especially with someone as talented as you in the kitchen."

"Yeah, we'll see. Maybe I'll just be a mom for a while first."

"And you can absolutely do that. This new job teaching at the university is going to double my pay and then some. And real estate is cheaper. We can start over and do whatever we want…and be whoever we want."

"Boring suburban parents is exactly who I want to be."

"Amen to that."

END OF BOOK 3

Please consider taking a few moments to leave an honest review on the website where you purchased this book. The review does not need to be long and in depth. Even a simple line or two will greatly help other readers decide whether or not they might enjoy this book.

For more information about upcoming releases or to follow this author on social media, please visit

www.alexcrowbooks.com

THE REBECCA BLACK TRILOGY

About the Author

As the daughter of a nurse, Alex Crow grew up surrounded by graphic medical journals and surgical textbooks. Her love for blood and guts developed at an early age and led her to a career in sports medicine.

After "retiring," and spending over a decade raising a family, Alex turned to her love of thriller novels and is now enjoying its creative outlet for her sick and twisted mind.

She currently resides in Maryland with her husband, two children, and adopted canine and feline children.

Milton Keynes UK
Ingram Content Group UK Ltd.
UKHW040136170224
437973UK00001B/55